These Wartime Dreams

Inspired by the Malory Towers and St. Clare's novels of Enid Blyton, Rosie Meddon spent much of her childhood either with her nose in a book or writing stories and plays, enlisting the neighbours' children to perform them to anyone who would watch.

Professional life, though, was to take her into a world of structure and rules, where creativity was frowned upon. It wasn't until she was finally able to leave rigid thinking behind that she returned to writing, her research into her ancestry and a growing fascination for rural life in the nineteenth century inspiring and shaping her early stories.

She now resides with her husband in North Devon – the setting for the Woodicombe House Saga – where she enjoys the area's natural history, exploring the dramatic scenery, and keeping busy on her allotment.

Also by Rosie Meddon

The Woodicombe House Sagas

The Housekeeper's Daughter
A Wife's War
The Soldier's Return

On the Home Front

Her Patriotic Duty
Her Heart's Choice
Ties That Bind

The Sisters' War

A Wartime Summer
A Wartime Welcome
These Wartime Dreams

ROSIE MEDDON

These *Wartime* Dreams

CANELO

First published in the United Kingdom in 2024 by

Canelo
Unit 9, 5th Floor
Cargo Works, 1–2 Hatfields
London SE1 9PG
United Kingdom

A CIP catalogue record for this book is available from the British Library.

Print ISBN 978 1 80032 663 7
Ebook ISBN 978 1 80032 662 0

This book is a work of fiction. Names, characters, businesses, organizations, places and events are either the product of the author's imagination or are used fictitiously. Any resemblance to actual persons, living or dead, events or locales is entirely coincidental.

Cover design by Debbie Clement

Cover images © Arcangel, Shutterstock

Look for more great books at www.canelo.co

Printed and bound in Great Britain by Clays Ltd, Elcograf S.p.A.

1

Exeter, England

May 1942

I. Marking Time

Chapter 1

'Huh. So much for coming back to save our belongings. Look at it all. There's nothing left. Those Jerry bastards have destroyed the lot.'

Sixteen-year-old Pearl Warren curled her fingers into the palms of her hands. She'd just about had enough of this war. What had Exeter ever done to upset the Germans? Nothing. Nothing whatsoever. Hadn't stopped them coming over and flattening the place, though, had it.

From the moment they'd been startled awake by the air raid siren, May had done her best to reassure Pearl and their other sister Clemmie that, even if this turned out to be a real attack – as opposed to another false alarm – Albert Terrace would be safe. Enemy bombers, she had maintained, grouchy at being got out of bed in the middle of the night, would only be interested in places like the airfield and the barracks, or the quayside and the railway depot. Just went to show, then, how much *she* knew.

It would have been bad enough had she been right, had the three of them come up from the shelter to find just the gasworks destroyed, or the pumping station gone. From what she could make out, though, German bombers had laid waste to the entire city: the Sovereign Hotel, where May had worked as a cleaner, looked to be little more than a blackened façade; halfway down Chandlery Street, the front of Mundy's the baker's stood in ruins, meaning that Clemmie would be out of a job, too. And she just knew the Plaza would be gone. Best part of a year it had taken her to persuade the manager there to take her on, to convince him she had what it took to be an usherette, that she was too talented to languish in the role of junior sales assistant in a ladies' clothing store. But now, even if by some miracle the Plaza *had* survived, she couldn't imagine the first thing on people's minds being an evening at the cinema – not if, like the three of them, they'd come up this morning to find their homes and jobs gone, too.

In the smoky brown dawn, Pearl exhaled a mixture of exasperation and despair. From the moment those first incendiaries had come whistling down – before the three of them had even reached the public shelter on Friar Street – she'd had a sense they were in for 'the big one' everyone kept saying was coming. Indeed, the longer they'd been confined to the shelter, the more she'd become convinced they wouldn't be returning home to find things as they'd left them. Nonetheless, despite four hours spent cowering from the explosions thundering overhead and their attempts to ignore the terrifying rumble of the ground shaking all around them, she still hadn't expected to come up this morning and find their home completely destroyed – to find the whole of Chandlery Street gone. In fact, when the raid had finally petered out, and the fracas going on above had been replaced by a silence as bone-chilling in its own way as the bombing had been, her thoughts had still centred upon what she would do first: have a much-needed wash and tidy-up of her hair, or put the kettle on and make a nice cup of tea. At no point had she envisaged emerging into a choking fog of brick dust and smoke. Nor had she imagined that, instead of filling their lungs with fresh air, the three of them would cough and splutter, the back of their throats crackling under a layer of grit, their eyes streaming uncontrollably from the acrid haze. Even once they had been let out of the shelter, it had taken her a while to grasp that not only was having a wash and a cup of tea going to be out of the question, but that they'd been left with nothing but the clothes they stood up in.

Her thoughts interrupted by the rush of collapsing masonry, she spun about, only to swiftly shut her eyes and turn back from the wall of dust hurtling towards them. When she felt it safe to look, she was aghast to see that Prentice's had collapsed, leaving a gap all the way through to the remains of Bagwell's the Printer's, where flames were still licking from upper storey windows and the heavily blackened front wall looked as though it, too, was about to come crashing down.

Unable to shift the taste of wood ash from her throat, she directed her attention back to the mound of rubble that had once been their home. Here and there were the remains of neighbours' possessions: the iron door from a kitchen range; a tin bath; closer to, a fire poker. Reaching across, she tugged it free and used it to stab at the debris. Ruddy Germans. What she'd give to flatten *their* homes, see how *they* liked it. Curse Hitler. Curse Göring. And curse this stupid war for ruining everything – she'd loved being an usherette. It might not have been what she intended doing for the rest of her life but being able to see the latest films over and over, especially the musicals, had been a joy: each new release brought the chance to study more actresses, to pore over their costumes, copy their hairstyles, their make-up. It had been through watching the leading ladies that she'd learned how to sashay down the aisles and glide across the foyer, exuding what she'd hoped was the same sex appeal as Jean Harlow – not for nothing known as the Blonde Bombshell. And then there was Rita Hayworth; she could watch her dance with Fred Astaire in *You'll Never Get Rich* until the end of time and still never tire of doing so. The Plaza was also where she'd learned the words to all of the latest songs, and where she'd picked up how to use a gesture or an expression to convey meaning. And now look at her: still five years short of adulthood and yet, already, thanks to this war, her dreams lay dashed.

With a despairing sigh, she dropped the poker and turned to where Clemmie was stood sobbing.

'What are we… going… to do? Everything's… gone. All of it. All of it…'

'Yeah.' There was no sense sugar-coating the situation. 'Ain't so much as a matchstick to be saved from this lot.'

The sight of everything laying broken was too much even for May, who, despite being a woman to take life's trials in her stride, looked as though she'd had all the stuffing knocked out of her.

'No,' the poor girl agreed.

Poor old May, when their mother had been taken ill and not long afterwards passed on, it had fallen to her to take care of everything from seeing the rent got paid and the laundry done, to putting meals on the table and keeping track of their food rations. But, no sooner had they got back on their feet when, like the bad penny that he was, Charlie Warren had shown up again. After an absence of God knows how many years, during which he couldn't have given a tinker's cuss what happened to his wife or his only daughter, and certainly not to his two stepdaughters, he'd simply moved back in and taken to scrounging or thieving from them as the mood took.

Moved back in. Dear God, her father. When the sirens had gone off, they'd left him, slumped, in his usual drunken stupor, over the kitchen table – which is where he would still have been when the bombs started. The fact only now registering, she shot a look to where May was standing with an arm around Clemmie's shoulders. Then, to make sure Charlie wasn't lurking somewhere, watching them, she cast about more generally. Satisfied that he wasn't, she said, 'You know… there is *one* good thing…'

May's expression, as she met her look, was one of puzzlement. 'Really? Not sure how you fathom that.'

'Well… you got to think we've seen the last of Charlie.'

The look on Clemmie's face suggested she doubted they could be so lucky. 'You think he were definitely still in there, then? You don't think he could have got himself out *before* the bombing started? He couldn't have… he couldn't have woken up after we'd left and took himself off to shelter someplace else?'

Withdrawing her arm from Clemmie's shoulder, May shook her head. 'Think about it—' Keen to hear what she thought, Pearl picked her way across the rubble towards her. 'When the three of us left, he was snoring fit to wake old Mrs Tuckett on the top floor. So, no, I reckon that skinful he had yesterday was his last, and that when he came stumbling in, cursing and lashing out as usual, it was for the final ever time.'

Relieved that May should agree with her, Pearl nodded. 'Yeah. There's *no way* he could have got out. He's gone. Dead and buried. And I, for one, shan't mourn his passing.'

'But—'

'Face it, Clem.' The more she considered the possibility, the more certain Pearl became. 'That foul-mouthed bastard might have been my father, but he was rotten through and through. And yes, I know you're not supposed to speak ill of the dead, but you're not supposed to tell lies, either. So, let's none of us pretend we'll miss him. You, Clem, might have been the one to feel the back of his hand most often but weren't none of us spared his wrath. It was me he swore at for fighting off the drunks he brought home. It was me he told not to be so prissy every time I complained about one of them putting a hand up my skirt or trying to reach inside my blouse. And if I can't forgive him that, then why would I mourn him? And you, May – don't tell me you weren't brassed off with him constantly helping himself to the coins from your purse.'

'Trust me,' May said stoutly, 'many's the time I could gladly have taken the carving knife to that man—'

'—or that you, Clem, weren't browned off with him sending you out with your own money for his fags or his booze.'

Clemmie's reply was barely audible. 'I daren't never disobey him.'

'See, that's what I mean. So, no, I shan't lose sleep over him being dead, and nor should either of you.'

Watching Clemmie dab at her tears, Pearl heaved a sigh of dismay. How on earth, given the torment that man had put the girl through, could Clemmie *still* feel sorry for him?

'It's true,' May said. 'He don't deserve to be neither mourned nor remembered.'

'Even so…'

'Look,' May went on, her words this time directed at Clemmie. 'You've had a shock. You're tired. We all are.'

'Besides,' Pearl went on, gesturing about her, 'we've more important things than the demise of Charlie Warren to worry about.' She supposed it was a *bit* of a pity about Dad – although a rather greater pity about the ten shillings he owed her. Still, at least her days of fending off the stream of lecherous old men he brought home were at an end. 'I mean,' she picked up again. 'What the hell do we do now? Where do we even go?'

May's response was accompanied by a weary sigh. 'Well, when we came up from the shelter, that warden told us we were to go up the church and wait there. So, I suppose we go and see what the arrangements are, see if a rest centre's been set up, like that time last month when those few stray bombs fell on Marsh Barton. I don't see as we have a choice. I mean, look about you. High Street's flattened. Fore Street's burned out. Even Bedford Circus is gone. There's nowhere left.'

That might be true, Pearl thought as she stared at the remains of the only home she'd ever known, but at least by bombing most of the High Street, the Luftwaffe had left little chance of her having to go back to shop work. On the other hand, if she was to avoid being sent to a job in a factory – thank God she was still too young for compulsory war work – she was going to have to be a sight quicker off the mark than every other young girl waking up this morning to find herself out of a job.

Her thoughts interrupted by the sight of something glinting in the rubble, she reached to pull it out; it was a tiny mirror in a metal frame, the likes of which old Mrs Duncan upstairs would have hung in her budgerigar cage. It being of no use to her, she let it go. 'So,' she said, brushing the dirt from her hands, 'that's what we're going to do, is it? Go up the church?'

May nodded. 'It is. We'll go and see what's what. And we'll do it now, early, before every other soul does the same and we're left to traipse here, there and everywhere in search of any old place that'll have us.'

'Which makes me proper glad then,' Pearl said, making no attempt to hide a satisfied grin, 'that on the way down the shelter last night, I thought to grab this.' Proud of her foresight, she held aloft her pink vanity case. 'Because at least I shan't be without my curlers or my toothbrush. Nor lipstick and mascara.'

'Yes, because let's face it,' May said, glass crunching under her shoes as she turned away from the ruins. 'Looking your best really ought to be your biggest concern when you've just lost your livelihood, your home, and everything that was in it.'

Following the path May proceeded to pick across the firemen's hoses snaking their way up from the river, Pearl gave a weary shake of her head. Those two might be her half-sisters, but they never had understood her; neither, between the pair of them, did they harbour a single dream. She, on the other hand, had plenty. And while she would be forced to concede that losing what May had described as *her livelihood, her home, and everything that was in it*, was thoroughly aggravating, it might also be the kick she needed to set about achieving her dream. This war couldn't last forever. And when it did finally come to an end, folk were going to need entertaining, cheering up. When they did, she would need to be ready.

Besides, it was a well-known fact that no one could keep a talented girl down for long. Sooner or later, the cream always rose to the top. Until then, however, she would keep her wits about her and her eyes open for anything – and any*one* – that might help her to realise her dream just that little bit sooner...

Chapter 2

'For heaven's sake, Pearl, would you just stop whining. You're driving me round the bend.'

'I wasn't whining.'

'See,' May snapped back. 'That's what I mean. It's got to the point where you don't even know you're doing it.'

'I *wasn't* whining. I was simply pointing out—' Spotting May's stony-faced expression, Pearl raised herself up from where she'd been slumped on her camp bed and decided against continuing.

It was now a little over a week since the night of the air raids. A week of sleeping on a camp bed in the church hall among a hundred or so other folk with nowhere to go; a week of having to wear the same clothes every day with little prospect of getting them washed; a week of accepting whatever meals the tireless volunteers from the Women's Voluntary Service's emergency kitchen could rustle up. It had also been a week of queueing to meet the requirements of officialdom: to register for temporary housing; to obtain replacement identity cards, ration books; to find out what help was available with regard to getting money for essentials. But, whereas their immediate needs were slowly being met, and the list of things for which they had to apply, or to obtain, was slowly shrinking, the number of hours in which they had nothing to do was growing. Unsurprisingly, forced to spend so much time with nothing but their futures to ponder had quickly brought them to bickering.

'Pearl, listen to me,' May picked up again. 'I know you're fed up. We all are. Not having a home—'

'Nor a job.'

'No, nor a job, is a hardship of the worst kind imaginable. It's not a fate I'd wish on my worst enemy. And if I could make things any different, I would. You know that. But I can't. So, how about you try an' be a little more patient? Maybe try an' show some gratitude for the kindness of strangers – for the roof over your head and a hot meal each day.'

Inwardly, Pearl groaned. 'It's all right for you—'

'Yeah? How d'you reckon that, then?'

'*You* lost a job you loathed.'

'Loathed or otherwise, I went and did it every day because my wage helped to keep us housed and clothed and fed—'

'So did mine.'

'I didn't say it didn't. We all three of us paid our way.'

'Difference is,' Pearl began, despite wondering as to the wisdom of what she was about to add, 'I *liked* my job. I liked going to work each day. It was fun and gay, a few hours' escape from the humdrum. And I was good at it, too.'

'I daresay we were all good at what we did, in our own ways. But the fact remains, there's no point griping. I can't conjure up somewhere for us to live in precisely the same way that I can't wave a wand and get each of us a job. We're on the list for rehousing but, same as everyone else, we've got to wait our turn. As regards work, well, it'll take time. Like that volunteer woman said to us the other day, as more businesses start to reopen, so there are bound to be more opportunities. In the meantime, going on about how fed up you are with it all don't help no one.'

Without meaning to, Pearl sighed. To describe her mood as fed up was an understatement, on a par with remarking that Gary Cooper was good looking, or that Billie Holiday had a nice voice. But if she had to wake up many more mornings in this dingy little hall, with the prospect of another day stretching emptily ahead, followed by yet another night spent cheek by jowl with some unwashed stranger, she was in danger of exploding. And yes, given how their home had been hit by a High Explosive bomb, she did realise that was an unfortunate turn of phrase. But she couldn't help how she felt, nor could she see any point hiding the fact.

To be fair to May, a camp bed in a church hall *was* preferable to sleeping out in the open – or, like a lot of people had taken to doing in order to stop looters pilfering what remained of their belongings, staying in their bomb-damaged home, where, at any moment, the roof might fall in. But surely, craving a decent night's sleep and the chance to conduct her ablutions in private – oh, and to have some underwear that hadn't been rinsed out in a washbasin five or six days running – wasn't unreasonable, was it? No. But, every time she dared even huff with exasperation, May shot her one of those looks that said *For God's sake, Pearl*. Either that, or else Clemmie would send her a sympathetic smile, only to spoil it by trotting out that other platitude currently driving her round the bend, the one about it being 'worse where there's none'. To Pearl's mind, yearning for a place to live, so that she might know where to look for work, demonstrated an eagerness to stop being a burden. Surely, a week on from the raid, she couldn't be blamed for simply wanting to get on with her life. Ordinarily, showing a bit of spunk was to be admired.

Feeling no less irate, but seeing no point in picking a fight with her sister, she let out a sigh. 'Happen I might go and have another stab at finding work. Even something temporary would be better than nothing.'

When she looked across to gauge May's reaction, she saw her frown change to a smile.

'No sense going back to the Savoy again, then? No chance they'll know when they might re-open and be in of need usherettes?'

Recognising May's suggestion as an olive branch, Pearl shook her head. 'Manager there said he didn't need the ones he already had. Said it could be weeks before they get the electric back.'

'Suppose so. Where else were you thinking of looking, then?'

It was a good question. Even had she the desire to go back to being a shopgirl – which she most definitely didn't – with so much of the High Street bombed out, there would be hundreds of girls for each vacancy, if not thousands. Having left school at fourteen, she wasn't qualified to work in an office; she was even too young to have to register for war work. That last fact, though, was a blessing; the thought of having to slave away, ten or twelve hours every day – or night – machining parachutes, or assembling parts for aeroplanes, brought her out in a cold sweat. For a girl with aspirations like hers, work like that would be a trial of the worst kind imaginable.

'I don't know where I'm going to look,' she said flatly. 'But since sitting here won't find me a job, I might as well at least get off my backside and go and look, wear through my shoe leather in hope.'

'Well, just have a care. And be back before supper or you'll go hungry.'

Straightening her skirt and hoping that her hair looked all right, Pearl nodded. 'See the pair of you back here later on, then.'

'As it happens,' May went on. 'I have to pop out, too.'

Having so far remained silent, Clemmie looked from one to the other. 'Then please be careful, both of you.'

Thinking Clemmie looked as though she might cry, Pearl sent her a smile. 'Cheer up. We're only going out for a while, not leaving you for good.'

At least, not yet, she thought as she set about picking a path between families perched gloomily around their few belongings. However, if May's secretive behaviour of the last few days was anything to go by, then despite the three of them having spent their whole lives together, she had an idea it wouldn't be long before Clemmie indeed found herself left behind. And while the prospect nagged at her conscience more than she might have expected, the only problems she had the power to solve were her own. Desperate situations called for desperate remedies, and the time had come to put her own needs first. And if that meant ending up at the Labour Exchange in order to get herself back on her feet, then so be it. She really was that fed up.

–

'And you're eighteen years old.'

Smiling at the woman behind the desk, Pearl nodded; admit she was only sixteen and she'd be sent way with a flea in her ear. 'That's right.'

'And you're not married.'

'No.' Honestly. Did she look like somebody's wife?

It was later that same morning at the Ministry of Employment Labour Exchange on Queen Street. Having had no idea how the place worked, Pearl had stood for a while across the street, from where, by watching the comings and goings, she had quickly established that men and women entered the building through separate doors. After that, it had been simply a matter of stepping smartly inside, approaching the first female comporting herself in the manner of an official, and enquiring how to go about getting a job. Directed to an office further along the corridor, she found a middle-aged clerk seated behind a small desk, and several other women apparently already waiting to see her. Taking a seat on the only vacant chair, she congratulated herself on getting this far. And now, having waited more than an hour and a half for her turn to be interviewed, she was determined to show herself in the best possible light, taking particular care to smile and appear friendly.

'Any typing qualifications? Or shorthand?' the woman enquired.

Since the answer, in this instance, didn't lend itself to displaying her true talents, Pearl set about changing the subject.

'What I was hoping for—'

'*Any typing or shorthand qualifications?*'

Trapped into answering, Pearl held her smile. 'No.'

Her spirits nevertheless taking a dent, she watched the clerk strike a diagonal line through an entire section of the form.

'Nature of your last employment?'

'Usherette. At the Plaza cinema.'

'Reason for leaving or wishing to leave?'

'It was destroyed by a fireball.' She watched as the woman wrote *Bombed out*.

'Employment prior to that?'

'Sales assistant in a ladies' clothing store.' There was no way including the word 'junior' would help her cause.

'Where?'

Pearl checked her impatience. The woman could at least *try* and hide her boredom. 'Countess Fashions.'

Having finished writing, the woman set her pen on her blotter and looked over the top of her spectacles to flick through a card index. Evidently finding the one she sought, she met Pearl's look.

'The hospital has urgent need of kitchen staff. Training will be given. Forty-five hours a week, uniform provided. You will work either the early shift starting at five o'clock in the morning, or else the late shift starting at midday.'

Pearl shrank back in her chair. Kitchen staff? Could this woman not see how wasted she would be in such a job? 'I was hoping for something a little less—'

'And so, Miss Warren, is every other young girl who sits in that chair. And as I point out to each and every one of them, there is a war on.'

'As my sisters and I know to our cost,' Pearl replied, all the while doing her best to appear eager and yet humble. 'But I was rather hoping for something where I might be dealing with people.' *Rather than potatoes*.

The woman flicked back through the cards in her little stand. 'Well, your dearth of qualifications and lack of any specific skill means I'm not supposed to offer you a choice.'

At that moment, going back to shop work regained a certain appeal. '*Please*. I really am very good with customers. I'm told so 'most every day.'

'However—'

'Yes?'

From a drawer in the pedestal of her desk, the woman pulled out a folder. 'Given your experience of serving customers, I suppose I *could* stretch a point. It's possible you might meet the criteria for this.'

Accepting the leaflet, Pearl ran her eyes over the front. On the cover was a drawing of a bus. On the rear platform of it, a young woman in a natty tailored trouser suit and jaunty cap was smiling gaily. *Keep the Country Moving. Help Win the War* the heading exhorted. *The Nation Needs Young Women to Train as Bus Conductors*. In smaller writing beneath the illustration, it went on to declare *Excellent Pay! Free Uniform!* And, beneath that, *Be the Friendly and Efficient Face of City & District Motor Services Ltd*.

Pearl raised an eyebrow. 'A clippie?'

'I've sent a couple of young ladies along just this last week. Why don't I telephone and arrange an interview? You clearly take pride in your appearance. And you certainly don't want for confidence. I have a suspicion you might do rather well.'

A *clippie*? Part of her wondered why she hadn't thought of it before; the other part wanted to laugh. But what did she have to lose?

'All right, then. Why not?'

'Excellent. I'll call right away and find out when they can see you.'

-

'Blimey, these dumplings are stodgy.'

'For goodness' sake, Pearl, keep your voice down.'

It was much later that afternoon and, in line with May's directive not to miss supper, Pearl was back at the rest centre. And while part of her was desperate to tell the other two what she'd been up to, she had no wish to put the mockers on it. What was it Mum used to say: 'discretion is the better part of valour'?

'All I meant,' she said, 'is that the ones you make are a lot – *were* a lot – nicer.'

'Yes, well,' May scoffed. 'No doubt having to fashion a gross of the things in a make-do kitchen is a darn sight harder than knocking up just a handful in your own. Besides, in our situation, it's a case of "worse where there's none".' Inwardly, Pearl groaned. *Back to the bromides.* 'Any luck with your search for work?'

Dropping her spoon into her bowl, Pearl let out a frustrated sigh. 'Do you think if I said I couldn't eat the dumplings they'd give me some more stew?'

'If you go up and tell them you don't rate their dumplings, I'd be surprised if they serve you anything ever again. Anyway, your search for work…'

'Actually, yes.' Thank goodness one of them had finally asked; she'd been about to burst. 'I do have something up my sleeve. But, since I have to go back for a proper interview and don't want to jinx it, I'm not going to talk about it until after I've been. But I'm sure I'll get it. I could tell.'

'*I* have some news—'

Having both spoken at precisely the same moment, Clemmie and May laughed.

'You first,' May directed as she scraped the last spoonful of stew from her bowl.

'I'm volunteering with the WVS.'

From across the table, Pearl noticed the warmth in May's smile.

'Well good for you,' May said. 'I thought you looked perkier when I came in. Was that this afternoon you joined up?'

Clemmie nodded. 'I bumped into one of the organisers and she asked me whether I could spare some time to help out, so I said I could. I mean, it feels only right. It's WVS volunteers who run this canteen. And the rest centre. And she told me that, since the bombings, they've also been helping out at the hospital with the casualties, and helping folk to get their belongings from their damaged homes and make them safe against thieves.'

'All well and good,' Pearl remarked. 'But not much use if they don't pay you.'

'I don't intend doing it forever. Just while I wait for a proper job to come along.'

'Take no notice,' May said to Clemmie. Reaching across the table, she patted her sister's hand. 'It's very kind-hearted of you. No doubt they need all the help they can get. And I'm sure they'll be as grateful for your time as we are for theirs. Besides, who knows what meeting new people might lead to – who you might meet that knows of someone with a vacancy?'

'Exactly,' Clemmie said. 'So, what's *your* news, then?'

'Well… I too have a job.' From her pocket, May withdrew an envelope and put it on the table. 'The letter offering it to me came this morning.'

Pearl stifled a gasp of surprise. This was a turn up for the books; there was May, urging *her* not to be so impatient, when all the time she'd been out there looking for work herself. Proper dark horse, she was turning out to be.

'This new job of yours in Exeter?' she asked, eager to know what May had got herself fixed up with. 'Only, I can't think there can be many hotels left taking guests.'

'Actually,' May said. 'It's not in a hotel, and it's not in Exeter. I'm going to be housekeeper to a farmer and so it will mean moving away.'

Blimey. That really *was* a turn up for the books: May leaving Clemmie, her little shadow? Well, as long as May wasn't expecting *her* to take on the task of looking out for her. Obviously, she would keep an eye on her; half-sister or not, they were all still blood. But, since Clemmie was clearly going to be the last of them to get work, she couldn't afford to get saddled with looking after her indefinitely – not with this clippie job in the offing. She was pretty certain she would get it. She had a feeling in her bones. That, and the fact that she knew how to turn on the charm when it was needed; she'd won over that woman at the Labour Exchange easily enough. All she needed to do now was summon a generous helping of it on the day of her interview – and then, for the sake of her conscience, hope it wasn't too long before Clemmie got herself fixed up with something, too.

Chapter 3

'Miss Warren?'

'That's me.'

Getting to her feet, Pearl smoothed a hand over her skirt. She would have liked to look smarter, but the emergency clothing coupons and the small amount of cash they'd been given at the relief centre had immediately been gobbled up by essentials like underthings, a nightdress, and a pair of shoes. Still, she didn't think she looked too bad; the skirt and jacket – a disappointingly dull shade of plain grey but, as an outfit, serviceable and hardly worn – she'd found by rummaging among the donated items at the WVS clothing centre. And thank goodness she had.

The woman smiled and indicated the door through which she'd just appeared. 'Staff Superintendent Kelland will see you now.'

For the first time, Pearl felt apprehensive – as though a flight of skittish butterflies had found their way into her stomach. 'Thank you,' she said, willing the sensation to subside.

In keeping with what she'd seen of the rest of the building, the office into which she was shown struck her as dreary and unremarkable, the furnishings utilitarian.

From behind the desk, a grey-haired man stood up to greet her. He wasn't, as she'd been expecting, wearing a uniform but an immaculate black suit, in his breast pocket, a starched white handkerchief.

'Miss Warren, good morning. Thank you for coming in today. I'm Staff Superintendent Kelland. As my title might suggest to you, it is my job to ensure City & District Motor Services has the appropriately skilled workforce to operate and maintain the service our passengers expect of us.'

The butterflies in Pearl's stomach all took flight at once. She was going to need more than a charming smile to win over a man like this. For a start, he looked old enough to be her grandfather – well into his fifties, if not a little more.

She cleared her throat. 'Good morning, Staff Superintendent Kelland. Thank you for seeing me.'

'Please, take a seat.'

Pearl sat down. 'Thank you.'

'Now, since the details provided to me by the Employment Exchange are somewhat brief, I shall start, if I may, by taking down some particulars.'

Pearl nodded. ''Course.' So far, so good.

Having confirmed her name, and that she was currently residing at No.1 Rest Centre, her interviewer looked up from his papers.

'I'm sorry to hear that. Where was your home?'

'Albert Terrace on Chandlery Street.'

He nodded. 'With your parents?'

As she went to reply, she spotted an opportunity. This early in the interview, tears would be over the top, but appearing to fight them back couldn't do any harm.

After a moment's hesitation, she reached into her bag for her handkerchief. 'I lost Mum a while back. But Dad was taken in the air raid. He was gassed in the last war and weren't able to serve this time round… else he wouldn't have been where he was. Now it's just me an' my sisters, waiting to be found somewhere to live.'

'I see.'

'Them raids cost me my job as well. Perhaps it says there,' she went on, indicating the form on his desk. 'I was an usherette at the Plaza. But as you most likely know, it was gutted by a fireball. When I found out what happened to it, I went straight round to see the manager at the Savoy… but, since he had no electric, he couldn't say when he would be reopening, and so he wasn't in need of no more staff.' She smiled weakly. 'It was such a shame. I loved that job. Checking people's tickets, showing them to their seats, you know, when they came in, all excited to see the film. Selling fag—cigarettes and confectionary, when we had any. Like I say, real satisfying.'

'I should imagine that being an usherette required you to work late into the evening.'

Pearl nodded. 'It was a long day. We'd start with the matinee, then the evening showing, sometimes a late one, too.'

'So, I suppose my question to you is how good are you at getting up in the morning? Your shifts would include both early and late turns.'

About to dismiss the superintendent's concern with a wave of her hand, Pearl instead plunged both of them into her lap. 'No fear on that front. I'm up with the lark. Always have been. But, if you take me on, from my first week's wages I'll buy a very loud alarm clock.'

Her interviewer smiled. 'I feel it only fair to warn you that six or seven hours on a swaying bus each day can be exhausting. And, on occasion, but especially when it's either particularly wet or horribly cold, not everyone will be polite to you. At times, your patience will be sorely tested. And with you being among our first female conductors, a certain type of passenger will think you fair game for all manner of lewd comments.'

Pearl laughed. 'Then I shall feel right at home. As an usherette, I had to contend with all of that and more besides.'

'I see from these notes that, prior to the Plaza, you worked as a sales assistant.'

'At Countess Fashions, yes. I saw just yesterday how that's been flattened, too.' As far as Pearl was concerned, it was good riddance. That stuck-up Mrs French had taken against her from the outset. In a way, she supposed it was a miracle she'd lasted in the woman's employment as long as she had.

'So, tell me, Miss Warren. Why do you think you'd make a good conductress for City & District?'

Pearl didn't hesitate. 'That's easy. It's all about the people, isn't it? People don't get on the bus because they want to go for a ride – because they like buses. They get on the bus because they've somewhere to be. And it's the job of the driver and the conductor – conduct*ress* – to get them there on time and with as little fuss as possible. Take someone who's got to get to the hospital. She's probably already anxious, so she doesn't want a lot of strife before she even gets there, does she?'

With some enthusiasm, Staff Superintendent Kelland nodded. 'She does not.'

'Well, I'm not the sort to flap. I also take pride in my appearance, which is important when you're the face of the company.' Being 'the face of a company' was a phrase Pearl had read in a magazine, in an article about an actress who had agreed to advertise a perfume; fortunate it should come to her at that moment – fortunate she hadn't turned the page without bothering to read it, the sight of so much writing and so few pictures initially putting her off. 'I'm quick with numbers, I get on well with pretty much anyone, and they seem to take to me, too.' *I'd also look eye-catching in a dark trouser suit and cap, especially with this hair.*

'You do come across as approachable,' the superintendent seemed forced to agree. 'In fact, I think you would do rather well. So perhaps I had better explain to you about our training programme, and about the assessment you would have to pass before we could confirm your contract of employment.'

Pearl tried to rein in her grin. No point looking simple; not when she seemed to have this in the bag.

The conductor training programme explained, Staff Superintendent Kelland picked up the telephone and spoke to someone. Moments later, a woman in a nurse's uniform arrived and took Pearl through to what turned out to be a small sick bay, to carry out a medical examination.

'Five feet nine inches,' she announced of Pearl's height. 'Eight stone twelve pounds,' she noted from the scales and then entered on her chart against *Weight in Stockinged Feet.* Consulting her tape measure, she recorded statistics of thirty-five, twenty-four, thirty-six. 'Still growing?'

Pearl nodded. 'I'm still having to let down the hems on my skirts. And I think my bust is still filling out. When I had to get a new brassiere recently, I needed a size up from last time.'

'You'll probably find you'll stop now you're eighteen.'

Christ. Yes. She'd forgotten she was supposed to be eighteen. 'No doubt you're right.'

'Most of our ladies find that being on their feet all day keeps them from putting on weight. Keeps their ankles trim, too.'

'I suppose it would.'

'Have you had chicken pox?'

'Yes.'

'Mumps?'

'Yes.'

'Measles?'

Pearl shrugged. 'Don't remember.'

'Scarlet fever, diphtheria, poliomyelitis?'

'Not so far as I know.'

'There's to be vaccination against diphtheria now, you know.'

'Goodness.'

'TB?'

'No.'

'Menstruation regular?'

'Pretty much.'

'Well, everything seems in order. Come with me and I'll take you back through to Staff Superintendent Kelland.'

'Right, then, Miss Warren,' the superintendent said once Pearl was seated back across the desk from him. 'Ordinarily, the next step would be for us to apply for references from your previous employers. However, with so many firms having gone out of business, and with the company in need of more conductors poste-haste, we're getting our new recruits on board while we await replies.' When Pearl nodded her understanding, the superintendent continued, 'Something of a formality anyway. By the time we've managed to get a reply to our request, you'll probably already be out on the open road, so to speak.'

Again, Pearl nodded. She didn't *think* she need worry what past employers would have to say about her. The manager at the Plaza had been more than satisfied with the way she conducted herself. And the only harmful thing snooty Mrs French at Countess Fashions could say was that, at the beginning, she'd had to warn her about answering back. *Just say 'Yes, Mrs French' and do as I tell you. Answer me back, whinge, or question an order, and you'll be out on the street without your feet so much as touching the ground. Are we clear?*

'Does that mean I've got the job?' Pearl asked. It seemed best to know where she stood.

'Yes, Miss Warren, I'm pleased to say that it does. What you lack in age would appear to be made up for by your experience of dealing with customers. You're certain to find that invaluable.'

Pearl couldn't stop grinning. 'Thank you. I won't let you down.'

'On that front, only time will tell. Now, since we have recently recruited three other young ladies, we have a training course scheduled to start Monday week. The ladies in question have already been kitted out with a uniform so how about—' the superintendent flicked through his Day Book '—you come back on Monday morning for your fitting, and start your training with the rest of our new recruits at nine o'clock the Monday after that?'

Pearl could hardly contain herself. Ten days from now, she would have a job. 'Sounds perfect.'

'In the meantime, we will write you a letter, setting out the terms upon which your employment will be based: pay, holiday entitlement, and so on.'

When the superintendent got to his feet, Pearl did likewise.

'Thank you,' she said, reaching to shake his hand. 'Truly, thank you.'

'And if, when you join us, you need assistance finding lodgings, please do ask. We have a number of landladies locally who help us out from time to time. It's important we know that our staff are settled, and able to get to work without difficulty.'

'Thank you. Yes. I'll remember that.'

Golly, Pearl thought as she was shown out through the staff entrance onto the side street adjacent to the depot. She'd only gone and got a job. Not any old job, either, but one with a decent wage and a week's paid holiday each year. And a smart uniform. And meals in a staff canteen. Granted, she wouldn't get to see all the latest films and musicals for free – but she'd be earning enough to pay to go and see them, if she chose. *And* the bus company would help her find somewhere to live. See, it had been worth putting herself out to go to the Labour Exchange, and then holding out for something better than peeling potatoes in a hospital kitchen.

In fact, the only problem she could see now, was how to tell poor Clemmie that she would shortly be doing the same as May – in other words, leaving her at the rest centre and getting on with life without her...

–

It was no good. She couldn't do it – not this morning. It was early the following Monday and, having only just seen May safely on her way to some farm, where she was to become housekeeper to a feller she'd never even met, Clemmie was already starting the new week in tears. To add to the girl's grief by telling her that she, Pearl, was about to go and get fitted for a uniform for the very same bus company that mere moments ago had taken May out of their lives, was something even she recognised as heartless. So, no, she would hold off breaking her news for now, even if the excitement *was* killing her. She would let Clemmie think that this morning she was just going for another interview, after which she would learn whether she'd been successful. That way, when she did tell her, it ought not to come as too much of a shock.

She turned to regard Clemmie's tear-stained face. 'Hey, c'mon,' she coaxed. 'Don't get upset. She'll be back. Mark my words.'

With a sniff, Clemmie met her look. 'I'm not so sure 'bout that. You know what a stickler she is for keeping her word. If she's told this farmer she can do the job, she'll make good an' sure to do it.'

Unwittingly, Pearl raised an eyebrow. 'Always assuming the place turns out to be what she was expecting. For all she knows, this feller could be tuppence short of a shilling. Or a German spy… or an axe murderer.'

'Stop it. Don't say that.'

'Well, you've got to admit, Clem, it's peculiar. I mean, who offers a woman a job in their home without even meeting her? Anyway, look,' Pearl said, spotting her opportunity and softening her tone, 'I have to go and see about this job again. They said if I called in today, they'd tell me if I've got it. But since I don't know how long it'll take, why don't you go on back to the rest centre and I'll see you there later on?'.

Clemmie's reply was accompanied by a disconsolate nod. 'All right. But be careful. Don't do anything rash.'

'You be careful, too.'

Feeling duplicitous, Pearl turned and walked away. She had no idea how Clemmie would fare on her own in the rest centre, nor anywhere else, come to that. She could only trust, as May must have done, that she'd be fine; what she couldn't afford was to allow herself to become preoccupied by worries about Clemmie while she, herself, was being shown how to be a bus conductress. Learning how to do a job like that was going to need her complete and undivided attention. No, best to hope that, by the time she got back from being fitted for a uniform, she would have come up with a way to break the news to Clemmie gently, after which all she could do was, well, leave her to it.

–

Trying on her conductress uniform was surprising fun. At the back of the square office building situated behind the bus garage was a small windowless room presided over by a no-nonsense seamstress called Miss Passmore. Running the length of one wall was what struck Pearl as a wardrobe without doors. At the nearest end were garments for men; further away, a smaller section for women. On the opposite side of the room were racks of boots and shoes, beyond that, a raised platform in front of a free-standing three-panel mirror with light bulbs on either side. There were also two curtained cubicles. This, Pearl thought, as she admired the set-up, must be similar to the wardrobe of a theatre.

Miss Passmore, having determined from the nurse's measurements that Pearl fell between two sizes, had given her two of everything to determine the best fit: trousers, shirt, jacket, overcoat. Then a sturdy pair of shoes and a cap. The number of garments was almost more than Pearl had ever owned at one time — far more than she currently had to her name. And when she came out of the little changing cubicle, and Miss Passmore instructed her to stand on the dais, Pearl had to withhold a gasp of delight. Her reflection looked so modern, so svelte and polished, the white shirt collar and dark jacket bringing a sharpness to the rich red of her hair.

'I don't often say this, miss, but that outfit was made for you.'

Pearl grinned. 'Never thought it would be so stylish.'

'Let me have a quick look at the waistband, though. Don't want it slicing you in half all day long, do we?'

Eventually satisfied that the various garments would serve Pearl well, Miss Passmore folded everything except the overcoat into a neat pile, which she tied with string. 'All this is your responsibility now. Minor repairs are down to you. More major mishaps you can bring to me. But constantly needing replacements goes against your record, you know, and could, in the end, cost you your job.'

'Oh, don't you worry about that,' Pearl said, draping the coat over her arm and accepting the bundle. 'I take real good care of my clothes.'

'Make sure you do. Now, since you're here, Staff Superintendent Kelland wants to see you.' At this news, Pearl tensed. Hopefully it wasn't because he'd discovered something awful about her. 'Come with me and I'll show you where to go.'

Staff Superintendent Kelland met her with a smile. 'All kitted out, I see.'

'Yes.' On his desk Pearl could see a file – *her* file, she presumed. For some reason, the sight of it brought a prickle of guilt.

'Firstly, since I knew you were coming in today, I saw no point in posting your letter of appointment. So, here it is.'

Printed in green on the top left-hand corner of the cream envelope were the words 'City & District Motor Services Ltd'; in the middle was typewritten her name. She'd never received anything so official looking. Well, unless she counted her ID card or her ration book.

Looking back up, she smiled. 'Thank you.'

'The only other outstanding item is your birth certi-ficate.'

Her birth certificate? 'Oh.'

'Purely to make sure everything's in order.'

'I… don't have it anymore.' When Staff Superin-tendent Kelland frowned, she hurried to add, 'Mum used to keep it in her wooden box, which was lost in the air raids, along with everything else we owned. The whole lot of it was reduced to rubble and ash.' It was noticing the distinct lack of sympathy in the superintendent's expres-sion that gave her an idea. 'It was one of the reasons I so badly wanted this job.'

'Forgive me, Miss Warren, but I don't follow.'

'I wanted to show Jerry that 'though he might have flattened our city and our homes, he hasn't destroyed our decent way of life. He hasn't broken us. We'll carry on. Be even more determined to defeat him and his evil.' Deciding she'd said enough, she met his gaze. 'Sorry,' she mumbled, adopting the appearance of contrition. 'But what he's doing to innocent people makes my blood boil.'

'Perhaps your birth certificate can wait. I'll make a note on your file to the effect that once everything is back to normal, you'll obtain a replacement.'

The wave of relief she felt was more muted than she would have liked. But at least she'd bought herself time to work out how to handle having lied about her age.

'Oh, yes, thank you. I will.'

'Well then, congratulations again on becoming a member of City & District. I'll see you on Monday, nine o'clock sharp.'

'Yes, sir.'

Once outside, Pearl walked sedately around the corner and kept going until she was out of sight of the entrance. Then, with her brand-new overcoat draped over her shoulders, her uniform bundle pressed to her body, with some difficulty, she tore open the envelope and pulled out the letter, her eyes running swiftly over the words.

She'd done it. She had a job with a wage that would allow her to rent lodgings somewhere. She would be independent, beholden to no one, free to live as she saw fit. She also now had a reserved occupation, which put her beyond call up for war work. She still had her dream, of course. Wartime or no, it was still her intention to escape the mundane for a glittering life on the stage. And yes, she knew it might take a while; she was nothing if not practical. But, today, she had moved one step closer to bringing it about. All she had to do before she could forget everything that had gone before, and take the next step towards being on the stage, was to somehow break her news to Clemmie…

Chapter 4

'Right, then, ladies. Your attention please for roll call.'

The girl to Pearl's left sat up straight. 'Here we go.'

When she had been shown into the training room and found it empty, Pearl had taken a seat at the end of the row of four desks feeling as though she was back at school. But the woman who had arrived next was clearly no schoolgirl. A quick glance to her now, seated at the far end, suggested she had to be at least thirty.

'Mrs Kathleen Fry.'

'Um… yes. Here.'

'Miss Edie Long.'

'That's me,' the girl next to Pearl hissed. 'Here, sir.'

'Miss Margery Seymour.'

The response this time was barely audible. 'Here.'

'And last but by no means least, Miss Pearl Warren.'

'Here.'

Trying to get comfortable, Pearl shifted on her wooden chair. Her new shoes were pinching her toes. And on the walk to the bus depot, the right one had rubbed her heel. She could only hope they softened up. When she took them off tonight, she would have to try and find some newspaper to stuff in the toes. For now, though, she had no choice but to grin and bear it.

'Very good, ladies. Now, as you already know, I am Staff Superintendent Kelland, and I am responsible for your training – for turning each of you into what most passengers would consider to be the face of City & District Motor Services. And by that, I mean a smartly attired, knowledgeable, and proficient conductress on one of our routes. During the period of your training, I shall address you as Miss or Mrs, and you will address me as Staff Superintendent – not "Sir" nor "Mr Kelland". That directive will continue to apply whether we are on board a bus, here in the classroom, or anywhere else within working hours. Please refrain from calling me "Staff" or "Super", as you might hear some of your more established colleagues refer to me. Everyone clear?' When four heads nodded, their instructor continued, 'Right, then since you have a lot to learn, let's get started.'

'Eyes down, look in.'

Pearl grimaced. If Edie Long wanted to lark about, that was up to her. For her own part, she was going to listen carefully.

'On the desk in front of you is an exercise book. It is there for you to note down the various steps in the procedures I shall demonstrate. By the end of this week, I guarantee you will not need to refer back to it, such will be the rigour with which you will practise. In the short term, however, you might like to jot down certain points as an aide-memoire.'

'A what?' hissed Edie.

'A reminder,' Pearl whispered back.

'Miss Warren, do you have a question?'

Pearl blushed. 'No, Staff Superintendent. Miss Long was asking me about the meaning of—'

'Aide-memoire?'

Pearl nodded. 'Yes, sir – I mean, Staff Superintendent.'

'And were you able to answer her?'

Pearl grew hot. 'I was.'

'Very well. But in future, Miss Long, if you do not understand something I say, please raise your hand and address your question to me. Miss Warren will not wish to be distracted. Moving on. This morning, we will learn how to punch a ticket.'

Relieved that Edie had been put right, Pearl picked up the lethally sharp pencil in front of her on the desk, opened her notebook, and wrote *How to Punch a Ticket*. From the corner of her eye, she saw Edie open her own notebook, glance across, and then proceed to write exactly the same thing, enunciating under her breath as she did so.

'How... to punch... a... tick... et.'

When Pearl cast her eyes over Edie's rounded writing, it was to see that she had spelled the last word 'tiket'. Tomorrow, she would try to sit next to someone else.

'First, I shall demonstrate how it is done, and then I shall call upon each of you in turn to try for yourself.' Pearl straightened up and watched. 'So, you take the strap. Pass it over your head so that it sits on your shoulder like so. By the adjustment of this buckle here, it can be made shorter or longer for your comfort. This piece of metal here, is called the plate, which needs to rest against the front of your body, like so.' In her notebook, Pearl wrote the words 'strap', 'buckle to adjust', and 'plate'. Beside her, Edie grabbed her pencil and did the same. 'Your punch,' the superintendent resumed, picking up a small metal box, 'slots onto the plate like this. At first it might seem quite heavy, but you'll quickly become accustomed to it. Adjusting the strap to vary where it hangs against your body will assist in that regard. Next, we need our ticket rack.' From the table in front of him, Staff Superintendent

Kelland lifted a wooden rack filled with tickets. 'Note how the tickets are different colours. Can anyone tell me what the colours denote?'

Margery raised her hand. 'The different prices of the fares.'

'Correct, Miss Seymour. The tickets are colour-coded to a specific value. Later, we will note down what those values are and how you determine where on the ticket to punch. But first we need to get to grips with holding the rack in one hand while punching with the other. Watch carefully what I do: ticket rack in the left hand, like so; with your right hand, remove the appropriate ticket from the rack, slot it in here like this, and give it a nice crisp punch down. A successful punch will bring a "ting" from the bell.' It looked, Pearl thought, straightforward enough. 'Mrs Fry, please come up.' Kathleen Fry got to her feet. 'No need to look so scared, I don't bite. And neither will the machine.'

Edie giggled. 'I should hope not. I only got five fingers on each hand.'

Actually, Pearl thought, you've only got *four* fingers. The other's a thumb.

In turn, each woman put on the strap, attached the punch, and perfected the art of making a hole in a ticket plucked from the rack. To Pearl's surprise, Edie was the one who took to it the quickest. *Large hands*, she thought, studying the size of them as Edie returned to her desk. For her own part, she found using her left hand to hold the rack trickier than she'd been expecting. It was a cumbersome thing that could have done with rounded edges rather than square ones.

'That's it,' Staff Superintendent Kelland offered encouragingly. 'Once you become proficient, you'll find yourself balancing the weight without a second thought.'

Their first attempts complete, they each had a second turn but, to her dismay, Pearl felt as though she was the one struggling most and was glad when they sat down to be shown something else.

'Good fun, isn't it?' Edie remarked when, a little after midday, the four of them were seated in the staff canteen.

Swallowing a mouthful of Woolton Pie, Pearl nodded. 'Not too bad so far.'

'What I can't seem to do,' Kathleen Fry said, leaning across the table to confide, 'is keep firm hold of the rack *and* punch the ticket. I know it's not difficult, but I seem to be all fingers and thumbs. I could hear Staff Superintendent Kelland tutting.'

'Oh, I'm sure he wasn't,' Pearl attempted to reassure her.

'I'm lucky, see,' Edie said. Setting her knife and fork on her plate, she held out her hands and spread her fingers. 'Big hands.'

Pearl tried not to laugh. Edie's hands truly were enormous. 'Where did you work before?'

'Granfer were a greengrocer. Quicke's on John Street. My cousin, Denny, left school and went to work for him. Then, couple of years back, he went in the navy. I was only kicking my heels at home and so I said I'd take his place, stopping with Granfer in his little flat up top. I did a bit of everything – serving in the shop, going up the wholesalers. It was lifting all of them crates an' sacks that gave me such long fingers.' Again, she splayed them in front of her.

Pearl's eyes went immediately to the calluses. An entire tub of Pond's would struggle to get that pair of hands looking decent again. 'Were you bombed out?' she asked.

'Yeah. You?'

'Yes.'

'Living back at me mum's now.'

'What did *you* do before?' Kathleen looked at Pearl to enquire.

'I was an usherette at the Plaza.'

Edie's eyes lit up. 'Cor, lucky you, getting to see all the films for free.'

'It was a perk, all right,' Pearl agreed. 'What about you, Mrs Fry? Where were you?' Of her three colleagues, Kathleen Fry was the one who intrigued her the most.

'Oh, for goodness' sake, call me Kath.'

'All right. Kath.'

'I was a housewife.' In that instant, Pearl hoped Kath wasn't about to say she was here because she'd been widowed. 'This is the first time I've been out to work since I married, obviously. But after Les got called up – that's Leslie, my husband – I didn't know what to do with myself. You see, we don't have children yet. When I wrote and asked Les if he'd mind if I got a little job, he wrote straight back and said he thought it a good idea. Apparently, his mum had written to him saying that, up in London, a niece of hers has recently gone on the buses. He said why didn't I see if I could do the same here. To be honest, with so many roads still closed after the raids, I didn't think the bus company would need anyone. And now I'm here, I'm not sure I'm going to be any good at it anyway. I mean, I've never done anything like it. I couldn't even get the ticket punched first time round. And as for those fare boards he said we're going to be learning this afternoon, well, even just looking at one gives me the willies. I never was quick at anything to do with numbers.'

'It's not the *numbers* that bother me,' Edie chipped in. 'I can add up quick as you like in here—' with her long forefinger, Edie tapped her temple '—it's the words what give me the trouble. "Edie could not spell to save her life," that's what the headmaster told me mum.'

'I think you'll be fine, Kath,' Pearl said. 'The staff superintendent obviously thinks you're capable, or he wouldn't have taken you on. And he does seem to explain things real careful.'

Kath looked unconvinced. 'Suppose.'

'What about you, Margery?' Having noticed how the fourth member of their little group barely spoke, Pearl was hoping to draw her in. 'What did *you* do before?'

'Oh. Well. When we had those air raids, I hadn't long finished secretarial college – had barely been presented with my certificates. I got passes in shorthand, typing, and bookkeeping. I had two interviews lined up. I'd even saved enough clothing coupons for a new blouse to wear for them. But then both of the companies were bombed out. At home, there's only Dad and me. And after all the scrimping and going without he did for me to go to college in the first place, I couldn't have it on my conscience to not go out and earn a wage, you know, pay my way. But nor could I bear the idea of joining one of the services and leaving him on his own. It seemed no way to repay him. So, when I saw the advertisement for this, and realised I could continue to live at home, I applied.'

'And here you are.'

'Yes.'

'What do you think of it so far?' Kath asked.

'There's quite a lot to it, isn't there?'

'I saw you scribbling away,' Edie said.

'It's the shorthand,' Margery said. 'Can't help myself. Someone starts talking and all I can think is how I would write down what they're saying.'

'Good practice, I should think,' Pearl observed with a smile before going on. 'You know what, I think I'll go and get a pudding. Strikes me I might need one to get me through the afternoon. Besides, I can't recall the last time I saw Manchester Tart.' She glanced at the clock. 'Just about got time to wolf it down.'

A little while later, back at their desks in the training room, the girls were each presented with a fare board and shown how to follow the columns and rows to work out a fare. To her relief, Pearl found it straightforward. As did Edie and Margery. But poor Kath couldn't seem to grasp it. She had, Pearl suspected, worked herself into such a tizzy about it beforehand, she was in too much of a panic to think straight.

Halfway through the afternoon, the class was given ten minutes to stretch their legs. And when they returned, it was to find that upon each desk sat a strap, a ticket rack, a punch and a fare board.

'Right,' Staff Superintendent Kelland said as the women took their seats. 'On your desk is everything you need to punch a fare. Please stand up and put on your equipment.' After a few minutes of fiddling, the women were stood ready. 'For the purpose of this first exercise, all of your imaginary passengers alighted at the first stop on your route.' Pearl smiled. *If only life were so simple.* 'One by one, I will give you a destination and, from that start point, I want you to work out the fare and correctly punch the ticket. When you're done, please hold out your ticket for inspection.'

When they'd punched what felt to be two dozen fares, most of them accurately, Pearl was astonished to find that it was five o'clock.

'That were fun,' Edie whispered as they were extricating themselves from their equipment.

'You did well,' Pearl replied. 'Only one wrong.'

'Yeah. An' I'm dead cross about that.'

She knew what Edie meant. She'd got one wrong, herself, too.

'Now, before we close for today, have you all noted down the colour code for the tickets?' When the women nodded, Staff Superintendent Kelland went on, 'Good, because tonight you have homework.' As though she was back in school, Edie groaned. Having apparently already got the measure of her, the superintendent went swiftly on. 'I want each of you to commit to memory the colour for each fare. When you come in tomorrow, we will start with a little test. By the end of the week, you must be able to pluck a ticket from your rack without the need to think about it. Tomorrow morning, I want you to be able to answer me with the same speed and accuracy as you would give me your date of birth or your address. Everyone clear?'

Everyone nodded.

On her way back to the rest centre a while later, Pearl felt like skipping. First thing this morning, she hadn't had a clue what to expect. But, once they'd got underway, and the butterflies in her stomach had settled, she'd found learning enjoyable. Hopefully, come Friday, she'd still feel the same way. She was also enjoying how, striding down the street in her dark worsted uniform, she was turning heads – a surprising number of them, actually.

Yes, she had a good feeling about this job. And now that Clemmie had been offered lodgings with the woman with whom she had taken to volunteering at the WVS, she had no need to feel guilty about leaving the poor girl behind. Once she passed her assessment – which she was already sure she would – then she would be able to find a place of her own. When she had that, and a pay packet each week, she would be free to turn her attention to her true aim in life: being on the big screen. Or at least, on the stage.

Really, Pearl supposed, as she continued striding confidently along, achieving a dream had a lot in common with making a bus journey: know where you want to go; work out which route will get you there with as few changes as possible and then, no matter how many other passengers board or alight along the way – or the distractions you might glimpse through the window – do not, *under any circumstances*, get off the bus until you've reached where you wanted to go.

Chapter 5

The remainder of Pearl's training course flew. By the end, she and her fellow trainees could calculate fares, accurately punch tickets, and list and use the various items of paraphernalia required while on duty. They had been taken down to the bus garage, where they had practised turning the front and rear blinds of a bus to show the correct destination, had practised trotting up and down the stairs with only one free hand, and had committed to memory how many times to ring the bell to signal to the driver: a single press when a passenger wanted the next stop; twice to communicate that the driver was clear to move off; three rings to indicate that the bus was full. They knew where to collect their ticket boxes from the cash office; how to reconcile takings and tickets at the end of the day; how to complete their waybill. This last task had caused poor Kath no end of difficulty, but she'd got there in the end. They'd also been shown how to handle difficult passengers and spot those trying to skip paying their fare.

'All that remains,' Staff Superintendent Kelland announced late on the Friday afternoon, 'is for me to inform each of you to which Inspector Conductor and route you have been assigned for next week when you will be out on the road.'

Pearl and Edie exchanged grins.

'I'm going to miss this,' Edie whispered. 'Being here with you three.'

Pearl knew what she meant. Having shared the ups and downs in the classroom, she'd come to feel genuine affection for her three colleagues. But, from now on, she would rarely see them, perhaps only when their meal breaks in the canteen happened to coincide.

'Me too,' she whispered back.

'Do you think we'll all pass?'

Pearl nodded. 'Bound to. Even Kath's found her feet. I'm sure we'll all be fine.'

Come Monday morning, though, when Pearl arrived at the bus depot and went to sign for her ticket box, she was trembling so much she could barely hold the pen.

'Check I've given you the right one,' the clerk behind the counter prompted her.

She checked the label on the end of the box to her lapel badge: F00107. 'It's the right one.'

''Course it is,' the clerk replied with a broad grin. 'But don't never assume.'

She smiled back at him. 'Thanks. I won't.'

'That's your Inspector Redway over there.'

She turned to where the clerk had nodded his head. 'Is he… nice?'

'All round good bloke. Son's a driver here.'

She moved aside from the counter, got herself set up with her punch and ticket rack, put her float into the pouch of her leather conductor's bag, checked she had everything she needed, and returned her box. Now to go and introduce herself.

'Conductor Inspector Redway?'

'That's right.'

She held out her hand. 'I'm Trainee Conductress Warren.'

'Pleased to meet you. Won't have a problem spotting *you* on a crowded bus, will I?' When she frowned, the inspector indicated her head. 'Not many folk with hair that colour.'

She smiled. 'No, I do stand out.'

'Right, well, come on then. Your driver's Reg Cudmore. You'll be in safe hands with him. He's been driving buses since before you were born.'

But that, Pearl realised, wasn't as long as he thought. 'Right.'

'He knows down to the second what time to pull out of this garage and be on the dot for the first stop.'

Slowly, Pearl relaxed. Everyone always said it was good to be a little bit nervous, but she wasn't so sure. She could do without everything she'd spent the last two weeks cramming into her head flying out of it the moment she had a real passenger in front of her.

When they reached the bus, Reg Cudmore sent her a wink, nodded to the inspector, and went around to climb in behind the wheel. Remembering the blind, she went to the front and peered up. Reg had already wound it to the correct destination. She walked around to the rear; that was correct, too.

Stepping up onto the platform, she said to her inspector, 'Blinds showing correct destination.'

'Very well.'

With a quick check in all directions, she reached for the bell. *Two presses; move off.* So far so good.

'Will the route be busy?' she asked, holding tightly to the pole as the bus pulled out of the garage and turned to the right.

'Until a few months back, Monday mornings were always busy,' Inspector Redway replied. 'Since those air raids closed so many roads, though, there's been fewer people travelling, the routes reduced accordingly. Starting to build up a bit again now, though. But this particular route shouldn't be too bad. Staff Super tries to break you in easy. In any case, first hour or so, I'll be watching your every step. After that, if you seem up to the mark, I'll back off a little, watch from a distance.'

With that, they pulled up to their first stop and three people boarded. Pausing to make sure they had tight hold, she gave two presses of the bell. And as the bus lumbered away, she cleared her throat and made her way towards her first passenger. 'Fares, please.'

'St James,' the elderly man said and handed her a couple of coins.

She checked the fare – penny ha'penny – slipped his coins into her pouch, pulled the ticket from the rack and punched the destination. *Ting.* Her first fare-paying passenger.

'Good morning,' she said to a woman already proffering her fare.

'Reading Road, love.'

She handed the woman her ticket. 'Thank you.'

'Barracks, please,' the next said.

'Tuppence change,' she said, handing him the coins and his ticket.

The man looked back at her. He was a smartly dressed older man, and when he'd got on, she'd noticed his limp. 'First day out, love?'

She nodded. 'Is it that obvious?'

'No, love, you're doing all right. It's just that if I'd seen that hair before, I'm fair certain I wouldn't have forgotten it.'

The bus stopped again; five people got on, three of whom went upstairs. She'd barely dealt with the first two when the bus stopped again, and four more got on. She was going to have to hurry up. As she trotted upstairs, she noticed the first woman passenger from downstairs get to her feet.

She reached to press the bell and heard the *ding*. Thankfully, when the bus drew to a halt and the passenger disembarked, no one was waiting to get on; she could finish collecting fares on the top deck.

'Barracks, please.'

It was then she noticed that the bus hadn't pulled away. Frantically, she reached to press the nearest bell. *Ding ding.*

'You're the one in charge of the bus, Trainee Conductress Warren.'

'Sorry,' she said to Inspector Redway, her insides squirming, her face burning with embarrassment. 'Yes. I know that.'

Thankfully, the inspector was smiling. 'Happens to everyone, first time out.'

Having collected all of the fares on the upper deck, she went back downstairs, relieved to remember which of her passengers had already paid. The bus stopped again; another two passengers got on, both starting up the stairs. *Bother these people, why couldn't they all sit in the same place? Ding ding.* At least this time, she'd remembered the bell.

The man who'd asked for St James made to get up. Realising she had no idea where they were, she ducked her head and glanced through the front window; the church of St James was ahead on the left. She stabbed the bell. *Ding.* She collected the fares from the newcomers. A new gentleman with a furled umbrella climbed aboard. *Ding ding.* Wishing he'd get a move on, she followed him up the stairs; three to collect, none of whom had the exact fare. She glimpsed the barracks ahead and stabbed the bell; at least two fares had asked for this stop. At the barracks, two more got on. *Ding ding.* She dived between them. 'Thank you.' *Ting.* 'Thank you, sir.' *Ting.*

At the traffic lights, she went down and stood on the rear platform. 'Golly,' she remarked, taking a chance to draw a breath of fresh air; the upper deck was already blue with cigarette smoke. 'And this isn't busy?' she said to her inspector.

'For this time in the morning, I'd say this is normal. But you're doing all right.'

She grinned. 'Apart from forgetting the bell.'

He grinned back. 'But you've remembered it every time since, haven't you? And you haven't forgotten which of the passengers have yet to pay. For a first day out, you're doing very well. Some trainees simply can't seem to remember a face – who's paid and who hasn't, and I have to prompt them over and over. It's not a skill you can teach, memory.'

'And you can't practise it in the classroom either,' Pearl said as the realisation dawned.

'You can't.'

The bus pulled away and, for Pearl, it was more of the same until, eventually, they reached the terminus for their route, the remaining few passengers disembarking and the bus's engine rattling to a halt. From the cab, her driver, Reg, jumped down and came around to the platform.

'How was that, then, maid?'

Largely from relief, Pearl laughed. 'Non-stop. Sorry about the bell back at the beginning.'

Reg shrugged. 'You're new. By the time we get back to the depot, it'll be second nature. You'll be pressing that bell in your sleep.'

She didn't doubt it. 'How long until we set off again?'

Signalling to Reg not to answer, Inspector Redway said, 'Check your schedule.'

Pearl tutted. Of course. She knew that. 'Yes.' Pulling the schedule from her bag, she scanned the timetable. 'Nine thirty-five.' She pushed back the cuff of her jacket and examined her wristwatch. 'Five minutes.'

'Correct.'

'Did I really do all right?' she asked. Seeing the look on the inspector's face, she went on, 'I'm not fishing for compliments or anything, but Staff Superintendent Kelland never told us how many times a trainee can do something wrong before falling short of the mark, you know, when it eventually comes to the assessment.'

'Bert Kelland's a good instructor. But there's no substitute for getting on a bus and having a go. Today and tomorrow, you'll make mistakes. You're not a machine. The thing to do is to learn from them. By Wednesday, you'll probably have made every error in the book at least once. Then you'll get into your stride, things like the bell will be second nature. You'll be quicker with punching, and more assured with reckoning change. You'll come to know the route, and have time to look out of the window to see where you are and know which stops are coming up next, as well as which stops are likely to be busy, and which are less so. It's why you spend so long out here with an inspector – to properly get to grips with everything, experience all there is to come up against, the best and worst of human nature.'

'Crikey,' she said, 'you make it sound like a battle.'

He grinned. 'Some days, peak times, when it's wet or freezing, when there's been a prang, or when some other jam leaves you sitting in a snarl up and behind for the rest of your run, you'll get the short end of everyone's temper, even though you're the last person at fault. Ain't that right, Reg?'

'*I'm* all right,' Reg replied with a laugh, 'I'm shut in my cab. But I see it all going on. And yes, some days the conductor can't wait to be back at the depot, young clippies like you, especially.'

'Hm.' She hoped they were exaggerating but suspected they weren't.

'Thing is, love,' Reg went on, stubbing out his cigarette under the toe of his boot, 'next time you're in the canteen, take a look around you. You'll see chaps who started on the buses the moment they were old enough and are still here now, trying not to count the years until they have to hang up their punch and spend their days trying not to get under their wife's feet. You're out on the road. You're in charge of the bus. You meet folks from all walks of life. And no two days are the same. Can't say that of all jobs now, can you?'

Pearl smiled. 'I suppose not.' No need to add that she had no intention of doing this forever more. To be fair, it had to be different for a man.

'Right then, let's turn the old girl around and point her in the direction of home.'

'I'll see to the blinds,' she said, anxious to demonstrate that she didn't need a reminder.

'Right you are, maid. Let's get back for a nice cuppa.'

Pearl yawned. It was her last day as a trainee conductor – well, at least, she hoped it was – because, this morning, she had her assessment. Pass that, and from Monday she would be taking the bus out on her own, just her and her driver. Did she feel ready for it? She supposed the fact that Inspector Redway had spent pretty much the whole of the last week riding on the platform and talking to passengers meant he'd felt confident he wouldn't need to assist or intervene. But if that was true then why, last night, had she struggled more than usual to get to sleep? And why, once she had finally nodded off, had she kept waking up? There was no reason for today to be any different from those that had gone before; realistically, she was unlikely to meet a challenge she wasn't up to. She'd certainly had her fair share of contrary passengers in the last few days, including one who had left behind an entire bag of groceries. Still, as Inspector Redway had said at the time, at least she now knew how to register lost property.

Hearing footsteps, she looked up; the driver coming towards the bus was Reg. She hadn't seen him for a day or two and was comforted to realise she would be making such an important run with someone familiar.

'Morning, maid.'

She returned his greeting. 'Morning, Reg. How are you?'

'Just dandy, love. Your big day, today.'

She raised her eyebrows. If people didn't keep drawing attention to the fact, she might not be so nervous. 'It is.'

Reg straightened his cap. 'Well, by all accounts, you've nothing to worry about. I overheard Inspector Redway saying you'll sail through.'

'Hm.' She wished he hadn't told her that. The only thing Inspector Redway had said to her yesterday afternoon, when they'd got back from their final run, was 'Just remember everything you've learned.' Something a little more encouraging wouldn't have gone amiss.

'Anyway, here's your inspector.'

When Pearl looked across, she frowned. Where was Inspector Redway? Was she to have a different inspector – today, of all days?

'Good morning,' the older man greeted her. 'I'm Conductor Inspector Bamfield.'

Forcing herself to stop frowning, she shook his hand, noticing as she did so that, tucked under his arm, he had a clipboard. 'Good morning, Inspector Bamfield.'

'Trainee Conductress Warren.' He peered at her lapel badge. 'F00107.'

'Correct.'

'This morning, I shall be carrying out an assessment as to your suitability for the permanent role of conductress with City & District Motor Services.'

She nodded. 'Yes.'

'At times, I shall observe from the platform. At others, I shall shadow you along the aisle. Carry out your duties as though I am not there. Should any passenger ask you who I am, tell them only that I am an inspector and that my presence today is routine.'

'Routine. Right.'

'To pass today's assessment, you do not have to complete a one hundred per cent fault free run. Everyone has the odd sticky moment – has need to consult their fare board, drops a coin, has a passenger ask them a question to which you could not be expected to know the answer. On one assessment I conducted, a passenger asked the conductor whether it was possible to go into the cathedral for a look around, or whether they could only go in if they were attending a service. The conductor in question thought he would be marked down for not knowing the answer.'

'Oh.'

'Now, is there anything you would like to ask me before I watch you complete your pre-departure checks?'

'Actually, yes.'

'Fire away, Trainee Warren.'

'Will you be assessing me on the whole run – there and back?'

'On this particular run, I am only required to assess you on the way out, followed by your cashing out procedure back at the garage. The ride back is just for fun.' Pearl smiled; fun for him, maybe. 'That said, should your run out be a marginal fail, I do have the option to continue to observe you on the return. The company very much wants you to pass and will give you every opportunity to do so. If your trainee inspector had doubts about your ability to pass, he would have reported as much to Staff Superintendent Kelland such that, this morning, rather than undergoing assessment, you would be back in the classroom.'

The news brought Pearl a modicum of relief. 'And when do you tell me how I've done?'

'As soon as we are safely back in the garage, and you have correctly tallied your waybill.'

'Thank you. It helps to know that.'

Inspector Bamfield peered across to the garage clock. 'Very well. From where does our route this morning commence, and at what time should it depart therefrom?'

'Our route is on diversion at the moment due to its normal start being closed on account of bomb damage. Our temporary start is at the railway station on Queen's Street. Our scheduled departure from there is at ten past nine.'

'Very well then. Carry on.'

'First I need to check the blinds.' He gestured her ahead of him before following her to the front of the bus and then to the rear. 'Then I usually pop up to the top deck to check there's nothing or no one up there that shouldn't be. While I'm there, I also open a couple of windows for the fresh air. I know that last thing isn't in the manual, but it can get stale up there real quick, and I don't think it's nice for the passengers who don't smoke. People are free to close the window if they're in a draught.'

'And then?'

'Then I usually peek into my bag to be doubly certain I've got everything, check the time, peer through to see that Reg – I mean, that my driver – is ready to depart, and then signal him to proceed.'

'Go ahead.'

With a discreet glance at her watch – if she wasn't careful, her eagerness to be thorough would make them late – she trotted up the staircase, checked between the seats as she passed along the aisle, leaned across to open a couple of windows and returned sedately to the lower deck. Then she bent to peer at Reg, saw him give her a thumbs up, and gave two presses of the bell. Well, this was it, she thought, as they trundled out of the garage. There was nothing she could do now except her job – and pray for an uneventful run.

As it turned out, most of her passengers were regulars; many of them with the exact fare ready in their hand.

Most said thank you without even looking directly at her. She greeted everyone with a 'Good morning', dealt speedily with their ticket and their change, and thanked them before moving on. By the time they'd made seven or eight stops, the bus was two-thirds full, but she knew by remembering people's jackets and hats or their hair who had paid, and from whom she still had to collect. Passengers boarded and alighted. She smiled at everyone regardless, assisted the elderly or the infirm, and politely directed a man with a cigarette to the top deck when he started along the downstairs aisle.

'You may smoke on the top deck, sir, or you may extinguish your cigarette and remain down here.' When he'd turned for the stairs, she thanked him and followed him up to issue his ticket.

At the termination of their route, she waited for the last passenger to disembark and then went straight to change the front blind.

'How did it go?' Reg asked as she was winding the handle.

'All right, I think,' she whispered back, anxious not to tempt fate. 'Nothing out of the ordinary.'

'Well, if he stays on the platform all the way back, you'll know you've passed.'

'I've only passed if my waybill tallies.'

'Has it ever been wrong?'

'Don't jinx it,' she said, wagging a finger at him. 'There's always a first time.'

Back at the depot later, her waybill in order, she went to the cash office.

'How did it go?' the clerk she had come to know as Cyril enquired.

She angled her head. 'Well, I'm about to find out, aren't I?'

'Good luck, love.'

When she left the counter, Inspector Bamfield went to stand in her place and watch while Cyril counted her cash and checked her paperwork. Unable to bear the wait to find out whether she'd passed, she wandered away. Surely, if she had failed, he wouldn't bother with her waybill, he would simply tell her what she had done wrong.

'Miss Warren?'

She turned sharply. 'Yes?'

'I'm pleased to inform you that you have passed.' For Pearl, it was as much as she could do not to hug the man. 'That was a faultless run. The perfect balance of efficiency and courtesy. Well done. As a result, your afternoon is your own. Check with the office before you leave, and they will advise you what time to report on Monday morning, when they will also have your employee pass for you. Staff Superintendent Kelland will instruct Personnel to write to you confirming that the terms of your contract are now permanent. Congratulations. And keep up the good work.'

'No need to ask how you did,' Reg said when she went back to the garage and discovered him leaning against the side of their bus. 'I can tell from that grin.'

'I did it,' she said with an enormous sigh of relief. 'I'm officially a conductress.'

'Off to celebrate?'

Her grin softened. Celebrate. Yes, she supposed some trainees would head out for a knees-up. But she had other plans. And the first of those involved going straight upstairs and asking to see someone from Personnel in order to request their help with finding somewhere to live. Get that sorted out, and then perhaps she really *would* feel like celebrating.

Chapter 6

'Good morning, Mrs Trude.'

'Huh. Blowed if I know what's good about it. Not unless, sometime last night, Germany surrendered, and nobody saw fit to tell me.'

'Well, if they did,' Pearl replied brightly as she reached the top of the basement stairs to arrive in the hallway, 'nobody thought to tell me, either. But the sky is blue, and the sun is shining, so I suppose that's something.'

'I'll give you *sun shining*. How many times have I told you not to clomp up and down those stairs like a ruddy cart horse.'

Sending her landlady a deliberately warm smile, Pearl leaned towards the mottled mirror on the wall beside the coat stand and adjusted the angle of her cap 'Sorry.' *You old witch.*

'Not everyone wants to be woken up at this ungodly hour. And for heaven's sake mind you don't slam that door on the way out.'

'Always try not to, Mrs Trude. See you later.'

'Hmmph.'

Knowing precisely what Mrs Trude would say next, Pearl took extra care closing the rickety front door while mouthing in time to the anticipated complaint: *Not if I can help it.* She truly was a miserable woman, a trait that was evident even before she opened her mouth to

63

speak, her lips invariably set in a hard and disapproving line. But Pearl didn't care; finally, she had a place to live, and it could scarcely be more convenient for work. That Mrs Trude had told the bus company she could provide neither breakfast nor supper for someone who worked such varied shifts, hadn't bothered Pearl in the least; she enjoyed going into work early to sit, nursing a mug of tea while chomping her way through two doorsteps of toast and marge, spread with whatever jam or savoury paste was to be had. As well as providing her with sustenance to last until her next break, it gave her the chance to get to know her fellow conductors and drivers.

Occasionally, she would be clocking on at the same time as Edie or Margery or Kath. By Kath's own admission, her assessment had been a close-run thing, her nerves on the day in question so jittery that, if it had been possible to mess something up, she had. Even her waybill hadn't tallied.

'Cyril had to take it off me,' Kath had explained over a cup of tea one morning shortly afterwards. 'Even then, I was tuppence short. Anyway, thank my lucky stars, I must have caught the inspector on a good day because he said that if I thought I could get a grip on my nerves, we could forget the first run and have another go. So, we did. I walked round the block to clear my head, and off we went all over again. I don't know what happened, but that next run went like a dream. And my waybill tallied straight off. I was so relieved, I can't tell you. I went straight home and wrote to Les. 'Course, I haven't heard back from him yet, but he'll be real proud, I just know it.'

Pearl had been pleased for Kath. It was a shame she didn't see her more often – or Margery or Edie – but, while she sometimes saw them getting ready to go out first thing, she rarely saw them at any other time. There was always someone in the canteen to talk to, though, and the food was pretty good: weekday offerings were usually a stew or pie, apart from Friday, which was always fish. Saturday was often something like bubble and squeak or corned beef hash, which the cooks in the kitchen called 'Use Ups'. Apparently, sometimes on a Saturday, there would even be an egg to go with it – a proper fried egg. Made her mouth water just picturing it. The food in the canteen was certainly better than anything she would have got from Mrs Trude who, judging by the boxes stacked in her lean-to, had some sort of arrangement with the Spam wholesaler.

To say that Pearl loved her job was an understatement. No matter the route, once she stepped aboard her bus, time simply flew; in the odd quiet moment, she would stand and look out at the city and watch the repairs being made to some of the buildings. Not that she had many quiet moments; since she'd passed her assessment, the person who scheduled her shifts had shown her no mercy, rostering her to the busy routes the same as everyone else. The first time she'd had a full bus – necessitating three presses on the bell to signal to her driver not to stop because there was no room – the looks of dismay and despair on the faces of the passengers waiting at the stop as they sailed past made her feel horrible; all those people who would now be late for work.

'Don't think about it,' one of the more senior conductors advised her as they sat chatting in the canteen one afternoon. 'You are the one in charge of the bus and it's your job to follow the rules. Ask yourself this. Which would be worse, feeling mean for leaving folk standing at the bus stop, or finding that, at the next one, there's an inspector waiting to board? If there is, then take it from me, the first thing he'll do is count the standing passengers. And if he finds you above the limit, he would be within his rights to give you a warning. That one moment of kindness could cost you your job in the same way as letting a friend ride for free.'

Pearl knew all of that. But, sometimes, on days when it was raining heavily, if two people got off and the third person in the queue was elderly, or wearing a nurse's uniform or the like, she would let them on, whispering to them as they boarded, *Just this once.* Other conductors, she knew, did the same.

One of the runs she liked best was Alphington to Whipton, partly because Reg often drove that route – given how kind he'd been when she was training, she had a soft spot for him. Another reason she liked the route was because it gave her a rare chance to see beyond the city itself. The open spaces and greenery around the outskirts were welcome sights after the browns and greys of the bomb-damaged buildings in the centre. She also liked the fact that people from the outskirts always seemed friendlier, often recognising her, and asking her how she was. She gradually came to recognise many of them, too.

On one mid-morning run back from Whipton, at the stop known locally as The Barracks, a man in army uniform got on. As he went to go upstairs and Pearl pressed the bell, he turned swiftly about and took a seat on the lower deck instead.

Accustomed to soldiers on her bus, she thought nothing of it and went towards him. 'Fare please.'

The joy in his smile caught her off guard; where he could have made it polite but perfunctory, it was genuinely warm.

'I've seen you before.'

She smiled back. 'I'm often on this route.'

'Couldn't forget that hair.'

Her smile ebbed a little. Remarks about the colour of her hair had already begun to wear thin – admiring or not. 'No one ever does. I'd be hopeless as a spy.'

He pressed his lips together as though trying not to laugh. 'Why?'

Was he simple? 'Like you said, you couldn't forget my hair.'

'So? You could be spying right this very minute, here, on this bus, listening to conversations and reporting back.'

'I don't imagine the powers-that-be are interested in the price of cauliflowers or the taste of margarine these days. Penny ha'penny, please.'

When he gave her the coins, he pressed them unnecessarily firmly into her palm such that she felt the warmth of his fingertips.

'I see you're not married.'

'Nothing wrong with your eyesight, is there? And no, I'm neither married nor looking to be.'

'Do you like music?'

When two women passengers near the front of the bus got to their feet and proceeded to squeeze past her, she reached up and pressed the bell. Waiting until they had alighted, and she had checked there was no one waiting to get on, she pressed it twice again.

'Doesn't everyone?'

'Friday night, I know where there's a band playing. They're top notch.' When she didn't reply, he went on, 'At the old ballroom. Perhaps you'd like to come? I could meet you there... at seven-thirty?'

Crikey, this one was forward. But then put almost any chap in uniform and he immediately thought he was God's gift.

Hearing someone move along the upper deck in the direction of the stairs, she glanced out the window and rang the bell.

To be fair, there was something about this man she liked. His smile? His immaculate appearance? His confidence?

Watching her passenger disembark, she considered his invitation. If she agreed to go, she could meet him there, meaning she didn't have to tell him where she lived. And afterwards, getting home from the old ballroom was something she could do under her own steam.

Onto the rear platform of her bus climbed a mother with three youngsters; the children wanted to go upstairs, the little one starting to wail when the woman caught hold of his wrist and dragged him along to the first available seat.

'Get in there and stop that noise. You too, Alan.' She motioned to the seat in front of her. 'Sit down and don't let me hear so much as a peep from either of you or we won't go to the park.'

Still reflecting upon her passenger's invitation, Pearl went to collect the family's fares. Tickets for one tuppenny and three halves issued, she returned to stand in front of him. 'All right then. Seven-thirty, Friday. Your treat.'

'Naturally.'

'So, what do I call you, then?'

'Sergeant Malcolm Clarke, at your service. More importantly, what do *I* call *you*?'

'You call me Sadie,' she said, borrowing her middle name. 'I'm Sadie Huxford. And you should know that if you're late, I shan't wait.'

'Sadie Huxford, for such beauty I shall be there at least ten minutes early.'

'Good for you.' When the bus pulled up and two men got on, she made to follow them up the stairs. 'Don't miss your stop,' she said over her shoulder as she reached to give two dings of the bell. 'It's this next one.'

Well, there was a nice surprise, she reflected as she paused a moment later to watch Sergeant Malcolm Clarke alight and walk away; her first proper date. Of course, he had no idea she was only sixteen. And she had no intention of letting him find out, either; in her uniform, she could easily pass for nineteen, maybe even twenty. It wasn't as though she proposed getting serious about him, he simply provided the chance for her to go out and have some fun. Oh, and an excuse for a new dress. Well, not a brand-new one, of course – she didn't have the coupons for that. But something hardly worn from that nice little second-hand place down near the Gaumont Palace would do just fine. And, if this first date led to another, then she'd certainly get good value from it, wouldn't she?

Chapter 7

Pearl was surprised by how nervous she felt – and how excited. She'd never been to a ballroom before. But then she'd never been anywhere on a proper date. It wasn't that she'd never been asked – many was the time a man had suggested taking her somewhere. The trouble was, they were usually old enough to be her father; indeed, a horrible number of them had been her father's friends, and of the sort she couldn't get away from fast enough. But there had been a couple of younger fellows; in her usherette's uniform, brown with gold piping and matching pillbox hat, she'd certainly attracted attention, especially when, during the interval, she'd stood, picked out by a spotlight, so that patrons could see where she was selling cigarettes. But looking glamorous had been part of the job; as the Plaza's owner so often reminded them, usherettes were there to make the patrons feel like they were the film stars.

She could always spot the men who fancied their chances. They weren't necessarily showy, nor even particularly confident; they would come to see a film, often with a girlfriend, and then come back a couple of nights later, alone. Or else they would come to the cinema by themselves, perhaps solely to keep warm, fall in love with the leading lady in the feature film and then, in the intermission, feeling love-struck, set their sights upon her instead. Either way, when they reached the front of the queue to buy cigarettes or confectionary – should the manager have been fortunate enough to procure such a luxury – they would whisper something along the lines of: *Has anyone ever said it should be you up there on the screen?* Or *You're so much more beautiful than...* at which point they would name the star of that night's feature. Some would be more direct. *Would you like to go out some time?* Or *Tell me, what do you do on your nights off?* She would always let them down gently, the reply she gave most often being a variation upon *That's really sweet of you, but I'm not allowed to date our patrons.*

Smiling fondly at the recollection, she felt a gust of wind lift the hem of her dress and, as she looked back up from flattening it against her legs, saw Sergeant Malcolm Clarke standing outside the entrance to the ballroom. As good as his word, he was early.

He came towards her.

'Wow. My lucky day. You look a million dollars.'

Lord alive. Would it be mean to tell him she heard such clichés every night of the week? Probably.

'Thank you.'

'That colour really suits you. What would you call it?'

She refrained from shaking her head in dismay. 'Burgundy.'

Her dress, which she'd bought from the second-hand shop, was a simply cut velvet affair with a sweetheart neckline and short sleeves. It had been a thrilling find and she'd known instantly that it would be serviceable for all manner of outings. It was new in, the proprietress had informed her but, at that price, wouldn't be there for long; she'd already had one woman try it on, only to find she couldn't get the zip done up.

71

'It makes you shine like a star,' her date said as he offered his arm. 'Shall we?'

'Please.' If they didn't get out of this wind sharpish, she'd be faced with having to tidy her hair.

Having paid the entrance fee, Sergeant Clarke went ahead of her and pushed open the door to an inner foyer. From beyond it, Pearl could hear music.

'Would you like to dance first or get some refreshments?'

What she really wanted to do was properly size him up, which was going to be tricky if the first thing they did was dance. 'I shouldn't mind a drink.'

'Then let's find somewhere to sit and you can tell me all about Sadie Huxford.'

Pearl withheld a groan. 'All right.' Yes, this one definitely fancied himself as suave.

Once in the ballroom proper, Pearl tried not to show her surprise. For a building that looked so dreary on the outside – the doors and windows boarded up against blasts not helping in that regard – the interior came as an assault on the senses. Around the perimeter of the cavernous room were plush banquettes in a deep red colour; in little groups in front of them, chairs with velvet seats were grouped about tiny circular tables. At the far end, the dance floor terminated at a raised stage, upon which was the band. Comprising ten or twelve musicians, they were playing something jazzy. On the floor, upwards of a dozen couples were dancing, their forms picked out in shafts of light in changing colours. She glanced up, but beyond the beams of light, was as dark as a night sky. From the blackness hung a mirrored globe. Rotating slowly, it seemed to collect the beams of light and scatter them to the four corners like fairy dust being blown from the palm of a hand. The effect was nothing short of magical. Even if it turned out that the best part of this evening was the setting, she would still be glad she'd come.

'How about that one?'

She jolted, having momentarily forgotten her date was there, and raised a smile.

'That looks good.'

Making straight for a table right on the edge of the dance floor, he pulled out a chair and gestured to her to sit down. 'What's your poison?'

Having never been asked before, Pearl tensed. What was the done thing in a place like this? What drinks could she even expect them to have? A glance at the bar suggested there was no shortage of choice.

'Gin and bitter lemon, please.'

'Coming right up.'

Thank goodness for remembering hearing Kath mention going to celebrate passing her assessment by taking the remains of an elderly bottle of Gordon's round to her neighbour's, where she proposed downing a couple of gin and bitter lemons. After quite boldly asking for one, she could only hope now that it would be to her taste. Her mum had never touched alcohol, and Charlie had only ever drunk brown ale. It had been seeing how a nightly excess of it turned him into an ill-tempered brute that had persuaded her to follow in her mother's footsteps and swear off alcohol altogether. But that was when she'd been about fourteen. Now she was older, she supposed it behoved her to develop a taste for something more grown up than orangeade.

In no time at all, her date was back, in one hand a tall glass containing a pale liquid and one of those little sticks

73

for stirring it, in the other, a dumpy glass with two fingers of a liquid the colour of honey.

He raised his glass in her direction. 'To the most exquisite beauty in the room.'

Determining not to let him see her squirm, she gave a polite nod, picked up her own glass, and took a sip. Her first impression was that it tasted quite nice – refreshing – but the longer it was on her tongue, the more she was reminded of pine needles. No, not pine needles: celery. Yes, that was it. While not undrinkable, the flavour was certainly unusual.

Sensing that he was watching her, she took another sip – best to try and appear accustomed.

'So, Sadie Huxford, how long have you been a clippie?'

She didn't like the word 'clippie', never had; it sounded cheap, unlike the name 'conductress', which suggested a more appropriate degree of authority. 'Not long.'

'You seem very proficient.'

'We have to undergo lengthy training, and then pass a test. It's not a job any old Tom, Dick or Harry can show up and do.'

'It most definitely isn't.'

'What about you? How long have you been in the army?' In possession of that fact, she hoped to be able to work out his age.

'A few years.'

Bother: such a vague answer was no help whatsoever. 'What did you do before?'

'I was in the family business.' In the hope he would elaborate, she didn't respond. 'My father sells motor cars. New ones. In west London. Do you know London at all?' She shook her head. 'He has a place in Earl's Court and another a few miles away.'

None of that told her anything about his age.

'Have you been overseas? With the army, I mean?'

'Egypt, mainly. I was there recently.'

She supposed it was where he'd got his tan; Egypt, she seemed to remember from geography lessons, was largely desert. 'Pyramids,' she said without meaning to. *Idiot.*

'That's right. And I shall be returning there very soon.'

Unsure how that made her feel, she nodded. Clearly, then, he didn't envisage a long-term thing with her. And while all she'd been hoping to get out of the evening was some fun, she was surprised to find his disclosure made her feel like a plaything: something to exclaim over while new, play with a few times, then leave on the floor and forget all about. Or tread on and break.

'The band is good,' she raised her voice a little to remark. 'The singer especially.'

'Very easy on the ear.'

'Yes.'

'Would you like to dance? When she starts her next number, I mean?' Perhaps, Pearl thought, in close proximity on the dance floor, he would be more talkative. 'Or would you prefer to wait for something a little less… old-fashioned?'

She shook her head. What little she knew of dance steps came largely from watching the same films, over and over. 'Old-fashioned is fine.'

'Then may I?'

When he held out his hand, she rose to her feet. God, how she wished her fingers would stop trembling; she could do without him knowing she'd only ever danced once or twice.

To her relief, once they were on the floor, he took charge, leaving her little choice about where to put her feet and in which direction to turn. As for the rest of him, well, that remained a puzzle. His build suggested he kept fit, perhaps playing a sport, the shoulders of his uniform fitting squarely, his build stocky but not fat. And although she always seemed to go for film stars who were clean shaven, she would have to concede that his moustache, being exceedingly dark, suited his face. Compared to the pasty locals, his tanned complexion gave him an air of the exotic, as did his cologne, which smelled musky and woody but also summery and fresh. When he addressed her, he didn't sound like an ordinary soldier but someone who knew what he wanted and how to go about getting it; she supposed it came from giving orders. But he wasn't plummy, like the officers in films always seemed to be. And from the way he kept looking at her, she had a feeling he was older than she'd first supposed – could even be well into his thirties. Middle-aged. Well, she wasn't entirely without a sly streak herself.

When the music ended, they applauded politely, but it wasn't until he escorted her back to their table that she realised she knew nothing more about him now than she had before they took to the floor. Regretting that she'd missed her chance, she picked up her glass and took a sip of her drink. She could see how it would be easy to develop a liking for it. At least, in the future, she would be able to ask for one in the knowledge that it wasn't vile.

When the next piece of music ended, a different singer took to the stage. Under the glare of the spotlight, she looked fearfully young – perhaps not even twenty. She also looked nervous. But when the band leader counted her in, and she hit the first note, Pearl's eyes widened in surprise. Her voice was more powerful than seemed right for so slight a creature.

'*She's* good,' she said.

Her date seemed genuine in his agreement. 'Isn't she just.'

'And I love this song.' Beneath the table, she tapped her foot.

'And I see you know all of the words, too.'

Unaware that, as she'd always done in the auditorium of the Plaza, she'd been mouthing the lyrics, she blushed. 'Sorry.'

'Don't be. You're clearly enjoying yourself.'

She wasn't sure, though, that the same could be said of him; at times, he put her in mind of an indulgent uncle taking his niece for an ice on her birthday. It did seem as though the age gap – at least, as she perceived it – was making her behave more like her unworldly half-sister, Clemmie, than the pouting siren she affected to be when she'd donned her usherette's uniform. And she knew which of those had more fun.

'Can we dance again?' she asked, looking up at him through lowered lashes.

She'd caught him off guard.

'To this or the next one?'

She laughed. 'To both.'

'Most definitely.'

'Shall we, then?'

They remained on the floor for so many songs she lost count. In the faster numbers, he cast her away, drew her back, twirled her under his arm until she felt giddy. She had no idea what they were dancing – if, indeed, it had a name – and in the slower numbers, when he pressed his hand into the small of her back, through the fabric of her dress she could feel not only the warmth of his palm but every ridge and button of his uniform. When he pressed

77

his head to the side of hers, she could feel moist breath in her ear, and could smell whisky.

The song ended. Around them, couples left the floor. Keeping hold of her hand, he led her decisively towards their table.

'Do you want the rest of your drink?'

She stared down at her glass. Something in his tone put her on alert. 'In a minute, perhaps.'

When he tugged sharply on her hand, she found herself snapped to his side. When his arm then slid around her waist; she tensed. His lips met the side of her neck; a shiver ran down her spine. 'How about we go somewhere... quiet.'

She fought to conceal concern. 'But I was enjoying dancing.'

His hold on her hand tightened. 'We can still dance.'

When he drew her away from the table and towards the door, her concern deepened. 'Where are we going?'

He strode on. 'I have a key to my brother's rooms. Last I heard, he was with his battalion in Greece.'

'But you said we could still—'

'Dear God, Sadie Huxford. I want you. And from the way you were responding out there—' With his free hand, he gestured back to the dance floor, now brightly illuminated. 'I assumed that's what you wanted, too.'

From the way she'd been dancing with him, he'd made *that* giant leap? Talk about taking two and two and making five. But how to refuse his suggestion without appearing naive? Or, worse, making him cross. 'Well, I—'

Immediately, his manner changed. 'Look, Sadie, I make no apology for being blunt. When a chance comes along, I take it. You're dazzling. Fresh. Different. It's a heady mix... and who among us knows where we'll be tomorrow, whether we'll even still be here? All I know right this minute is that I want you. And unlike some chaps who'd conceal the fact and lure you away under false pretences, I don't do that. I'm honest about what I want. We can have a great night, no pretence, no promises. But if that's not what you want, if you're not the fun and decisive woman I took you for, then well, mea culpa. So, what's it to be? Are you coming or not?'

Burning with mortification and disappointment, Pearl stared at the floor. Men. They were all the same. Women said they were, and now she'd seen it with her own eyes.

'I'd rather stay here and listen to the music.' It seemed a more adult thing to say than simply 'no'.

'That's a shame. A real shame.'

'Perhaps.' As responses went, she felt pleased with that one. It was enigmatic, like something from a film.

'Do you want me to see you home?'

She shook her head. 'It's not far. I won't leave it long.'

'All right. Well, goodbye, then, Sadie Huxford.'

When he walked stiffly away without looking back, she returned to their table, sank onto her chair, and exhaled in relief. More than anything, she felt foolish. It wasn't that she'd wanted to go with him but hadn't dared, she had genuinely wanted to stay and dance. It would have been fun.

Drawing a breath, she looked up and glanced quickly about. On the stage, the band were returning to their instruments. At nearby tables, couples were sipping drinks and chatting. Some of them must have seen what happened; if they had, at least they weren't gawping or tittering. But what did she do now? She really would like to stay and hear more of the music. It was one of the things she missed most about working at the Plaza. Perhaps, then, the best thing would be to wait until the lights dimmed again, and then make her way to a less prominent seat.

She picked up her drink – there was half of it left – and, glancing about, moved towards the wall. The couches were largely occupied with couples on dates and anyway, she might be safer closer to the bar, from where she could attract attention if she needed. Sizing up the available seats, she spotted a woman on a stool at the far end. Alongside the woman's glass was what appeared to be a notepad and pen. Perhaps she worked there.

'Excuse me.' Closer to, the woman was older than Pearl had expected, fifties, maybe. 'I was wondering… would you mind if I sit next to you?' The woman looked back at her but didn't reply. 'I was with a date… but he wanted to leave, and I didn't. I wanted to listen to the music.' As though that by itself was insufficient, she went on, 'That last girl in particular was very good.'

'Here,' the woman said with a fraction of a smile as she moved a silky wrap from the adjacent stool and draped it across her shoulders. 'Have a seat.'

Having hoisted herself onto the stool, Pearl put down her glass and wriggled herself comfortable. 'Thanks. I feel less conspicuous here.'

'You were with the chap in uniform,' the woman remarked. 'And yes, I know that doesn't exactly narrow it down.'

Pearl blushed. 'I was.'

'Well, good for you for standing your ground. Wanting to listen to the music tells me you've a discerning ear.'

A discerning ear? Was that the same as having good taste?

'I love it when music moves me.'

'I rest my case. I'm Sylvia Murrin, by the way.'

They shook hands.

'Pearl Warren. And I'm sorry if I'm disturbing you.' As she spoke, she noticed that on the bar was a newspaper, upon which she could see listings for the latest film releases. '*Back-Room Boy*,' she said. 'That was one of the last films I saw before the air raids.'

The woman glanced at the newspaper. 'Any good?'

'Arthur Askey plays the lead. It's quite funny. The audience laughed. But then I think people laugh at anything even mildly funny these days, you know, for the relief. I prefer musicals.'

'So do I.'

'I like anything with Fred Astaire. But I also like Deanna Durbin, Eleanor Powell… I enjoyed *Lady Be Good*.'

'"Fascinating Rhythm".'

Pearl grinned. 'I love that song.'

'George Gershwin was a genius. He was only thirty-eight when he died, you know.'

'I didn't.' She would remember it from now on, though.

'He wrote that particular song in the early twenties. He wrote the music, and his brother, Ira, wrote the lyrics. George didn't give him an easy time of it, with such an unusual rhythm.'

'I've tried singing it,' Pearl said, and then immediately wished she hadn't. 'It's real hard to get right.'

The woman's look turned quizzical. 'You sing?'

'A bit. Not professional of course. Though it's my dream to someday.'

Sylvia indicated her notepad. 'I come here to listen to new singers. Roger – he's the manager of this place – is renowned for giving less well-known performers a chance. Over the years, I've picked up one or two new pupils.' When Pearl frowned, Sylvia went on, 'Amongst other things, I teach singing.' Pearl straightened up. *A singing teacher?* 'I'm proprietor of the Timothy & Sylvia Murrin School of Music. I teach singing, and my late husband used to teach music – piano, woodwind, brass, drums. Not strings. He was a jazz man.'

'Goodness.'

'Unfortunately, he died a couple of years back. And thanks to the war and conscription, I haven't been able to find a replacement – as a teacher, I mean, not as a husband.' Pearl grinned. This woman was nice. 'The handful of people I've interviewed have either been far too young and therefore likely to get called up and leave me in the lurch again, or else over the hill and more into the classics. I'm starting to think I'm doomed to offering just singing lessons. Well, unless the war takes an unforeseen turn and musicians come flooding back.'

'So…' Pearl's thoughts were in a whirl. 'You take someone you think can sing and train them to sing better?'

'That's the aim. Unfortunately, the pool of talent is a shallow one. I spot someone with potential only to find they already have representation, and I have to back off. Others I approach mistakenly think they are good enough as they are – that they'll make it without proper training. And then there are those who might have what it takes but lack the means to pay for lessons.'

'I suppose so.'

'This last week, I've been looking for singers to join an orchestra putting on shows. My husband, Tim, used to lead a dance band. After he died, the band kept going, one of their number, the saxophonist, taking on the job of getting them bookings. They'll play anywhere – as long as the fee covers their expenses, that is – but they're always short of decent singers.'

Pearl felt a ripple of excitement. 'What kind of shows do they put on?'

'Oh, you know, the usual – anything from a function to a concert party at an army camp.'

'I see.' Golly, how she wished her heart wouldn't race so.

'Well, as I say, I sing a bit.' Dear God, what was she doing? The woman's eyes, Pearl noticed, were a steely shade of blue grey. And frighteningly piercing. 'I've been told I have a good voice. I can hold a note. And I know the words to hundreds and hundreds of songs.'

'Do you read music?'

Blast. How she wished now that she'd paid more attention in music lessons at school rather than flicking through women's magazines under the desk.

'Never got the chance.'

'How old are you?'

There was too much resting on this to lie. Or was there perhaps too much resting on it not to? 'Eighteen.'

'In a reserved occupation?'

'Bus conductress.'

The woman looked impressed.

'Pearl, did you say your name is?'

'Pearl Warren.'

'You live in Exeter?'

'Lodgings near the bus garage.'

'All right. I'll hear you sing.' From her clutch bag on the bar, Sylvia pulled out a business card. 'This is me. I suppose you work all week.'

Oh dear. Another obstacle. 'Shifts, yes. But I can—'

'Sundays?'

In a wave of relief, Pearl shook her head. 'No. These days, only a few routes run on Sundays. And the men like them for the overtime and to get out of going to church.'

'All right. Ten o'clock, next Sunday morning. More than five minutes late and I'll move onto the next girl. Understand?'

Pearl nodded vigorously. 'I do. Yes.'

'Think of a couple of songs you know well, recent ones, if possible. If they're from musicals, so much the better. A slow one, and something upbeat.'

Pearl slid off her stool and extended a hand. 'Thank you, Mrs Murrin. I'll be there.'

'Call me Sylvia.'

'Sylvia.'

'Watch out going home.'

'I will, yes.'

Once outside, Pearl found the stiff breeze had dropped to leave the air balmy and smelling of the river. Well, she thought, that was a turn up for the books. From the ashes of a disastrous evening that had left her feeling embarrassed and furious in equal measure, had sprung the most marvellous and unlikely of opportunities. Could this be her chance? Could she genuinely become a singer? It was a long shot, she knew that. But, by getting what amounted to an audition, the chance did at least exist.

Still unable to believe what had just happened, she started in the direction of Mrs Trude's. What should she sing? Ooh! Something from *Babes in Arms*; there were a couple of good numbers in that musical. 'My Funny Valentine'. She knew all the words to that song. And how about 'The Lady Is a Tramp'? It had to be almost impossible to go wrong with anything written by Rodgers and Hart. Well, whatever she chose, she would practise and practise until she was as good at it as the original singer. Maybe even better, because, of the few decent chances she'd had in life, this one had to be her best yet. And she simply mustn't mess it up.

II. Harmony

Chapter 8

'Now, you know where you're meeting them.'

'The drill hall. Seven o'clock.'

'And who to ask for.'

'Jack Bassett. Saxophonist.'

'He's tall. Thinning on top.'

Pearl laughed. 'And there was me thinking the saxophone would be the giveaway.'

'Pearl,' Sylvia said wearily. 'Listen to me. It might only be a village hop, but you need to take it seriously. There's a lot resting on it – for both of us. If Jack likes what he hears, he'll talk to me about what else you might be able to do. I've told him you're keen. But eagerness alone isn't enough. You need to be disciplined and professional. As the only woman on tonight's bill, all eyes will be on you. For heaven's sake, let it be for the right reasons.'

'I will. I promise.'

'Good. Because my reputation's at stake here.'

'I know.'

'Now. You've got your music.'

Pearl waved the leather folio case Sylvia had loaned her. 'And a few coins for a drink—'

'Not pop.'

'No, no bubbles. Bad for my throat. And I've got my powder compact and lipstick for a quick repair if I need it.'

'Whatever you do, don't forget to warm up.'

'I won't. Since you showed me those exercises, I do them even before I go out on my bus. Since I do a lot of talking to passengers, I thought it couldn't harm.'

'It never harms to warm up.'

'No.'

'Right then. Good luck. But most of all, try and enjoy it. No matter how much you're trembling, the moment you hit that first note, you'll forget the audience is there.'

'So you keep telling me.' When Sylvia opened the front door to let her out, Pearl cast a final glance at her reflection in the hall mirror and then breezed past her down the path. 'Goodnight, then. And thanks, Sylvia, truly.'

'Pop in tomorrow. I'll be expecting a blow-by-blow account.'

'On my way home, I promise.'

Setting off along the pavement, Pearl wished she knew how to calm the butterflies in her stomach. Tonight, she was going to sing with Sylvia's late husband's band – The Tim Murrin Dance Band – and couldn't remember ever being so nervous. It wasn't only the fact that she'd never done anything like it before, it was the fact that so much hinged on how well she did. Sylvia had said the band looked upon bookings like this one tonight as an opportunity to run through new material. Apparently, the dance was being put on by the parish council and, at best, would host two hundred people. Moreover, since those attending would be dancing – rather than there to listen to her sing – this fellow Jack Bassett had agreed she could do two numbers with them, in the manner of a trial. The rest of the pieces would be either instrumentals or else sung by a chap called Ron Bachelor who, according to Sylvia, was an old crooner, way past his best. But, as Sylvia had gone on to add, beggars couldn't be choosers; with so many male singers and musicians away at war, bands had to work with whomever they could get. And that was where she, Pearl, came in. Do a good job tonight, and a permanent slot with them might become hers.

Her audition for Sylvia felt like such a long time ago now, Pearl reflected as she strode along the street, her feet keeping to the four-four beat in her head. It had gone surprisingly well; her rendition of 'The Lady Is a Tramp' better than 'My Funny Valentine', but she had been pleased with both.

'You show promise,' Sylvia had observed afterwards. 'There's no doubt you have a good voice and, just as importantly, a feel for the music. Almost anyone's voice can be trained and developed. But if you can't instinctively engage with the rhythm and melody, feel it resonate through your body, then all the training in the world won't make you a great singer.'

Pearl had been thrilled by Sylvia's remarks, especially to learn that she had what was important. Until then, she'd always assumed everyone 'felt' music.

'So...' she remembered getting up the courage to venture.

'So, you have something we can work with. You have the basic ingredients. The question is, do you have what it takes to learn the rest? I liken it to making a cake. Anyone can put sugar, butter, and so on, into a bowl. Most people can even accurately weigh them out in the right proportions. But not everyone has the skill to combine them reliably, time after time, to produce the perfect cake – or has the experience to know when something looks amiss, and the ability to put it right. In your case, you're going to need to learn to read music – you won't be able to pick up *everything* by ear – along with the basics of using your voice. You'll need to learn about posture, breathing, registers, techniques.'

Pearl hadn't been put off; whatever it took, she was prepared to do it. So, when Sylvia had suggested she try out with The Tim Murrin Dance Band, she'd jumped at the chance. In that first week after her audition for Sylvia, she'd crammed in five singing lessons, one each evening on her way home from work, and had taken every chance between them to sing: in her room ('If you're going to keep that up, you and me are pretty quickly going to fall out,' Mrs Trude had warned her one morning); on her bus as they trundled each day to the route's first stop ('What was that you were singing back there, maid?' Reg had enquired on one such occasion. 'Couldn't make it out for the din of the engine.'). She had even sung as she strode each day to Sylvia's for her lesson, attracting looks from passers-by that ranged from amusement to mild alarm.

Waiting now at the kerb for an empty milk float to rattle past, she pressed her lips together and inhaled through her nose. Learning how to breathe for the purpose of singing had made an astonishing difference to the sound of her voice; she could hear it for herself. Moreover, just as she'd never thought to reflect upon her breathing, she'd also never given thought to the need to warm up her vocal cords. In fact, she hadn't even known she had any. Already, she had learned so much.

Unfortunately, that first week of lessons had drained every penny from the little pot on the mantlepiece where she set aside whatever she could spare each week from her pay packet. As a result, this last week, she had only been able to cover the cost of two lessons, and only then because Sylvia had shaved a bit off the price and given her homework – learning the basics of reading music – in lieu of showing her at the piano.

Nevertheless, here she was, on her way to her first public performance, and she still couldn't believe it. She wasn't being paid, of course; she was doing this for the experience, and to show the band what she could do in order for them to decide whether she might be a good fit.

Looking up from her musings, she spotted the drill hall ahead on the right. The sight of it made her throat constrict. And what she definitely didn't need now was a tight throat. Nor did she need to start out in a panic.

Ahead on the left, the church clock was showing ten to seven; she had time to calm herself down. With a glance back over her shoulder, she stopped walking and put the folio case on the ground. Planting her feet to match the width of her hips, she dropped her shoulders, raised her chest a little, and levelled her head. As Sylvia had shown her, with thumb and forefinger, she gently felt for her voice box and ran up through a scale. 'Do-re-mi-fah-so-la-ti-do.' Perhaps a *bit* tense, but not as bad as she'd feared. She removed her hand and brought the soft pad of her thumb to rest beneath her lower jaw. 'Do-re-mi-fah-so-la-ti-do.' Sylvia had told her to watch in a mirror as she exercised but, tonight, she didn't have that luxury. And anyway, her muscles didn't feel especially tense. She opened and closed her jaw a couple of times. It seemed free enough. She'd be fine – and in which case, she'd better get over there or she'd be late.

Not finding anyone in the little entrance porch, but spotting the door to the main hall standing open, she went in. Ahead of her, on the stage, the band were moving chairs, setting up music stands, and unpacking instruments. A quick glance revealed a trumpet, double bass, trombone and drumkit. To the side stood an upright piano, against which leaned a guitar. Oh, and there was the saxophone. Golly, now she was really nervous.

Inhaling slowly for courage, she started towards the stage. As she drew near, she could see that it was made up of separate wooden sections pushed together and that, on one of them, stood a microphone. *Her* microphone.

'Excuse me,' she said, approaching the chap who most closely resembled Sylvia's description. The man turned towards her. 'Are you Jack Bassett?'

'That's right. You must be Pearl.'

She reached to shake his hand. 'I am.'

'Well, if your voice is as powerful as your looks, we're in for a treat. Is that your music?'

With a nod, she unzipped the case. 'These are the versions I've practised with Sylvia.'

He flicked through them. 'Yep. They're the ones. So, the running order is this. We open with two instrumentals. Ron does his numbers. We take a short break. Immediately after that, you do your two. If you want to head off when you're done, that's fine. If you want to hang around afterwards, that's fine as well. Out the back,' with his head, he gestured to a door to her right, 'is a little room where we put our cases, and so on. Once we're underway, you're welcome to use it to warm up.'

She nodded. 'Thanks.'

'If you want to go and take a look now, call out before you go in. Mike was using it to get changed. He's on trumpet and comes by bike.'

'I'll do that.'

'Right-o, then. Give us five minutes and we'll use your first number as a warm-up. How does that sound?'

She didn't know whether to panic or relax. 'Sounds fine.'

'Out the back, you'll find a jug of water and some glasses. Maybe go and have a sip or two.'

'Is there a mirror?' she asked.

Jack thought for a moment. 'The ladies' is probably your best bet for that. Through there.'

'Then I'll be back in a minute.' When she went through a door on the other side of the stage, she was taken aback by the stench of disinfectant; despite having taken no more than two bites from the Marmite sandwich Sylvia had insisted on making for her, the odour of pine was powerful enough to turn her stomach. In the ladies', the smell was worse, so she wasted no time in leaning towards the mirror and inspecting her face. Already, her nose had developed a shine; it did that when she was nervous. Hastily, she pulled her compact from the pocket on the side of the folio case, flicked it open and, staring at her reflection, dabbed powder across the bridge of her nose and then down over the tip. There. That was better. Fingers trembling, she stuffed the compact back into the folio case and hurried back to the hall. Did she have time for a breath of fresh air to clear her lungs of the disinfectant? On the stage, the band were settling down. No. By the look of it, they were ready to start their warm-up.

Jack looked across at her. 'Fit?'

With a nod, she deposited her folio case at the edge of the stage, climbed the single step and crossed to the microphone. How on earth was she supposed to sing while she was trembling so badly? She supposed by making a start.

'Ready.'

'Four bar intro.'

She signalled her understanding with another nod. And, as the piano and double bass began to play, she swallowed, drew a deep breath, and counted herself in.

It was over in no time. With no recollection of having sung a single word, she realised she was rounding off the last note, the tinkling from the piano fading away behind her, the hall completely still. With no idea how she'd done, she turned slowly about. Nine sets of eyes were staring back at her.

'Was it… all right?'

On the musicians' faces there seemed to be disbelief. And when Jack began to applaud, the others joined in.

'Have you honestly never sung with a band before?'

Wishing he would simply tell her how she'd done, she shook her head. 'Only with Sylvia on piano. And then only for the first time just recently. Usually, I just sing to myself.'

'Do it like that for real later on, and you'll be upfront every night. Seriously, girl, that was a joy. How old are you?'

'Eighteen.' She'd given it as her age so many times just lately that she'd begun to believe it.

'I mean, I'm not saying you can't improve. With more consistent breathing, you'd sound even stronger. But, well, old Sylv was right. She's sent me girls before, but you're by far and away the best.'

'I could tell you were going to be good,' the pianist interjected, 'from the first note.'

'Almost missed mine, I was so surprised,' confessed Jack.

'Thank you,' she said. It went through her mind to wonder whether they were having her on. 'To be honest, it was all a bit of a blur.'

'Getting lost in the music is something even professionals sometimes struggle to achieve. I tell you, keep on like that, and you'll go far. Now, go out the back, keep your body nice and loose and your voice gently warm. Maybe have a leaf through some of the music, get a feel for what we play.'

'I will,' she said, and went to retrieve Sylvia's folio case before making her way out the back.

Once out of their sight, she exhaled heavily with relief. Where she'd pulled that performance from she had no idea. She'd like to say she'd enjoyed every second of it, but the truth of the matter was that she couldn't remember a single word she'd sung. She recalled hearing the drummer and anchoring herself to the beat. And she had a vague recollection of the saxophone – of Jack – swooping in. Still, best not to dwell on it too much: she still had to do it for real.

Finding the little room Jack had directed her to, she went in and, scanning the assortment of instrument cases and other paraphernalia, pulled from beneath the table the only free chair. In the quiet, something Sylvia had said came back to her: it was after she'd sung for her that first time, and it was something along the lines of: *If you can't instinctively engage with the rhythm and melody, feel it resonate through your body, then all the training in the world won't make you a great singer*. Having until now only sung with Sylvia playing the piano, any feel for the music had been fleeting, little more than the odd flicker when she'd correctly hit a tricky note. But by getting as lost in the music as she had tonight, she understood now how intoxicating it could be, and knew she wanted to feel that way again. Growing up, she'd always considered her singing voice better than those of her classmates, but to be admired for it, as she had been just then, made her more determined than ever not to waste it. Charlie used to say she took after his mother – his Irish side – who, according to him, were all musically gifted. Odd she should remember that now.

The euphoria from her run-through subsiding a little, she sighed. Well, whoever she had to thank, she was immensely grateful. Getting lost in the music had completely seen off her nerves, which, in turn, had enabled her to stop worrying and allow herself to be swept along by the song. All she had to do now, was exactly the same thing all over again…

–

'I can't put in words how it felt. I've never known a sensation like it.'

It was the evening after her performance at the drill hall and, as promised, Pearl was back at Sylvia's, relaying what had happened. Sadly, try as she might, there was much she still couldn't recall or even explain – the proceedings as much a blur to her almost twenty-four hours later as they had been the moment she'd finished her final song.

'The feeling when it goes well does rather defy description, doesn't it?' Sylvia replied. 'Other than to perhaps call it rare and precious.'

'That's about the measure of it.'

'My advice? Use the memory as a spur. Don't try too hard to define the feeling. Let it remain mysterious and magical. Trying to pin down how to get it back – to summon it to order, if you will – is to risk losing all chance of it happening again. If you feel it sometimes but not others, don't become obsessed with how to get it back. Perform to your best, and it will come by itself.'

While Pearl could see what Sylvia was getting at, it wasn't what she wanted to hear. She didn't want the feeling – if that was even the right word for it – to turn up by chance; she wanted to learn a routine she could go through, or a technique she could adopt, to summon it at will – Sylvia did, after all, talk endlessly about technique. But looking back upon the two songs she'd performed last night, she realised it was only during the second one that she'd felt the sensation return. She'd been expecting it during the first, had been watching out for it, but it was only when she'd given up trying to get it back again that it had reappeared. Perhaps, therefore, Sylvia was right; she'd certainly been in the business long enough to know what she was talking about.

'So,' she said, deciding not to get wound up over the matter, 'you've spoken to Jack.'

'He dropped by on his way to work this morning. Given that last night was your first time, he thought you were tremendous.'

'Then what happens now?' It was only any good being tremendous if it led to her securing more appearances, as she'd learned they were called. Enjoying singing was one thing, earning money from it, a different matter altogether. And she did so badly want to make a living from it. Being a clippie was fun, but she'd much rather sing for a living.

'Now, we go back to lessons.'

Pearl frowned. 'But the band do want me to join them again?'

'Jack's open to the idea, in time.'

'But—'

'He agrees with me that you have a good voice but also feels that, to make the best of it, you need to understand more about breathing.'

'Breathing.'

'Don't scowl so. I know it sounds dull. But, until you are able to breathe properly, without the need to think, much as you do to stay alive, you won't progress. What you *might* do, if you're not careful, is ruin your voice by singing from your throat.'

'Right.' It wasn't what Pearl had gone there hoping to hear; she'd been hoping to learn that Jack wanted her to replace Ron Bachelor. And as soon as possible.

'You also need to work harder at learning to read music. Your repertoire at the moment is non-existent—'

'I know loads of songs.' To her shame, she realised she'd sounded petulant.

'I don't doubt it. But you'll have to learn new ones, songs to fit whatever type of booking the band is playing. And to do that, you have to be able to read the score.'

What a bloomin' nuisance. Learning what all those lines and squiggles meant was proving to be the most tedious thing she'd had to do since being forced to learn how to multiply fractions.

'So, what do I do?'

'Firstly, you decide whether or not you want to bother.'

'With *singing*?'

'With performing.'

'I do.'

'Next, you decide whether you want it badly enough to put in the hours. And by that, I don't mean simply coming here once a week and expecting to spend the entire hour singing. I mean spending your time practising posture and breathing. I mean exercising your vocal cords, your jaw, your tongue, your lips. I mean persisting with learning to read music. You should be pestering me for the chance to come here in your free time and sit at that piano, playing like a child of six.'

'Can I *do* that?' she asked. 'Come here, I mean?'

'If I'm not teaching.'

Despite the way her spirits seemed to be plunging ever deeper, Pearl felt a jolt of recognition. 'You didn't send me to sing with The Tim Murrin Dance Band because you thought I was ready for bookings, did you.'

Getting up from her chair, Sylvia smiled. 'I did not.'

She wanted so badly to be wrong that discovering she was right simply made Pearl feel even more disconsolate. 'You might have said. Bit mean of you, sending me there and getting my hopes up like that.'

'Had I not got your hopes up, you wouldn't have wanted to go. And you wouldn't have sung with such a passion to impress.'

Having been on the point of saying *You don't know that*, Pearl fastened her lips. If Sylvia was prepared to help her do whatever it took to succeed, then she was going to need to knuckle down and accept that Sylvia knew best.

'Happen you're right,' she said. 'But is there *any* chance I'll get to sing with Jack and the band again? While I'm still learning, I mean.'

Extending a hand, Sylvia patted Pearl's arm. 'I'd say there's *every* chance. After all, a special appearance now and again for me to gauge your progress couldn't do any harm, could it?'

To Pearl's mind, it could do no harm at all. In the meantime, the only way to bring about the progress she so badly craved was to stop feeling miffed and ask how soon Sylvia could fit her in for some more lessons.

Chapter 9

'So, how long have you been coming to Sylvia?'

With no clue as to the identity of the young woman addressing her, Pearl moved past her along the hall. There being no free pegs on Sylvia's coat rack, she settled for hooking the collar of her jacket over the top of an olive green gaberdine and then turned back to meet the woman's look; for a stranger, it was disarmingly frank.

'Not long.' Without knowing who she was, Pearl felt disinclined to give too much away; the woman's dark hair, and the olive tint to her complexion, made it seem unlikely she was a member of Sylvia's family. Assuming instead that she was another of her pupils, she said, 'You?'

'Four or five months. D'you sing?'

Continuing to take in the woman's appearance, Pearl nodded. Whoever she was, she had unusually large eyes. 'I do.'

'For a living?'

Why the inquisition, Pearl wondered. 'No. But I'd like to.'

The woman's expression softened. 'Oh, me too. I'd do anything to get a part in a show somewhere. But where's that going to happen round here, eh? Thanks to them bloody Germans, there's not a single theatre still putting on a show.'

Earlier wariness cast aside, Pearl joined the woman's lament. 'I *know*. And the only cinema to survive *still* doesn't know when it'll be open again. Bad luck all round.' The mention of cinemas made her realise how badly she missed working at the Plaza. Being a conductress was fun, but the best part of being an usherette, apart from the luxury of working indoors, had been seeing all of the latest films.

'You managed to get *any* bookings?' the girl asked. If pushed to guess at her age, Pearl would have said twenty, maybe a year or two more.

'Sylvia says I'm not quite ready. Last week, I went and sang with The Tim Murrin Dance Band.' There was no need to mention it had been only the two numbers, and only then, it turned out, so that Sylvia might get a second opinion about her.

'They're good aren't they? I like Jack. Got a nice way about him.'

About to agree, Pearl changed her mind; when it came to getting bookings – or appearances, as she ought to start calling them – she was only now realising she would be in competition with other singers. Naturally, Sylvia would have other pupils, as would any teacher worth their salt. But, until now, she'd overlooked how most of them would be as desperate for opportunities as she was. Best, then, to play her cards close to her chest.

'He did seem nice, yes.'

At the sound of someone coming down the stairs, she turned to see Sylvia, in her hand a piece of paper.

'This is the address— Ah, I see the two of you have met.'

Pearl and the girl nodded.

'I'm Ivy, by the way,' the young woman said and held out a hand.

'Pearl.'

Handing the piece of paper to Ivy, Sylvia went on, 'I suspect you have a cavity that needs filling. So, don't hang about. Act now, and you might avoid losing the tooth. Besides which, you can't sing with one side of your jaw in pain. And if you're in pain again, don't wait so long to have it looked at.'

Ivy's expression was sheepish. 'I won't.'

'A singer – indeed, a performer of any sort – must look after her body. It is, after all, the tool of her trade.'

'I'll go tomorrow.'

'See that you do.'

'Word of advice,' Ivy whispered to Pearl as an aside. 'Don't bother trying to hide anything from her. If there's something up, she'll sniff it out in an instant.'

'Thanks.' Perhaps this girl was all right. 'Duly noted.'

'Right-o, then, see you next week, tooth permitting.'

Once Ivy had left, Pearl followed Sylvia through to the room referred to as The Studio. Recently added to the side of the house, it was the antithesis of the Victorian dwelling to which it was attached. Modern and brightly lit, it had bare white walls, a sprung wooden floor, and a high ceiling from which spotlights illuminated a shallow stage. At one end of the latter stood a grand piano, at the other, a drumkit. To one side of the room, a number of guitars were positioned on stands, behind them, a rack housing all manner of percussion instruments.

'So,' Pearl said, kicking off her shoes and placing them neatly inside the door. Sylvia didn't allow heels on her polished floor. 'Ivy is one of your pupils.'

Sylvia lowered herself onto the piano stool. 'She started coming around about Easter. She has an interesting voice, contralto, full and rich but in need of training.'

'I see.' Perhaps, then, Pearl thought – the term contralto suggesting Ivy's voice was deep and low – when it came to auditions, the two of them might not be in direct competition after all. She hoped not.

'Anyway, enough about Ivy. Come. Show me how you ensure your throat and jaw are relaxed and then we'll warm up.'

Pearl felt her insides sag under the weight of her disappointment. *Bloomin' warming up.*

More frustration was to come, more than half of her hour-long lesson swallowed up with exercises of one sort or another: posture; breathing; exaggerating different sounds. Unlike being at school, where, in most lessons, she had sat trying to make the big hand of the clock speed up, in Sylvia's classroom, Pearl found herself willing it to do the opposite. There was so much she needed to learn, and she was impatient to get on with it; only then would Sylvia let her try the sort of songs she knew from musicals – songs that would be of use to her in an audition for a show. Naturally, the basics were important; Sylvia had repeatedly drummed that into her. She was also more than happy to *put in the work*, as Sylvia called it; mastering the basics would get her closer to her dream. But, golly, she was anxious to get there, especially now she'd met Ivy, and had been jolted into realising that she wasn't alone in having the ambition to be on the stage. And all of that was without reckoning on the cost of these lessons. Coming on top of everything else, they were stretching her purse to its limits.

Eventually, with barely a quarter of an hour of the lesson remaining, Sylvia put a piece of music on the stand.

'We're going to try this. It's a popular piece for beginners. Follow your score while I play.'

How Pearl wished now that she'd done more of her homework. 'All right.'

'There,' Sylvia said when she'd played to the end. 'Were you able to follow?'

'Near enough.' It wasn't *too* much of a lie; she had *more or less* reached the end of the score as Sylvia played the final chord.

'Very well, now we'll break it into phrases. I'll play the melody, like this.' Pearl watched Sylvia play single notes. 'Then you'll sing it. Then we'll play it together.'

Finally, she was singing. And eventually, albeit in choppy fashion, she managed an entire verse and a chorus before going wrong.

'It's harder than I thought,' she confessed when Sylvia handed her a glass of water.

'Sip it. Don't gulp. You did well. By the end of next week's lesson, you will have perfected the entire song. Now, for your homework—'

'Couldn't I take the music and practise this?' With her hand, Pearl indicated the score on the stand.

'Not this time. This week, you need to continue with your exercises for posture and breathing. And yes, I know it's dull. But you have to master—'

'The basics. Yes,' Pearl said. 'I understand.'

'Good. Then I'll see you next week.'

Humming the melody of the song she'd been learning, Pearl went out to the hallway where, to her surprise, she found Ivy sitting on the bottom stair, on her lap what she recognised from seeing Sylvia's copy as that week's issue of *The Stage*.

'Oh, good,' Ivy said, getting to her feet. 'You're done.'

Pearl reached for her jacket. 'I am. Did you come back to see Sylvia?'

'Actually, no. I was waiting for you.'

'Me?' Pearl frowned.

'Had anything to eat?' By way of response, Pearl shook her head. 'Fancy rock an' chips from Reid's?'

The thought alone made Pearl's mouth water. 'All right. If we go back to my lodgings, we can make a cup of tea to go with it.'

'Don't suppose you've got bread and marge as well?'

Pearl laughed. She liked this woman. Her directness was a joy. 'Afraid not, cheeky.'

'Worth asking.'

'Lead on, then. But no starting on the chips before we get home. Oh, and we'll have to eat in the garden. I can do without the pong of grease getting on my things.'

As they stepped outside and Pearl closed Sylvia's front door, Ivy cast her eyes to the sky. 'Fair enough. It's not a bad evening.'

At the fish and chip shop, they had to queue. 'Busy for a Thursday night,' Pearl remarked once their order had finally been taken.

'It's always busy,' said Ivy. 'You know they used to have two places.'

Pearl shook her head. 'I didn't. But then I haven't lived round here long.'

'The other one had sit-down tables – proper restaurant with waitresses and tablecloths, the lot.'

'Don't tell me,' Pearl said, her stomach choosing that moment to rumble. 'It was bombed.'

'Yep.' Turning her attention to the lad wrapping their order, Ivy called across, 'Got any vinegar?'

'Sorry. Fresh out.'

'What, none at all?'

'Nope. Might have some tomorrow, though.'

'Trouble is,' Pearl said drily, 'by tomorrow, our supper will have gone cold.'

'So,' Ivy said, once she'd stopped laughing and they were back out on the street, 'where do you live?'

'From here, down St David's Hill and then cut through to Queen's Terrace.'

'What is it you've got there? A room?'

'In the basement. But it's not as grim as it sounds, and perfect for me on my own. What's more, right outside is a lav, and since there's another one upstairs, none of the other lodgers trouble to come down and use it, so I have it all to myself.'

'Nice.'

'I can also get out into the garden.'

'Even better.'

'Which no one else ever uses either. Anyway, in a minute, you'll see for yourself.'

'Right you are.'

When they reached the house in Queen's Terrace, and Pearl went to put her key in the lock, she gestured to Ivy to be quiet. Closing the door softly behind them, she tiptoed along the hall until she reached a door, where she motioned Ivy ahead of her down the stairs. Arriving at the bottom, she let herself into a room on the right.

'This is me.'

'Your landlord don't like you having visitors?'

'Land*lady*. And I've no idea. But she's difficult about everything, so I'm sure she'd find reason to object.

Anyway,' Pearl said. Crossing to the right hand of a pair of windows, she twiddled the catch and, with some difficulty, pushed up the bottom sash. 'You all right eating from the paper, or are you one of those people like my sister, who insists on a plate?'

'Put fish and chips on a plate?' Ivy's question was posed with a laugh. 'When there's perfectly good paper that can go straight in the bin after?'

'Come on, then. I'll climb out and you can pass me the food.'

The patch of garden abutting Pearl's window had been left to run wild: what had once been lawn now resembled a meadow; for want of pruning, a pair of apple trees had a frenzy of branches growing in bizarre directions; dandelions and thistles had colonised the gravel path. Mess or not, though, to Pearl, it was a sanctuary.

'You got fairies living out here?' Ivy asked as the pair of them lowered themselves cautiously onto a dilapidated wooden bench and set about unwrapping their suppers.

'Wouldn't surprise me. There are definitely hedge-hogs.'

'How did you come by this place?'

'Through my work. When they realised I'd been bombed out and was living in a rest centre, the supervisor of manpower offered to help find me somewhere.'

'Jammy. You on war work, then?'

'Reserved occupation.' She still liked the way that sounded; how it gave her an air of importance.

'Yeah? Where to?'

'City & District.'

'I saw a woman clippie the other day,' Ivy said. 'Smart uniform.'

'Yup. For the most part, it's a good job full stop. What about you?'

Ivy bit off the end of a particularly fat chip. 'Up the hospital.'

'You're a nurse?' A more unlikely nurse Pearl struggled to imagine.

'Don't be daft. No, I'm in the kitchens. Five in the morning till one o'clock dinnertime, five days on, one day off. Only good thing is getting a breakfast at six, and a hot meal when I come off.'

Pearl withheld a smile. If, when she'd gone to the Labour Exchange that day, she hadn't held out for something better, the two of them might already have met. 'My shifts can be either earlies or lates. I prefer the early runs. Always ask for them if I can.'

'Yeah. Can't say I *enjoy* the five o'clock start, but it does mean I get to go out in the evenings.' Something of a necessity for a would-be singer, Pearl thought as she broke off a section of battered fish and popped it into her mouth. 'The late shift wouldn't do for me,' Ivy continued. 'It's midday till eight.'

'This is good,' Pearl said, gesturing to her meal. 'I must remember where we got it. Not that I can afford a treat like this all that often, what with the rent for my room and paying for singing lessons as well.'

Ivy gave a dismayed shake of her head. 'I know.'

'Where do *you* live? Somewhere around here?'

'Used to. Now I'm somewhere else.'

The vagueness of Ivy's answer made Pearl wonder what she was hiding.

'With family?'

'Friends.'

'Oh.'

When they'd finished eating and had wiped their fingers on Pearl's handkerchief – Ivy, she noticed, didn't have one – they climbed back through the window into Pearl's room.

'Didn't no one think to put a door in down here then?'

'I think there was one once upon a time,' Pearl replied. 'But someone must have bricked it up. The house next door has one. I peered through the fence.'

'But yours is the only room down here.'

'Uh-huh.'

'And with twin beds—'

'One of which, as you can see, is handy for dumping clothes.'

'I've always thought wardrobes overrated.'

As Pearl laughed, she noticed that Ivy was working her way around the room, inspecting her belongings. She thought it a bit of a nerve. 'Anyway, thanks for suggesting the fish and chips.'

Having returned the mirror on the chest of drawers to the angle at which she'd found it, Ivy spun about. 'Maybe we should make a thing of it – after your lesson each week. I could wait after mine and then we could go and get supper.'

'I suppose.' If she'd come across as wary, it was because that was how she felt. Ivy seemed nice enough – like someone with whom she could have a laugh – but she knew from experience how easy it was, in a fit of bonhomie, to agree to do something and then find yourself wishing you hadn't. Ivy might turn out to be a great friend, but she might also turn out to be trouble. For certain there was something about her she couldn't put a finger on, a caginess. 'Let's see how it goes,' she said, anxious not to close down the opportunity altogether. 'I don't know how I'm going to get on in the longer term. I'm not even sure I'll be able to stick to the same day each week, you know, with work. My shifts aren't set like yours are.'

'Yeah. All right.'

Now she'd put Ivy in a huff. 'But I'm definitely having my lesson on Thursday *next* week. So, I'll try an' get there a bit early to be sure of seeing you when you finish yours. We can decide then about supper.'

'Yeah. If you like. Well, I'll be off then. Leave you to it.'

Was Ivy angling to be invited to stay? For two people who had only just met, it seemed a bit forward.

'All right. I'll see you out. Then I've got the glamorous job of slop washing some smalls, or else I'll be wearing the same pair of socks for longer than is strictly fragrant.'

'A job you're welcome to.'

When Ivy had left, Pearl went to the window and stared down the garden. Were she and Ivy going to be best pals? Or was there a chance that, in competing for singing jobs, they might end up as adversaries? She hoped not, Ivy seemed like fun. And she wouldn't mind a few new friends – as long, of course, as they weren't the sort who came bringing trouble or got in the way of her dream…

Chapter 10

As July wore on, Pearl's wariness about Ivy's character faded. She even began to feel mean for having doubted her in the first place; Ivy had turned out to be warm and open, possessed of boundless energy, and full of good ideas. Every Thursday, after her lesson with Sylvia, Ivy would wait for Pearl to finish hers and then, since both girls were usually ravenous, they would go in search of something to eat: on one occasion, they stopped to buy the last two pasties from a baker who was closing up; another time, Ivy led her to a tiny cafe, where the only thing on the menu – and, apparently, the only thing *ever* on the menu – was Pie of the Day with mash.

On this particular Thursday, however, food was the last thing on their minds because, tonight, both girls were taking part in a concert being put on at a nearby convalescence hospital. At the end of Ivy's lesson the previous week, Sylvia had called Pearl into the studio to explain the news to the pair of them together.

'The concert,' she had said, 'is to be held in the hospital's dining hall. By all accounts, it's not overly large, but then I don't suppose your audience will be, either. Walking wounded, I imagine, plus, no doubt, some of the staff who care for them. You'll be singing with Jack and the band, so there's no need for nerves. Since you've both sung with them before, look upon this as a chance to gain further experience.'

'But it's ages since we sang with them,' Ivy had pointed out.

Pearl had agreed. 'Ages.'

'Which is why I have arranged for you to sing the same numbers you performed with them previously.'

Only two songs? And the same ones, at that? To say Pearl was disappointed was an understatement.

Struck by a thought, she'd asked, 'Is there not a duet we could learn?'

Ivy had pounced on the idea. 'Ooh, yes. That would be good.'

'Perhaps another time.' To Pearl, Sylvia's reply had sounded like something her mother would have said, *another time* being a way to soften the fact that she had no intention of agreeing – neither then, nor at any point in the future. 'There isn't sufficient time before the concert to get up to standard on a new song. And I shouldn't want either of you being under prepared. It reflects badly.'

In a way, now that the day of the concert had arrived, Pearl was glad she hadn't had to learn anything new, the butterflies in her stomach already in a high-old state of apprehension. Having had no chance to practise with the band beforehand, the girls had run through their songs accompanied by Sylvia on the piano – to Pearl's mind, hardly the best of preparation.

'How did this concert come about?' she asked Sylvia, as the three of them now stood waiting for the bus to take them to the army camp where the hospital was located.

'Jack's niece volunteers there. Not on the nursing side, I shouldn't think. But it was her idea to bring the patients some entertainment.'

'Are there going to be other singers?'

'Ron Bachelor will do a couple of numbers – you remember him, don't you?' The girls nodded. 'And the choir from the girls' school are going to be singing something. At one point, there was talk of a couple of variety acts, but I'm not sure that came off.'

When they arrived at the hospital and were shown to where they would be performing, it was quickly apparent that Sylvia had been right about the size of the room: it wasn't just *not overly large*, it was small and dark, with low ceilings.

'The sound in here will be terrible,' Ivy hissed as the two of them stood surveying the set up.

The quality of a room's sound was not something Pearl had ever stopped to consider; it was a realisation that made her feel foolish. 'Even so,' she said to disguise the fact, 'I'd rather sing somewhere with terrible sound than not at all. And I don't suppose our audience will mind. I imagine they'll simply be pleased someone has made the effort.'

'That's true. Shame there's no stage, though.'

On that point, Pearl had to agree. 'You're right. Stood down here, we're in danger of not being seen. Still, can't be helped. We're not here for ourselves, we're here to bring music to injured soldiers.'

Before long, the concert got under way and the two of them, along with Sylvia and Ron, squeezed their way to one side of the dining hall to watch the girls' school choir perform a piece Pearl recognised from her own schooldays: 'Sumer is icumen in', an ancient song of the countryside, which they proceeded to perform, as she remembered having done, in a round. The girls' voices were pretty, their harmonies charming, and in their bottle green school pinafores they looked fresh and innocent, even if a couple of the older girls in the back row did keep eyeing the soldiers stood at the rear of the hall.

Discreetly, Pearl turned to study their audience for herself. Sylvia had been right to suggest they would be the 'walking wounded'. With the exception of a couple of men who each had an arm in a sling, those standing at the back of the hall appeared uninjured. In front of them were several rows of upright wooden chairs, upon which were seated men in dressing gowns: a couple had bandaged heads, another couple must have had injuries she couldn't see. To the front were the patients in wheelchairs, many of whom had a leg in plaster. In all, there had to be thirty or forty patients and a dozen nurses and orderlies.

When the girls' choir had sung their third and final song, the applause for them was genuinely warm.

'I'm up then,' Ivy whispered and squeezed her way towards the stage.

In her stomach, Pearl felt her butterflies stirring. 'Good luck,' she whispered back.

When the girls' choir had filed from the room, The Tim Murrin Dance Band moved to replace them, Jack Basset bringing a microphone, with which he then proceeded to tinker. Evidently satisfied, he nodded to Ivy, who stepped forward to join him.

'Ladies and gentlemen, we are The Tim Murrin Dance Band, and singing for you first tonight is Miss Ivy Snell.'

As the audience applauded, Jack counted in the band. And when Ivy delivered the opening line to 'Begin the Beguine', Pearl felt a ripple run the length of her spine; Ivy's voice was rich and smooth, and for someone with such an unprepossessing build, surprisingly deep. There was also, she noticed now, a huskiness to it. Ivy really should give up smoking; huskiness might sound sultry but, as she knew Sylvia had more than once pointed out to her, wasn't conducive to a long career on the stage.

As Ivy continued to sing, Pearl studied her friend's appearance; if she was being critical, she would say that she ought to wear a little more make-up. Her complexion was clear but sallow; a light sweep of rouge would emphasise her cheekbones. A stroke of eyeliner would look good on her, too, as would more mascara. And she really ought to wear a different shade of lipstick; the one she was wearing tonight was too orangey for the tone of her skin. If she was going to wear that dark green dress, a shade of ruby red would be better. In fact, deep red worked well with almost any outfit.

Hearing the closing notes of Ivy's song tinkling from the piano, Pearl joined the generous applause from the audience. Almost immediately, the band's pianist, accompanied by the clarinet player, began Ivy's next number, a song called 'Fools Rush In', the Anne Shelton recording of which Pearl remembered from a couple of years previously, her mother always singing along whenever it came on the wireless. Her mum had loved listening to the radio. When she died, though, May announced that the wireless set was to be sold; not only was there no money for something as frivolous as getting the accumulators charged every week, but the proceeds were needed in the here and now to buy food. She would never forget the day she'd come home and found an empty space on the shelf where the set had always stood – nor how she'd torn into May, railing at her for being heartless. More lately, of course, she'd come to appreciate that her sister hadn't had a choice. She'd missed hearing music, though – at least she had, until she'd gone to work at the Plaza.

Fools rush in… She wondered now whether Mum sang along with Anne Shelton's lyrics because the title had struck a chord; while she would never have admitted as much to her daughters, Pearl knew her mother rued marrying Charlie. *At least had I remained a widow*, she recalled hearing her one day confide to a neighbour, *I wouldn't now be carrying the shame of having been deserted*.

Pearl directed her gaze back to Ivy. As she held a note, she closed her eyes. She was good; the words to the song delivered with feeling. She must remember to put a bit of passion into her own singing. Dear God, yes! She'd forgotten she had to get up there next. Dratted butterflies: having momentarily settled, they were now flitting about all over the place.

'If it's all right with you,' Jack said, when she moved to replace Ivy in front of the band, 'we'll do "My Funny Valentine" first – another slow number on the back of Ivy's will set up "The Lady Is a Tramp" as our big finish.'

'All right.' Belatedly, Pearl realised she should have gone outside and warmed up; they might have run through their numbers at Sylvia's but that felt like ages ago. Well, there was nothing she could do now – she would just have to remember the oversight as a lesson for next time.

Her rendition of 'My Funny Valentine' was by no means her finest. Anyone with an ear for music would hear how, when she held a note, there was a tremor to it. It didn't help that so many faces were staring directly at her; each time she looked out at them, all she saw were eyes pinned directly upon her own. When she'd sung with the band last time, the ballroom had been largely in darkness, the spotlight upon her too dazzling to allow her to pick out individual faces. Besides, that particular audience had been dancing, not sat listening. The applause as she finished, though, suggested her audience were neither snobs nor critics. But she could do better – a lot better.

After allowing her a moment to catch her breath, Jack directed the band for her next number. And, as she stood counting time, she had an idea; she would assume the persona of the character in the song. She would act the part. She would *perform*. She'd seen enough musicals to know how it was done. This particular song was about a young woman who didn't care what people thought of the way she behaved. She would become that woman: confident and carefree.

Hand on hip, she turned sideways to the microphone. The first line of the song left her lips. Ahead of the second, she turned back to her audience; as she delivered the next, with her hand, she signalled indifference. Now all eyes really were glued to her. And she loved it. Her only regret, when the song came to an end, and the audience roared their approval, was that it was all over so quickly.

'Ladies and gentlemen, Miss Pearl Warren.' When Pearl acknowledged the audience's continued applause with a little wave, Jack moved to stand beside her. 'Tremendous stuff,' he said into her ear. 'Carry on like that and we might have to give that number regular billing.'

'Wow,' Ivy greeted her. 'You're quite the dark horse, aren't you?'

Feeling her cheeks burning, Pearl affected nonchalance. 'All I did was play to the audience.'

'Never had you down as sassy.'

Sylvia's response was less effusive. 'You took a risk. On this occasion, it worked. But no more surprises. If we rehearse a song in a certain way, that's how you go up there and perform it.'

At that moment, Pearl didn't particularly care what Sylvia thought. After all, Sylvia had been the one to point out that, while she could teach her to sing, she couldn't achieve her dream for her; only hard work and determination could do that. And she was right. Besides, she realised now, her dream had never been solely about singing; she wanted to *perform*. Sylvia could say what she liked but her rendition of 'The Lady Is a Tramp' had brought the biggest applause of the night; she was still tingling from it now. Moreover, Jack had said she was tremendous. And since Jack was the one who got the bookings, she would trust him to know. On the other hand, to fall out with the one person who could set her on her way to stardom would be daft. So, if Sylvia was expecting her to show some contrition, she could do that, too; this acting lark had its uses.

'With a different audience,' she said, her tone demure, 'I wouldn't have taken the risk. But I do understand what you're saying.' There. Contrition. But neither hint nor promise that she would refrain from doing the same again – should the chance one day present itself…

–

'Golly, I'm cold.'

'Me too. It's been so dreary these last weeks you could be forgiven for thinking it was autumn rather than summer.'

'Yeah. Not the best weather to hang about a draughty tent waiting to sing.'

It was now late July, and the girls' success at the concert party for the convalescing soldiers had brought them an invitation to take part in further shows.

'I suppose what we do might loosely be called a variety show,' the pianist with The Tim Murrin Dance Band – a man by the name of Cliff Rowse – had explained when he'd first approached them about taking part. 'We put on an hour or so of light entertainment for servicemen. I'm afraid,' he'd gone on to point out, 'it doesn't pay. But if the venue is somewhere far flung, then the army or whomever usually sends a couple of trucks to pick us up and bring us back.'

What he'd failed to mention, Pearl had quickly come to realise, was the nature of the venues, popular among them, chilly halls with rickety stages fashioned from whatever materials were to hand – leaving whoever was performing scared half to death of falling through it – and tents in army camps, occasionally, but rarely, with the luxury of a curtain hung to provide a 'backstage'. Somehow, though, it was always fun. The show, which had informally taken on the moniker The Twilight Troopers, featured a randomly changing selection of acts that included Murray the Magician, who, through sleight of hand could make items disappear, only for them to turn up somewhere unlikely seconds later; a comedy sketch featuring two actors dressed as hapless German airmen trying to pass themselves off as British – and which regularly brought the house down – and a chap who impersonated famous people. As Cliff had observed, with that fat cigar stuck in his mouth, the mimic's impression of Winnie was uncanny.

'I know it's only a couple of nights a week, but this concert party lark is killing me,' Ivy groaned after they'd had to wait almost an hour one night for their transport back into the city. 'I'm in danger of falling asleep over the vegetables.'

Pearl knew what she meant; while she didn't have to start work as early as Ivy did, the late nights were nevertheless beginning to take their toll. 'You're not going to give up, though, are you?'

'Not on your nellie. Too fond of the perks.'

By 'perks', Pearl knew Ivy was referring to the little bits and bobs they got given: on air force bases, they were brought drinks by good-looking airmen; from those army camps that were home to foreign servicemen, they came away with chocolate, soap, and cigarettes; from hospitals, or village halls where the audience mainly comprised evacuees, they came away with people's genuine gratitude for the brief reprieve from homesickness or hardship and drear.

'Performing for people is fun, though, isn't it?' Pearl said, as they sat now, on the wall at the bottom of Sylvia's front garden, waiting to be collected for that particular night's concert. Had she been on the lookout for a boyfriend, Pearl reflected, she couldn't have asked for a better assortment of candidates from whom to take her pick.

'Yeah. Not many folk get to laugh as often as we do.'

Pearl grinned. 'Even if it is often for the wrong reasons.'

'That awful piano that time. Do you remember? Poor old Cliff did his best, but it was so out of tune, all I could picture as I stood trying to hold a note, was him sat in the corner of a pub, hammering away on a beer-stained upright. I kept expecting him to break into a round of "Knees Up Mother Brown".'

'That *was* a night best forgotten,' Pearl agreed. 'And then there was last week, when Stan from the comedy duo took a step too far backwards and fell off the stage.'

'The audience thought it was part of the show.'

'It got the biggest laugh of the night.'

Pearl sighed. Yes, they did have some fun. And at least she was getting to perform several times a week. Her desperation for something more, though, was as strong as ever. In fact, the longer it went on with their appearances being solely voluntary ones, the more she'd started to fear getting stuck in a rut. While she knew it was a lot to ask in the middle of a war, she longed to sing on a proper stage; to be part of a regular billing – earning recognition, building a reputation. Not to mention being paid for her efforts.

Beside her, Ivy groaned. 'Where the devil's this ruddy truck got to?'

'Should have worn a jacket,' Pearl replied, glancing to the slinky fabric of Ivy's dark green dress.

'I didn't think I'd need one. It's supposed to be summer. I can't imagine Anne Shelton waiting about to get a lift from an army truck.'

'No,' Pearl agreed. 'Nor Billie Holiday. Nor Judy Garland.'

'Bit bold to draw comparison with Judy Garland, aren't you?'

Since it was unusual for Ivy to sound scathing, Pearl turned to regard her. 'Bold?'

'Those women are stars.'

'So? That's what I'm going to be some day.'

'Well… I know that's what you *want* to be,' Ivy said. 'It's what I want, too. I just think maybe you should—'

'What? Set my sights lower? 'Cos I don't see how that's going to help.'

'All I'm saying—'

'Name one good reason why I couldn't become… say…' Pearl wracked her brain for someone well-known to support her case. 'The Forces' Sweetheart.'

'Already taken.'

Pearl wasn't ready to give up. She had plans. She was going to be famous.

'Just because the *Daily Express* says people chose Vera Lynn to be the Forces' Sweetheart, doesn't mean I can't be one, too. Or take over from her. For a start, I'm more… sultry. Men who've been away from home a long time hardly daydream of the girl next door, do they? They want something a bit more… exotic.'

Ivy shook her head. 'If you say so. But if you want my opinion, aiming to be *something more exotic* is asking for trouble. And I definitely wouldn't let Sylvia know what's going through that daft head of yours.'

'Wasn't planning on telling her. Or anyone else for that matter—'

'Wise.'

'You're free to follow *your* dream in the same way as *I'm* free to go after *mine*.'

'Fair enough. But don't come crying to me if it all goes wrong.'

'I shan't have to because it won't. Anyway,' Pearl said – sometimes, Ivy seemed to delight in putting her down, 'here comes the truck.'

'About bloody time. Come on, then, I can't wait to get out of this wind. Goose bumps aren't my best look.'

As she accepted a hand up into the back of the truck and then edged her way along to sit on the sideways-facing bench, Pearl smiled. Ivy could think what she liked. If you wanted to achieve anything in this life, you had to aim high and be dogged in your pursuit of it. It was about the only thing her headmaster had ever said that had struck her as worth remembering.

—

'Golly, we're going to be late home again.'

'I know. It's lovely that they wanted us to stay for a bit of a party, but if I were to close my eyes right this moment, I could fall asleep standing up.'

'Yeah. When I said to you earlier that I might not be able to keep on with these late nights, I wasn't altogether joking. Must be getting old.'

It was later that same evening and, having just performed at a temporary army camp on the outskirts of Exeter, Ivy and Pearl, along with Stan and his actor pal, and Murray the Magician, were being driven back into the city. Their pianist, Cliff, had already been dropped off.

'Doesn't the hospital have a later shift you could work?' Pearl raised her voice over the din of the truck's engine to ask. The idea that Ivy might give up these concerts put a damper on her own enthusiasm.

'There is one, yes, but then I wouldn't get away in time to do the shows.'

'Oh. Yes. I see.'

'And next week we're doing three.'

'I know.' Pearl had to admit that, as much as she looked forward to these performances, they certainly took it out of her, coming as they did after doing the early run on her bus.

'I mean, even once I get dropped off, I still have to walk fifteen minutes or so.'

Pearl frowned. 'Really?'

'Yup. And the place where I live ain't particularly peaceful either, not like where you are. It's hard enough getting to sleep at the best of times, without the couple downstairs rowing and throwing things. I'm surprised they've anything left to smash.'

'Golly.' It had never occurred to Pearl to wonder about Ivy's living arrangements. 'Haven't you family you could go to?'

The truck having come to a halt at a junction, Ivy waited to reply until it had pulled away. 'Nope. Dad came back from the last war, married Mum, made me, and then got sick and died. He'd been gassed in France, see. Then, when I was three, Mum died. I don't remember neither of them. I only know as much as that because it's what the neighbours told the authorities.'

Pearl wished now that she hadn't asked. Poor Ivy. What a sad thing. 'I'm sorry. I didn't know.'

'I don't talk about it,' Ivy went on, 'because when folk hear my parents died when I was small, they usually go on to ask if I went to live with an aunt or uncle. When I tell them I was sent to a children's home, they don't know what to say. To be honest, nowadays if anyone asks, I just say that yes, I went to relatives.'

'Oh, Ivy.' In her throat, Pearl could feel the hardening of a lump.

'I always supposed that when no one came forward to claim me, the authorities had no choice.'

In the darkness, Pearl reached for Ivy's hand. 'I'm so sorry. I had no idea. Are your lodgings really that bad?'

When Ivy didn't immediately reply, Pearl wondered whether it was because she was crying. Over the rumbling of the truck, it was impossible to hear, and in the pitch black, she couldn't see clearly enough to be sure.

'To be honest, that's something else I'd prefer not to talk about.'

No, she didn't sound as though she was crying.

'Then come and live with me.'

'What?'

'As you've seen for yourself, my room's got a spare bed.' To Pearl, it seemed the obvious answer. 'I mean, clearly, I'd have to ask Mrs Trude. And you'd have to pay your way, she'd charge double for two of us. And though I've not the least idea how far it is to the hospital, if it turns out to be too far to walk, we could see about getting you a bike.'

From within the pitch black came an explosion of laughter. 'Pearl Warren, you certainly are one of a kind. You'd really let me come and live with you?'

Pearl wasn't sure whether to take umbrage. 'I offered, didn't I?'

'You certainly did. I just want you to be sure you mean it.'

In the darkness, Pearl nodded. 'You'd do the same for me, were the boot on the other foot.'

'Then yes,' Ivy said with a squeeze of Pearl's hand. 'I'll come after work tomorrow afternoon… if that's all right.'

'I'll have to catch Mrs Trude in the morning. And I warn you, she's a nosy old bag.'

'No matter,' Ivy said with a light laugh. 'So am I.'

Pearl felt a wave of relief. 'Then it's settled.'

Now, with a bit of luck and, perhaps, one less worry, Ivy could keep singing with The Twilight Troopers – not to mention anything else that came their way as a result.

Chapter 11

'And how was *your* day, dear?'

'Oh, you know, darling. Much the same.'

It was surprising, Pearl thought as she bent to untie her shoelaces, how quickly she and Ivy had settled to sharing her room. Individually, they both had their quirks, Ivy's turning out to be the way she found the humour in situations – the way they had taken to greeting each other every evening a case in point. But, even when the alarm clock Ivy buried beneath her pillow went off at four-fifteen, five mornings out of every six, and the poor girl stumbled about getting dressed, Pearl didn't mind; she simply turned over and went back to sleep until her own alarm startled her awake again an hour later.

She found Ivy's company enjoyable, which brought home to her how much, without until now realising it, she had come to miss the sisterly companionship of Clemmie and May. She hadn't seen either of them in ages now. In fact, the last time she'd seen Clemmie was before she, Pearl, had come to lodge at Mrs Trude's. She had a vague recollection of flying out of the rest centre on her way to work one morning, only to bump into Clemmie coming in the opposite direction, heading, she assumed, to a spell of volunteering with the WVS. Oh, and Clemmie had left with one of the other volunteers a slip of paper upon which she had jotted May's address. *I expect May would love to hear your news*, she had written beneath details for a place called Fair Maids Farm. She remembered because the name had struck her as daft for a place that was no doubt perennially knee-deep in mud. Where that little piece of paper was now, she had no idea. Most likely long gone.

To distract herself from the unexpected wave of guilt brought on by the realisation of how she had neglected her sisters, she looked across at Ivy. Perched on the sill of the open window, she was blowing cigarette smoke out into the garden. Finally, the cool and indifferent weather of July had moved on, with August showing signs of behaving more like summer. The unfortunate knock-on effect was that, instead of shivering with cold while they waited their turn to perform under some or other tent, they now perspired in the stuffy heat. A couple of nights ago, she would swear she'd actually felt her foundation sliding down her face.

'This place tonight,' Ivy said, looking back at her. 'Is this the one Cliff said has a proper stage?'

By now stood in her underwear at the wash basin, Pearl turned on the tap. Waiting for the water level to rise, she said, 'I think so. To be honest, they've all become a bit of a blur.'

'I know what you mean. One canvas roof is pretty much like the next. Audiences the same. Here, tell me,' Ivy went on, stubbing out her cigarette in the little metal dish she'd brought with her when she'd moved in. 'You ever tempted to go out with any of the men who're always asking?'

'You know you should give that up, don't you?' With her head, Pearl gestured to the ashtray. As she watched,

Ivy emptied the contents out of the window. 'If you're serious about singing.'

Ivy shrugged. 'Happen I like the throatiness it lends.'

'That's all well and good but at what cost in the long run? Sylvia said—'

'Pearl, do me a favour and let it go. Please? I don't need *both* of you on my back about it. I know I should give it up, all right? But I don't want to. I find it… soothing.'

'Well, it's *your* voice,' Pearl replied with a shrug of her own.

Tonight, The Tim Murrin Dance Band had been invited to play for soldiers at one of the barracks. To the girls' delight, they were each to sing four numbers; in consultation with Sylvia, Jack had deemed they were ready. The news had apparently put Ron Bachelor's nose out of joint, but everyone else had been pleased.

'Soldiers want something pretty to look at,' Jack had said when the two of them had gone along earlier in the week to practise with the band. 'They also want to hear some of the newer numbers, and that's where you two come in. So, ladies, glamour is the order of the night.'

'You buying us evening frocks, then?' Ivy had quipped.

'If only, love,' Jack had replied.

'I mean, these concerts are war work, aren't they? Essential to the morale of the troops?' With a wink to Pearl, Ivy had gone on, 'So, shouldn't we be allowed frocks above and beyond what we've got coupons for?'

'Find a way to bring that about,' Jack had retorted with a grin, 'and I'll back you all the way. But otherwise, get up here to the microphone. Sylvia assures me your two new numbers are ready to go. So, let's hear them.'

Returning from her reverie to find herself staring into the washbasin, Pearl dried her hands and dabbed some deodorant under her arms. 'Poor old Ron – losing some of his act.'

'Lucky us, more like. Now we've started doing four songs each, it'll be hard to put us back to just the two, don't you think? Although, to make good an' sure of that, happen we should press Sylvia to learn another two each, as well.'

'Ivy Snell, I do believe you're mounting a takeover.' Slipping her burgundy dress from its hanger, Pearl pulled it over her head. 'We do need new frocks, though, don't we?'

'*I* certainly do. Yours is a darn sight newer than mine. And mine wasn't new to start with.'

'Neither was mine. Tell you what, how about on your next day off we make a trip to that little second-hand shop down near the Gaumont?'

Ivy sighed. 'My day off's tomorrow. And I'm not exactly flush. But I suppose I *might* be able to scrape together enough for something simple. You forget, you earn more than I do.'

'You get war wage,' Pearl remarked, smoothing her dress down over her hips.

'You still earn more than me.'

'Well, I say we at least go and look. I'm leaning towards something full length this time.'

'Who isn't? You finished at the basin?'

'Yep.'

'Then once I've freshened up, will you help me do my hair? Next to yours, mine always looks scruffy.'

'I'll do your hair if you let me put some make-up on you.'

Turning on the tap, Ivy groaned. 'All right. But bear in mind I don't suit pretty-pretty.'

'Don't fret. I won't do pretty-pretty. What we're going for tonight is *film star*.'

Ivy responded with a laugh. 'Huh. Good luck with that.'

'No harm aiming high.' For Pearl, aiming high had become something of a mantra; if she believed she could do it, and put herself out, she was certain to reap the rewards. From the moment the Luftwaffe had left her and her sisters homeless, she had determined to make the best of the situation. And since she didn't seem to be doing too badly so far – why change her attitude now?

–

The venue for the night's concert turned out to be a considerable step up from the draughty little halls and hastily rigged canvas affairs to which the girls had become accustomed. But then, tonight, they were singing with the whole of The Tim Murrin Dance Band – not just with Cliff on piano.

'I could get used to this,' Pearl said as she and Ivy were shown into a room at the back of an auditorium filled with wooden benches and a stage with a proper curtain.

'A treat, for sure,' Ivy responded as she followed her in through the door and stood glancing about.

'Look, there's even a mirror.'

'Ah, here you are.' At the sound of Sylvia's voice, both women turned to see her standing, hands on hips, in the doorway. 'I can't hear much warming up going on.'

'Only just got here,' Pearl hastily excused the pair of them.

'That's as maybe. But now you've had a good look around, I suggest you get straight to it. I'll go and find Jack and get the running order. When I come back, I expect to hear you both exercising.'

The moment Sylvia left the room, Ivy mimicked her tone. '"*I expect to hear you both exercising.*"'

Pearl smiled. Ivy's impersonation was spot on. 'She only wants us to do well,' she defended Sylvia before proceeding to press under her chin with her forefinger. 'I don't feel tight or tense, do you?'

Ivy, though, was ferreting about in her handbag. 'Not so as I've noticed. But I wouldn't mind a— Curse it. Don't tell me I've left them at home.'

In the knowledge that Ivy was referring to her pack of cigarettes, Pearl sighed. 'Perhaps it's no bad thing if you have. Come on, let's make a start or we'll be in trouble.'

'Oh, for heaven's sake, woman, lay off.'

Taken aback by Ivy's sharpness, Pearl turned to regard her. 'Really? That's the mood you're in? Before we even start?'

Ivy gave a doleful shake of her head. 'Sorry. But you know how tetchy I get when I haven't got any fags, more so when it means I'll have to go cap in hand to Fat Harry and scrounge one.' Fat Harry was Ivy's nickname for the band's drummer, who happened to be as slim as a rake.

'So? What's the problem? You've done it enough times before.'

'The problem is that he keeps asking me out.'

'Then keep saying no.'

'I do.'

'Then ask yourself how desperate you really are for a smoke. Now, for goodness' sake, come on, let's start warming up.'

Whilst they were bickering, Sylvia reappeared, in her hand a sheet of paper. 'Right, I have the running order.'

Craning to see over Sylvia's shoulder, Pearl ran her eyes down the list; a few instrumentals to start, after which Ron was doing his set. Then there were a couple more instrumentals followed by a short break. After the interval, the band were doing one number and then Ivy was on. Following the schedule to the bottom, Pearl withheld a gasp: Jack had given her top billing! If she hadn't already been riddled with nerves, she would be now; Jack had chosen her to close the show. Goodness, what an honour. Regrettably, the downside to performing last was having the best part of two hours in which to wait about, growing evermore terrified. The prospect already had the dratted butterflies in a twitchy mood.

'Golly,' she whispered. 'If Ron's nose wasn't already out of joint, it will be now.'

'I wouldn't read too much into it,' Sylvia was quick to remark. 'Jack simply feels that, given tonight's audience, you two will go down better.'

'What are we going to do until we go on?' Pearl asked, her question directed to Ivy.

'If you'll give me a moment to go and get a ruddy fag off someone,' Ivy hissed once Sylvia had left the room, 'we can go outside for some fresh air, maybe take a bit of a stroll. You've told me before how that helps calm you down.'

Pearl shook her head. 'It does. But tonight, it might be tempting fate. Knowing my luck, I'll trip and sprain an ankle or break a wrist.'

Ivy frowned. 'Why on earth would you do that?'

'Nerves. I'm nervous.'

'You should take up smoking.'

'Oh, ha-ha,' Pearl scoffed. 'You got your monthly? Only, you're awful snide tonight.'

'Sorry,' Ivy apologised for the second time. 'Ignore me. I'm tired.'

'Well, if we're last to go on, there's no point warming up yet. So, come on, you go and find a cigarette and then we'll pop outside for a bit.'

'Hallelujah. That's the first sensible thing you've said all night.'

Eventually, from where they were leaning against a wall, out of sight of the entrance, the girls heard a man's voice over a microphone, followed swiftly by the opening notes of the band's first number.

'They've started,' Pearl whispered.

'Look, how about later, when we're done here,' Ivy ignored her to say, 'we do something?'

Why the deliberately casual tone, Pearl wondered; what, exactly, did Ivy have in mind?

'Such as?'

Ivy's shrug was no less casual. 'Maybe… see if a couple of good-looking fellas want to spend some money on us?'

Pearl gave a despairing shake of her head. 'Good-looking or not, I can't think where they'll find to do that. For a start, it'll be past ten. And it's Thursday. Nothing's open on a Thursday.'

'There's always the late showing at the Savoy…'

Pearl turned to study Ivy's expression. Was the girl serious? 'So, let me get this straight. You want to pick up a couple of men we don't know from Adam – your only yardstick seeming to be that they're good-looking – and then spend a couple of hours with them in a dark cinema. I mean, is the Savoy even open again?'

'I happen to know it is, yes.'

'No thanks. Tomorrow might be *your* day off, but it's not mine.'

'Fair enough.'

'Come on,' Pearl said as she watched Ivy drop the butt of her cigarette and stub it out beneath the toe of her shoe. 'Let's go back inside. I'm thirsty.'

'All right. I'll see what's to be had on the drinks front.'

Alone in their little dressing room, Pearl began her warming up exercises. After a few minutes, though, she paused. What on earth had happened to Ivy? How far had she gone for a glass of water? She went to the door and looked out; both directions along the corridor were empty. With a shrug, she went back to stand in front of the mirror and tried to remember where she'd got to in her exercises. Oh, yes.

As she was finishing the last of them, Ivy came bowling in, her face oddly flushed, in her hand a glass containing a drink the colour of straw.

'Where on earth have you *been*? I was beginning to think something had happened to you.'

'Here, try this.'

'What is it?'

'Cider. First decent stuff I've tasted since before the war. Go on, you'll like it.'

Irritation welling, Pearl resisted the urge to shout – at times, Ivy Snell could be thoroughly exasperating. 'You said you were going for water.'

Ivy held her grin. 'This is better. Trust me, not only will it moisten your throat, but it will put an end to your nerves as well.'

'No, thank you.'

Ivy continued to hold out the drink. 'Come on. Don't be such a wet blanket—'

'I am *not* a wet blanket.'

'For once in your stolid little life, let your hair down. Take a chance. Try something new.'

'I *said* no thank you.' *Stolid?* What did that even mean? 'Where did you get it, anyway?'

'There's a bar.'

There would be. And trust Ivy to find it. For someone who claimed she wanted a career on the stage, she took very little care of herself. She could only suppose she wasn't as committed as she made out.

'Well, for your own good, I suggest you don't let Sylvia catch you with it. Any minute now the interval will be over, and there's only one number before you go on.'

'Ladies.' At that, through the door came Jack Bassett. From the corner of her eye, Pearl saw Ivy shove the glass to the back of the table and then perch in front of it. 'Ready, both of you?'

'Could you tell me where I might get a glass of water, please?' Pearl took the opportunity to ask him.

'Of course.' He beckoned with his head. 'Come with me. Can we fetch you anything, Ivy?'

Turning to see Ivy shaking her head, in exaggerated fashion Pearl mouthed to her, *Get rid of it.* 'Perhaps I'll bring you back a glass anyway.'

'As you wish.'

When Pearl returned carrying two glasses of water, it was to see that Sylvia was back.

'All right?' Sylvia enquired.

Pearl exhaled heavily. 'Bit nervy, truth to tell.'

'That's no bad thing. It means you're not taking anything for granted, which usually ensures you properly prepare.'

'Oh, yes, I have done.'

'Then once the music strikes up, you'll be fine.'

Pearl wished she shared Sylvia's conviction.

'Hopefully, yes,' she forced herself to concede. 'It's just that this do tonight seems rather more professional than a concert party by The Twilight Troopers.'

'You know Jack well enough by now to appreciate that no matter the event or the venue, he treats every perform-ance the same. So, for what it's worth—' at this point, Sylvia turned her look upon Ivy '—my advice would be that *you* treat it seriously, too. Jack told me he's of a mind to take the band's music in a slightly more modern direction—'

'No more Ron Bachelor crooning?' Ivy interjected.

Sylvia regarded her evenly. 'I didn't say that. But I do know he thinks a younger female singer might broaden the band's appeal.'

For Pearl, the news triggered two thoughts. Firstly, Jack was right about Ron; his style of singing was old-fashioned. Secondly, Sylvia had said Jack thought a younger female *singer* might broaden the band's appeal – which, to her mind, implied one singer, not two. If that was the case, then she had to do everything she could to make sure that *she* got chosen over Ivy. For a start, there was the money to consider; she knew from one of the other band members that for a proper appearance, the band received a fee, which Jack apportioned between them. So, if she could replace Ron, then, presumably, she would get his share. More important still was the matter of publicity; her name would appear on posters; local entertainment writers would mention her in their reports for their newspaper. Agents might get to hear about her.

'Did you hear what I said, Pearl?'

She snapped her attention back. 'Sorry, I was miles away.'

'I said that if the two of you are ready, we'll go and wait in the wings.'

Wait in the wings. Yes. Of course. That would be helpful anyway – would give her the chance to see how the audience took to Ivy.

When Ivy pushed herself away from the table, Pearl was relieved to see that the glass of cider had disappeared. 'Break a leg,' she said, bringing a hand to rest on Ivy's arm.

'Same to you.'

Ivy's gaze, she was dismayed to notice, looked decidedly glassy. Please God, she willed, don't let Ivy have downed that entire glass of cider.

With the band winding up to the finish of their instrumental, Pearl leaned forward for a glimpse of the audience. They looked to be enjoying the music. And Ivy, if she was on good form, would warm them up even more. So, if she, Pearl, couldn't go out and get them on their feet with her closing number – which Jack had chosen as 'The Lady Is a Tramp' – then she might as well forget any and all notion of becoming a proper singer and start looking among the audience for a husband instead.

-

The roar was deafening. Hands were clapping; feet were stamping. Voices were roaring. *More!* She was bringing the house down, and she loved it. So loud was the noise from the audience that she failed to hear Jack arrive to stand beside her.

'Take my hand,' he bellowed into her ear. And when he clasped her fingers and raised her hand above her head, she treated the audience to yet another bow.

'We haven't rehearsed an encore,' she said, all the while beaming at the cheering servicemen.

'No,' Jack shouted back. 'We must work on that for next time.'

Next time? Was she to be Jack's choice of singer then? The possibility that she might be, added to the sensation that she was floating twelve inches off the ground. The audience had loved her performance. And Jack was talking about the future. Surely, now, she was on her way.

Still grasping her hand, Jack looked beyond her and beckoned to the wings; she turned to see Ron Bachelor strolling on to share the applause, and Sylvia propelling Ivy towards them. Ron bowed deeply; Ivy went to Jack's other side, and once again he raised Pearl's hand high above her head.

And then Jack was leading them off the stage. The band were patting her shoulder; Sylvia was giving her a hug.

'Congratulations.'

'Well done.'

'Wow.'

'They loved you.'

'Good job, Ivy.' Jack's praise for Ivy, Pearl couldn't help but notice, was more muted – warm, but not gushing.

'It sounded to me, Ivy,' Sylvia remarked as they made their way back to their dressing room, 'as though you hadn't warmed up. It took you most of your opening number to get going.'

The face Ivy made suggested she didn't care. '*I* didn't think so. After all, it's not the kind of number you go into all guns blazing, is it? It's a warm-up in itself.'

'I'm aware of that.' Sylvia's reply sounded unusually clipped and, fearing that Ivy was inviting trouble, Pearl moved away to collect her jacket from the coat hooks and busy herself checking the contents of her handbag. 'I rather meant that your voice sounded cold and thin.'

'I'll try not to let it happen again.'

'Please see to it that you don't.'

'Well,' Pearl said brightly when their exchange concluded. 'Since we have to walk, I suppose we'd better head home.'

Sylvia glanced at her wristwatch. 'You won't catch a bus?'

Pearl shook her head. 'The late services don't run now. Since the regulations for fuel were changed to include buses, the company have had to cut back. No route over twenty miles round trip operates after seven, and all the city routes stop at nine. Shanks' pony for us, I'm afraid.'

'Well, be careful,' Sylvia warned.

'We will.'

Once out of earshot, Ivy grabbed Pearl's arm. 'Uptight old cow.'

'Who?' Pearl asked, shocked by the venom in her friend's tone.

'Sylvia. "*It sounded to me, Ivy, as though you hadn't warmed up.*"'

'Well, you hadn't. And I did warn you Sylvia would notice.'

'Yeah, well—'

'And anyway,' Pearl went on, looking around to get her bearings. 'Where are we going? This isn't the way we came in.'

'Well done. No, it's not. We've got two hot dates.'

Pearl stopped dead. '*What?*'

'There's a couple of corporals want to take us for a few drinks. If they're as nice as they seem, I thought that, afterwards, we could get them to take us on to the late showing.'

Despite doing her best to swallow her irritation, Pearl knew it was to no avail. 'Ivy, no. I'm sorry but I'm dead on my feet. I couldn't go out now even if I wanted to, which, for the record, I don't.'

'Oh, for God's sake,' Ivy remonstrated. Taking Pearl's arm, she attempted to tug her onwards. 'For once in your life, don't be so prim. There are two dashing men in corporal's uniforms, their pay jangling in their pockets, who want to take us out. I know you've got to work in the morning, whereas I've got the day off, but you can't live like a nun. You've got to have *some* fun—'

'Um, excuse me, ladies?'

At the sound of a man's voice, the girls spun about. Approaching them along the corridor was a crumpled-looking little man in a dinner jacket.

'Yes?'

'Probably wants your autograph,' Ivy whispered.

'Miss Warren. Miss… er… Snell.'

'What can we do for you?' Ivy asked.

Pearl, meanwhile, was taking in the chap's appearance: above his cummerbund, a shirt button was undone; his forehead was beaded with perspiration; his hair was untidy and in need of a good cut. As for his age, well, it was hard to tell. He showed no signs of grey but then, these days, men used all sorts of tricks to look younger, even resorting to boot polish if push came to shove.

The stranger proffered a business card. When Ivy took it, the man offered a second to Pearl.

'My name is Gordon Gold.' His accent, Pearl noted, marked him out as not from locally. 'As it says on the card: *Gordon Gold, Agent to the Stars*.'

'That's a very bold claim, Mr… Gold.'

'I'm a bold man, Miss Snell. Wouldn't survive five minutes in my business if I wasn't.'

Glancing at the stiff little business card, Pearl suspected a prank. Agent to the Stars – and yet, here he was, at an army camp, talking to the two of them?

'An agent for singers – for performers?' Ivy asked.

'One and the same. I saw your show. To be honest, I was tipped off to come. Took a good deal of palm greasing to get into this place, though, I can tell you.'

'Who tipped you off?' Pearl asked. As much as she wanted to believe this was happening, something about it didn't feel right.

'That, I cannot divulge.' Pearl studied his expression; she knew it wouldn't be Sylvia who had 'tipped him off'. Nor would it have been Jack. One of the other members of the band, perhaps? Even that felt unlikely – after all, what would be in it for them? 'What I will say,' Gordon Gold went on, 'is that having seen your acts, I should like to represent you. Both of you. Come to London and I'll make you stars. With voices like yours, you'll be picking and choosing what you do. I'll get you big shows. Top billing. I'll get you into recordings – with *your* looks, maybe even into films, musicals. I'm telling you, you've got what it takes.' His spiel delivered, he paused before continuing, 'I detect doubt. I see you looking at me and thinking, how can he be so sure? Or... why should I believe this man's flannel? So, ask yourself, why would I lie? What would be in it for *me*? If I don't make you money, *I* go hungry, too. And you can see from my waistline that I'm not exactly starving.'

'We'll think about it,' Pearl said sharply. It was the only way she could think to stop him from going on. 'But now, if you'll excuse me, I've been on my feet all day, I'm dog-tired, and I just want to go home.'

'Of course, Miss Warren.' With a nod to Ivy, he went on, 'Well goodnight, ladies. When you've had the chance to sleep on what I've said, telephone my assistant. She'll make an appointment for you to come and see me in town. I'll show you some of the stars I represent, show you the work I've got for them.'

'We'll do that,' Ivy said. In her tone, Pearl detected breathy excitement.

'Yes,' she added, concerned now with nothing more than simply crawling into bed. 'We'll do that.'

'Wow,' Ivy breathed when Gordon Gold returned whence he'd come. 'Well, now you've *got* to come out tonight.' When Pearl frowned, Ivy went on, 'To celebrate our good fortune. An agent – from London, no less – wants to represent us, get us bookings. This is it. Our dreams are coming true.'

'Credit where it's due,' Pearl fought off a yawn to say. 'He did seem eager. I vote we talk about it tomorrow.'

Ivy dropped Pearl's arm. 'You're really not coming for a drink? You're really going to duck out on some fun?'

In her exhaustion, Pearl sighed. 'I am. I'm going home. And I'd like you to come with me. But, since I don't think you're going to, and since I'm not your mother, I'll settle for saying goodnight and for seeing you in the morning.'

Ivy, too, let out a sigh. 'All right. If that's what you want. But don't wait up.'

'No chance.' With another yawn, Pearl followed Ivy out into the balmy night air, and then stopped to watch her cross the grass to where two cigarette ends were glowing in the darkness. If Ivy wanted to go carousing with two men she didn't know, that was down to her. For her own part, though, she reflected as she turned with an exhausted sigh in the other direction, the only thing she wanted to do right now was crawl into bed and fall asleep.

–

Walking up the hill towards the bus garage, Pearl succumbed to her second yawn in a dozen paces. It was the morning after the concert at the barracks, and she hadn't had enough sleep – nowhere near enough. Having not arrived home until well after eleven, the first thing she'd done was push up the window to let in some fresh air; since Ivy had moved in, her room – and everything in it – continually bore the smell of cigarette smoke.

Mindful of the need not to 'show a light', she had stood in the darkness, applying Crowe's Cremine to remove her make-up and reflecting on the evening's surprising turn of events. To be honest, it was all a bit of a blur. She recalled casting her eyes over Jack's running order, and her disbelief at seeing that she was to close the show. After that, she remembered nothing more than the roar of applause when she finished her last song, and feeling a rush of… a rush of what? Warmth? Elation? Affirmation?

Whatever it was, once she'd got into bed – and no matter that she'd felt both physically exhausted and mentally drained – she'd been unable to settle. This morning, with the benefit of distance, she could see that her wakefulness had been down to a longing to do it all again. There was also, though, a lingering sense of unease. That funny little man – that Gordon Gold character – had appeared out of nowhere. He claimed to have watched them sing, but she couldn't recall seeing him in the audience; in full evening dress, he ought to have stood

145

out like a penguin in a field of khaki. It wasn't that she doubted he'd been there, it was more that the manner of his approach had felt peculiar – furtive. Why hadn't he come backstage the moment the show had finished? She supposed it was possible he had but, upon seeing them with Sylvia and not knowing who she was to them, had decided to wait and catch them alone. The odd thing this morning was that, by rights, she should be overjoyed by the discovery that an agent wanted to represent them; on the surface at least, it was everything she craved. So, why wasn't she?

As she crossed the road, she saw a City & District bus chugging towards her. When it gave a toot of its horn, she realised the driver was Reg. During the air raids back in May, the bus garage experienced a near miss, leading the depot superintendent to decree that, until further notice, no bus was to remain there overnight. Instead, each driver was to take his vehicle home; should there be further raids, the chance of the entire fleet being lost would be minimal. There having been no further raids – nor even false alarms – Pearl had to wonder how long the practice would continue. As Reg slowed to pull up at the kerb and gestured to her to get on, though, purely from a selfish standpoint, she was relieved the directive was still in force.

Grateful to have a lift the remainder of the way, she boarded the platform and sank onto one of the sideways facing seats by the door. For now, she would try to forget about Gordon Gold. Later, when she finished her shift, she and Ivy were going to the second-hand dress shop again in the hope of finding something new to wear on stage. They could talk about Gordon Gold then. *Three o'clock* it had been when Ivy had come in this morning.

She knew the time because, in her fuddle-headedness, she had mistakenly thought Ivy was getting up to go to work.

'Have… a good day,' she'd mumbled, as had become her habit.

'Go back to sleep,' Ivy had whispered, as had become hers.

But then, of course, when she'd been awoken by her alarm at quarter past five and seen that Ivy was sound asleep, she'd realised to her horror that Ivy hadn't long been in.

'All right, maid?' Reg greeted her when they'd pulled into the bus garage and were crossing the forecourt to clock in.

She nodded. 'Thanks for stopping.'

'Late night?' He gestured her ahead of him to punch her card.

'Later than I'd have liked, yes. But only tomorrow to get through and then it's Sunday.'

Climbing the stairs to the ladies' cloakroom, she sighed. Perhaps she should simply stop fretting about this Gordon Gold and suggest they just go and see him. She didn't dislike being a conductress; if she had to work for 'the good of the nation in this time of war', she could do a lot worse. But, if she waited for Sylvia to tell her she was ready to audition for roles in musicals, she could be stuck taking fares forever.

Opening her locker, she exhaled yet another sigh. Yes, she'd made up her mind. If this afternoon Ivy still felt as she did last night, then she would suggest they telephone Mr Gold's assistant and make an appointment to go and see him. Other than their time and their effort, what did they have to lose?

III. Discord

Chapter 12

'I'll pay you back.'

'It's all right, there's no need. I had a little put by—'

'But it's like I said, I hadn't reckoned on us not being able to get here and back in a day – you know, to us needing to stop over in a boarding house. And I'm already losing a day's money as it is.'

'Truly,' Pearl said. 'I told you not to worry about it. I know it's a bind that we've had to stay over, but you've told me you'll pay me back and I believe you. Ordinary times, we could have got here and back no trouble. I'm just glad that chap in the ticket office thought to mention how unreliable the trains are these days. I never gave a second thought to them not running properly. But anyway, we're here now.'

'Yes. This is it. Our big day.'

Rather than sounding bubbly and bright, Ivy's tone appeared doubtful. Perhaps, Pearl reflected, she was just a bit jittery. Her own nerves had been jangling since the moment she'd opened her eyes. 'Our big day,' she agreed. 'Yes.'

''Though I don't mind saying how I'd always pictured being more… well, more excited.'

'Maybe *next* time we come to London,' Pearl said in a bid to distract from her own bad case of second thoughts, 'we'll be staying somewhere smarter than this place.'

It was the week after the concert at the barracks and, having had what turned out to be an extremely brief discussion about the merits or otherwise of Gordon Gold, the girls had quickly come down in favour of at least hearing him out; the manner of his approach might have been peculiar, they had agreed, but that didn't, by itself, make him a poor agent. As Ivy had gone on to point out, that he was an agent at all, let alone one interested in representing the two of them, was nothing short of a miracle. And gift horses, she'd gone on to say, were not to be looked in the mouth.

To that end – and with Ivy having won the argument about who, of the two of them, would sound more professional – they had traipsed to the telephone box on the corner, Pearl's stomach knotting so hard at the prospect of speaking to him she'd begun to hope that, when they got there, the kiosk would be out of order. Even once she'd gone in and closed the door behind her, she'd stood, for what felt like an eternity, fingering Gordon Gold's card while trying to summon the courage to dial the operator and ask for his number. To make matters worse, once her call had been put through, the telephone at the other end had rung and rung, until, just as she'd been about to replace the receiver and press button 'B' for the return of her coins, a rather bored sounding woman had come on the line.

'Gordon Gold. Agent to the stars.'

By that point, Pearl was in such a stew that she'd completely forgotten what she'd planned to say.

'Oh. Yes. Hello,' she'd finally mumbled. 'Good afternoon. My name is Pearl Warren. When he was in Exeter the other day, Mr Gold gave me – and my friend, Ivy

Snell – his business card, and asked us to telephone and make an appointment to see him.'

'Warren, you say?' To Pearl, it sounded as though the woman at the other end was chewing.

'That's right. Pearl Warren and Ivy Snell. Mr Gold came to hear us sing in a concert at the—'

'Hold the line.'

Using her foot to wedge open the door and allow in some fresh air, Pearl had covered the receiver with her hand to tell Ivy – pacing up and down outside – what was going on. 'I think she's gone to check with him.'

'Eleven o'clock next Wednesday,' the woman had returned to say.

'Eleven o'clock Wednesday,' Pearl had repeated, shooting a look at Ivy to see her respond with a thumbs up. 'We'll be there. Thank you very much. Goodbye.'

'Yes!' Ivy had yelled, deafening Pearl as she'd wrapped her in a hug. 'We're on our way. This is it.'

If this lodging house was indeed 'it', Pearl thought as she stood there now, surveying the shabby little room with its sooty fireplace, water-stained ceiling, and moth-eaten candlewick bedspreads, then God help them. Even penny-pinching Mrs Trude shelled out for a daily woman to keep her lodging house clean.

Against her better judgement, Pearl perched on the corner of the stool in front of the dressing table. The three-panel mirror standing on top was so badly mottled, it couldn't even claim to be ornamental, let alone func-tional. 'What do you think Mr Gold will want to ask us?'

Ivy shrugged. 'I've been wondering that myself.'

'Perhaps we *should* have told Sylvia,' Pearl said, recalling Ivy's adamant stance that they refrain from telling anyone about their plans, but especially Sylvia, who, she claimed, would only try to talk them out of it.

Ivy's tone this morning was no less resolute. 'And as I told you last time you said so, I happen to believe that would have been a mistake. "You're not ready. You don't have enough experience. All in good time." Honestly, Pearl, I can hear her now.'

Deep down, Pearl suspected Ivy was right. Nevertheless, a growing part of her still wished they'd got Sylvia's blessing. 'Maybe,' she said. 'But at least she knows how these things work – would have been able to help us prepare. As it is, here we are, with not the least clue what's going to happen. I mean, will he want us to audition – you know, to sing for him? Only, if so, we should have brought our music.'

'He's an agent. He'll have music.'

'But what if it's a song we don't know?'

'*You're* all right. You know every number from 'most every musical in recent years.'

'Not well, I don't.' Ivy did have a point, though. Look through enough scores and she was bound to find something she could have a go at.

'*I'm* more concerned he'll ask who we've sung *with*, where we've performed, that sort of thing. I mean, we don't exactly have much to brag about.'

'That's another of my fears,' Pearl replied. 'And what if we were supposed to bring a stage outfit. Oh, dear God, what if he sees how unprepared we are and—'

'If he'd wanted us to do a full-blown audition, that secretary woman would have said so.'

'I'm not sure *she* knew what day of the week it was. Sounded half asleep to me.'

'Well, anyway,' Ivy picked up again. 'Unprepared or not, we're here. So, all we can do is make the best of it. By the way, will you do my eyes for me? You said you would.'

Pearl smiled. ''Course. Though the light in here is truly awful. Sit there and I'll do my best.' When Ivy moved to the stool, from her make-up purse Pearl withdrew two palettes, one of eyeliner, the other of mascara. 'What did you decide to tell them at work yesterday?'

'Oh, you'll like this,' Ivy said and started to grin. 'Not long before I was due to finish for the day, I took a gulp of water, held it in my mouth to make my cheeks look big, doubled over, groaned, shot back up, motioned frantically towards the door and fled.'

'Crikey.'

'When I got to the ladies', there was this other girl already there. No idea who she was. So, anyway, I dived into one of the cubicles, spat the water down the toilet and retched for all I was worth. Hurt my throat, actually.'

'Hold still. You can keep talking but just try not to move about so much.'

'Then I went to the basin, made the front of my hair wet, splashed some water down the front of my overall, and went back to the kitchens, all apologies.'

'And they didn't see through you?' Sometimes, she had to admire Ivy's wiliness. 'And *don't* shake your head when you reply.'

'See through *my* acting? Hardly. "Oh dear, love," says my supervisor. "Perhaps you'd best go on home. And if you're not right in the morning, don't come in. Don't want you spreading sickness round the wards, do we?" So, I mumbled something about going home to bed and staying off food for a while.'

'They won't be surprised you're not in today, then.'

'That's right. Costly, though, having to go without a day's pay. Not something I can make a habit of – which means today had better amount to something or I'll be in even more dire straits than usual.'

'Do you want me to pat some powder over your nose?'

'Do I need it?'

'You might, before the morning's out.'

'Go on, then. Might as well go the whole hog. For a ha'p'orth of tar, and all that.'

'*I* had to plead with the controller to switch shifts. I made out I had toothache and that a dentist was able to see me at short notice. I've got to do a Sunday shift now to make up for it.'

'Shame.'

'It is,' Pearl agreed.

'Still, if this morning goes well, happen it won't matter. Happen we won't be doing our jobs much longer anyway. And wouldn't *that* be nice.'

'Lovely. Right. There you are,' Pearl said as she took a step backwards. 'You brought lipstick, didn't you?'

Ivy nodded. 'I got that red you told me to.'

'Good.'

'Something else that cost me dear.'

'Look upon it as a— What do you call it?'

'An investment.'

'That's it. An investment. Anyway, come on, then,' Pearl said with a glance to her new wristwatch. It was only a second-hand white metal one with a plain face and simple black hands, but she'd bought it from her first pay packet and was extremely proud of it. 'I'm going to pop along to the lav and then we'd best be going.'

'Got the directions?' Ivy asked when, a few minutes later, they emerged from the boarding house onto the street.

Pearl unfolded a slip of paper. 'Say what you will about that place, the landlady was as helpful as can be. Wrote it all down for me.'

'If it wasn't for my old copy of *The Stage*, we would never have found her. *Rooms for actors in boarding house. Ten minutes' walk from Shaftesbury Avenue.* Saved our bacon.'

'It did. Anyway, she says that, from Piccadilly Circus, we have to go up Shaftesbury Avenue as far as Wardour Street – apparently, we'll know it from the bomb-damaged theatre on the left – then follow that as far as Peter Street. From there, we go right onto Berwick Street, past the next lot of bomb damage and then it's one of the little alleyways off that. She said she didn't know exactly which one but that, by then, we should be close enough to find it.'

When the girls reached Piccadilly Circus, they paused to look around.

'Bit of a let-down if you ask me,' Ivy remarked of it.

'No doubt it's better without everything boarded up – and when they were able to have all these lights on.'

'Happen it was.'

They were more impressed with the theatres on Shaftesbury Avenue.

'Look at all these places, right next door to one another,' Pearl said.

'Never thought to see so many in the same street,' Ivy agreed. '*Escort: A Play of the Royal Navy,*' she went on to read from the billboard outside the Lyric Theatre. 'Nice enough building but, to me, the play sounds as dull as ditch water.'

'*Flare Path*,' Pearl read from the poster at the Apollo, next door.

'Never heard of it.' After a moment, Ivy added, 'You know, I really do ache to be a part of all this.'

Pearl turned to regard her. 'To be on stage in a theatre?'

'Not necessarily in a play – but definitely part of all this performing lark. I've always wanted to be in a show, especially in London. I can scarce believe I'm even here...'

Pearl knew what Ivy meant. Standing there today, looking around in awe at what she'd heard referred to as 'Theatreland', had fired her own burning urge. Yes, it looked pretty dreary and depressing now but she could just imagine it when the war was over, and all these buildings were lit up, and the streets thronged with theatregoers, excited about the spectacle they were going to see – or animated in their praise for it afterwards.

Wandering past the Apollo, she looked up, spotting by chance that they'd reached Wardour Street. 'We go up here.'

'That's Queen's Theatre,' Ivy said with a gesture to the bomb-damaged building on their left. 'I remember two years ago when it was hit in the Blitz reading afterwards that although the whole front of the building is gone, and the rear stalls are missing, they still use it for rehearsing.'

'Really? I shouldn't like to work in somewhere half derelict.'

'I suppose they'll eventually rebuild it. But not any time soon, I shouldn't think.'

Pearl was impressed that Ivy knew so much. Perhaps she had underestimated her, perhaps she genuinely was keen to be a part of all of this.

'Oh, look,' she said as they walked on, 'that poor church, all burned out. How sad to see it like that.'

'No sadder than anything at home,' Ivy countered.

'I suppose not. It's just that, at home, I've got used to the sight of certain places standing in ruins.'

'Yeah. Amazing how quick you get used to something not being there anymore.'

A short distance along Wardour Street, they found Peter Street, then Berwick Street. After that, it was a question of looking for names on the narrow alleyways.

'Here,' Pearl said, staring up to where, on a plain brick wall, a heavily soot-blackened sign read *Tranter's Passage*. 'It's along here.' In precisely the same manner as they had when the two of them had stumbled upon the boarding house, Pearl's spirits sank. Tranter's Passage was no more than a narrow cut between buildings, the uneven cobbles stained green where downpipes disgorged rain from the rooftops.

'Are you sure this is right?' she heard Ivy enquire from behind.

She turned over her shoulder. 'There's a door ahead. Maybe that's it.'

The first thing she noticed as she drew level with it was how most of the black paint had peeled away to expose the bare wood beneath. She glanced up: over the door, a panel of glass was obscured by grime; above that, hung a light. With a sigh, she looked back down; fastened to the spalling brickwork was a tarnished brass plaque engraved with the name Gordon Gold, underneath, the words, 'Talent Agent'.

Arriving beside her, Ivy scoffed. 'Can't see him attracting much talent down here.'

Her own unease deepening, Pearl turned to study Ivy's expression. 'Do you still want to go in?'

'Well, I certainly didn't come all this way to turn around and go straight back home again.'

Ivy had a point. Even so, Pearl couldn't imagine how someone with premises in such a dank alleyway could possibly be any good. But, since they'd spent a considerable amount of their hard-earned wages to get there, she supposed it behoved them to at least see the thing through – make up their minds on the facts.

Drawing a breath, she reached out and turned the handle. 'Come on, then. Let's see what he's got to say for himself.' Beyond the door, Pearl was confronted by an uncarpeted staircase. She waited for Ivy to follow her in and then started up it. At the top, she came to a halt and, in the dim glow cast by the unshaded bulb above a second door, looked about for a bell. 'Should I knock, do you think?'

When she turned to Ivy, two steps lower down, it was to see her shrug.

'No idea. Can't hurt, though, can it?'

She knocked twice. Her breathing, she noticed as she waited for a response, had grown rapid and shallow. And she'd come over so cold she was almost shivering.

'No one's coming,' she whispered back down the stairs.

'Knock again,' Ivy instructed. 'A bit harder.' Still, Pearl's knock went unanswered. 'What time is it?'

Pearl examined her wristwatch. 'Ten to eleven.'

'Perhaps he's not here yet then. Try the handle.'

Beset by misgivings, Pearl nevertheless complied, pushing open the door, stepping inside, and beckoning Ivy to follow.

Beyond the door they found themselves in a windowless hallway lit by yet another dim bulb. On one side of the passageway's short length were several doors, the first of which stood partly open.

She cleared her throat.

'Hello?' When no one answered, she pushed the door wider and went into the room beyond. 'Hello?' She edged further in. As rooms went, it was peculiar; a window on the far side gave onto rooftops while, closer to, panes of glass, angled like the roof of a lean-to, revealed a sliver of blue sky sandwiched between the brick wall of a neighbouring building and yet more roofs. Beneath the skylight was a desk upon which sat a large and solid-looking typewriter and a telephone. Balls of screwed-up paper littered what remained of the surface. Away to the right, the far corner of the room had been sectioned off by the construction of two partition walls, the top halves of which comprised frosted glass. Upon the glazed panel of the door, stencilled in black capital letters was the name *Gordon Gold*.

'At least we're in the right place,' Ivy stepped out from behind her to say.

Her pronouncement should have made Pearl relax. In reality, it simply compounded her nerves. 'Hm. So, where is he?'

With that, they heard a door slam, followed by a heavy tread on the stairs.

'Someone's coming.'

If they were going to leave, Pearl thought, now was the time to do so. Even without suggesting it, though, she knew how Ivy would respond. Instead, she reminded herself of what was at stake and drew a breath. 'Good.' The sooner this ordeal was over, the better. It wasn't that she'd lost the desire to perform, it was more that she would prefer to go about it with someone *wholesome* – someone a bit more like Sylvia.

With that, through the door came Gordon Gold, puffing from the exertion of having climbed the stairs.

He paused momentarily to consider their presence.

'Well, good morning,' he eventually said, his mouth breaking into an oily smile. 'I'm so glad you decided to come.'

Chapter 13

To Pearl's dismay, Gordon Gold looked exactly as she remembered him, his smarmy manner and the way he sized them up, making it hard to ignore that he made her feel unclean.

'We did knock,' she said, feeling the need to explain why they had let themselves in. 'But when no one answered, we just… came in.'

Beside her, Ivy nodded. 'But the place was empty.'

A flicker of irritation crossing Gold's face, he set down his briefcase, reached to hang his mackintosh on the coat stand and then disappeared back into the hallway.

'Joanna?' When there was no answer, he called again. 'Joanna!'

Eventually, a female voice acknowledged him. 'Uh-huh?'

'There are clients in the outer office.'

The unseen woman responded in a sleepy drawl. 'They're early.'

'Oh for— Never mind. Is there any coffee?'

'Nuh-uh.'

'Tea?'

'Maybe.' To Pearl, the woman sounded as though she was pulling on clothing. 'But there's no milk.'

'Then take something from petty cash and go and get some.'

'Okey-doke.'

As Pearl and Ivy stood exchanging looks, Gold returned.

'Ladies, forgive the disarray. Jo-Jo had a… booking… last night that kept her out late.' Pearl forced a smile. 'But that needn't concern you.' He bent to lift his briefcase; barely twelve inches from the floor the latch shot undone, the case springing open to reveal several manila folders. Hoisting the case to his side, Gold strode towards the office in the corner. 'Please, follow me.' Once beyond the door, he gestured vaguely. 'Take a seat over there. I'll just clear a space and then I'm all yours.'

'We're in no rush,' Ivy said, indicating with her eyes that Pearl should join her in sitting down.

'No,' Pearl agreed, settling onto the second of the two chairs. 'None at all.'

Once seated, Pearl felt marginally less tense. If she'd found the manner in which this interview had got off the ground – or this audition, or whatever this was supposed to be – off-putting, she clearly didn't have what it took to make it in this world. Besides, it probably wasn't as bad as it seemed; Gold hadn't actually been late, and his office had only been empty because his assistant had been working late. She knew how tiring evening appearances could be, especially after eight or more hours at the day job. The main thing was that any minute now, they would get down to business; from this point forward, it was up to her to appear professional and charming.

The office into which Gold had invited them shared the same view out over rooftops – or at least, a grimy version of it, the panes of glass giving the impression of going uncleaned since long before the war. The walls were panelled to waist height with dark wood and painted a dirty cream colour above. From the centre of the ceiling hung a dusty chandelier. On the desk stood a telephone, a perpetual calendar on an onyx base, and a large hardcover book that might have been a diary. In front of the desk stood two hardback chairs; against the wall behind her, a leather Chesterfield that had seen better days; in front of that, a low table. Upon the latter, someone had made a fan-shaped display of theatre programmes. The sight of them lifted her mood; presumably, they were for shows in which this man had clients.

'Well, then, ladies,' Gold looked up after a moment to remark. 'Let me first say how delighted I am that you decided to come. It's not often I venture so far from town in search of talent. It was a fortuitous day on both sides.'

'I hope you didn't think us offish the other night,' Ivy replied. Her enunciation, Pearl noticed, was a number of notches up from her usual.

Determined not to let her do all the talking, Pearl cleared her throat. 'But with you turning up out of the blue like that, well, let's just say we were caught off guard.'

Gold glanced between them. 'Let me tell you a little secret.' Instinctively, the girls leaned forward in their seats. 'I've always rather enjoyed the part where I approach someone for the first time. I get a frisson of excitement when I see a young woman who has what it takes, and I confess to rather enjoying seeing her reaction when I introduce myself.'

'You mean, when a girl has what it takes to make it in the entertainment business?'

To Pearl, Ivy appeared to have come over all breathy and excited; it didn't become her. For her own part, she had determined to appear keen but professional – perhaps even a little aloof – but definitely not awe-struck.

'Let's start with some details, shall we?' From the top drawer of his desk, Gold withdrew a sheet of foolscap, followed by a second, and placed them side by side on his blotter. From the breast pocket of his jacket, he withdrew a fountain pen. 'Renée Harper Hanson gave me this,' he said, holding it out for them to see as he unscrewed the cap, 'when she signed the contract for her first leading role. Of course, she's in Hollywood now.'

Ivy was clearly impressed. 'Gosh.'

Beside her, Pearl frowned. Renée Harper Hanson was a name she didn't know; perhaps, in America, she was on the stage rather than in films.

'That's her up there.'

The girls turned to look. Above the Chesterfield was a framed head-and-shoulders shot of a woman who appeared to be in her mid-twenties. Her chin was resting on her folded hand, blonde hair tumbled artlessly about her face. In the corner of the photograph was a swirly signature. While not beautiful in the accepted sense, she would certainly turn heads on Exeter High Street.

Ivy seemed even more impressed. 'Wow.'

'Anyway, back to the two of you.' From there, Gold proceeded to note down details, starting with Ivy. 'Ivy Flora Snell. We might swap that about,' he said, angling his head to stare down at what he'd written. 'And Snelling sounds better. Snell is too short. Don't take offence,' he looked up at Ivy to remark. 'Ivy Snell is pithy and to the point. Great for a librarian. But Flora Snelling has more of a ring.'

'Flora Snelling,' Ivy repeated reverently. 'Ooh, yes. I see what you mean.'

When she turned to Pearl for confirmation, Pearl smiled. 'It does have a ring to it.'

From there, Gold asked Ivy about her height and weight. While still noting her answers, he said, 'Stand up. Start at the door and walk across to the window.' He glanced up from making notes to watch her walk. 'And return.' When Ivy was back where she'd started, he said, 'This time, without shoes.' As far as Pearl could see, Ivy removing her shoes made scant difference to her boyish gait. 'Take some lessons in deportment. I assume such things are to be had in the wilds of Devon?'

'Um...'

When Ivy looked at her, Pearl shrugged; she wasn't even sure what the word meant.

'If there are no stage schools, you might find a dance teacher – ballet teacher in particular – worth asking.'

'Yes,' Ivy said. 'I'll find out.'

'You can sit back down now.'

'Thank you.'

'Unpin your hair for me.'

When Ivy turned to Pearl this time, her look was a wary one. 'But I'll never be able to—'

'I need to see you with your hair down. Producers always want to know about hair.'

'Here,' Pearl said, getting to her feet. 'Let me help you.'

Between them, they pulled out the pins securing Ivy's Victory roll and placed them on the desk. Given the amount of lacquer Pearl had applied to hold the sausage curls in place, Ivy's hair didn't immediately drop down. 'I'll... um... fluff it up a bit for you.'

'Fine,' Gold said with little more than a cursory check of Ivy's hair. 'You might want to lose a little weight.'

Having bent to replace her shoes, Ivy sat up straight on her chair. 'Weight,' she muttered. 'Right.'

'Not a great deal. But losing a little off your face will highlight your cheekbones. Directors like cheekbones. And they might go for your colouring – the olive tint of your skin won't be something they see every day. Not everyone will like it, but you might get roles that a more traditional English rose complexion wouldn't suit. Do you smoke?'

Pearl noticed Ivy blush.

'I'm trying to give it up.'

'Don't. Directors like it. Makes a woman look sexy.'

Ivy brightened up. 'Sexy. Right.'

From there, Gordon Gold cast his scrutiny upon Pearl.

'Pearl Sadie Warren,' she replied when he asked for her full name.

'Pearl's nice,' he said as he wrote it down. 'But you deserve better than Warren. Leave it with me. I'll come up with something more exotic, more alluring.'

'All right.' She had hoped to have some say in the matter. But never mind.

'Height?'

'Five feet nine inches. I was recently measured for my job.'

'Weight?'

'Eight stone twelve pounds.'

'The sort of willowy that makes even a willow weep,' Gold remarked as he continued writing. 'What do you do for a living?' He glanced back at his notes. 'I imagine you don't have to register for war work just yet.'

Pearl shook her head. 'I'm a bus conductress. It's a reserved occupation.'

'Could hardly be better,' Gold acknowledged her reply. 'As well as head and shoulder shots, we can get you in your uniform. *From clippie to stardom.*' As he spoke, he spread his hands in an arc in front of him. She could only suppose he was envisaging a theatre poster, or perhaps her name on the marquee above the entrance. 'I can see it now.'

'Do you want to see me walk?' she asked, preparing to get up from her chair.

He continued writing. 'I saw all I needed to when you walked in.'

It wasn't the reply she'd been expecting. 'Oh. What about my hair?'

'With that colour, I imagine it looks sublime however you wear it. You could have it cropped into one of those ghastly flapper styles and directors would still fall over themselves to cast you.'

'Oh.'

'But don't.' When he looked directly at her, he went on, 'Cut it, I mean. In fact, look after it. It's going to be your selling point. Well, that and your voice. When the god of creation was doling out talent, young lady, you certainly hit the jackpot.'

'I did?'

'Take it from me.'

Pearl bristled. With Ivy sitting right next to her, she wasn't sure how to respond to such a flurry of compliments. She'd always known her hair drew attention – had hated the fact when she was little. *You take after your Irish gran*, Charlie had once told her. *You won't feel that way when you're grown up*, her mother had reassured her the day she'd come home from school in tears, having yet again been called Carrot Top. *The name callers will be jealous then.*

'So, what happens now?' Ivy broke the momentary silence to ask.

'What we do now is get together a portfolio for each of you.'

'You'll take us on, then? To your talent agency?'

'I'm minded I can find work for you. Do you act?' Gold's question was directed to Ivy.

Pearl noticed her friend's expression become downcast. 'Not really...'

With a wave of his hand, Gold dismissed her concern. 'The situation, ladies, is this.' Again, both women leaned forward in their chairs. 'I can take you onto my books. I don't have anything to offer you right away. Times are uncertain. Besides, there's a lot we need to do. Once you sign, I'll get you booked in for some head and shoulder shots.' He gestured to the wall. 'Like that one of Renée. Samuel takes care of photography. His studio's off Old Compton Street. His rates are reasonable.'

The girls exchanged looks.

'So... we have to pay him.'

'You pay me, I pay him.'

'Do we need gowns for the photographs?' Pearl ventured. She hoped not. She was stretched for money as it was.

'Not for now. Your first shot is always one with bare shoulders. You'll just take off your blouse or whatever.'

For the second time in quick succession, Pearl bristled. 'Right.'

'But I'll book you in for hair styling and make-up beforehand. Samuel likes to work with Julia. I'll book them both together at his studio. That way, you won't have to trail around the West End all made up.' Pearl debated whether to tell him she was more than capable of doing make-up for both of them. 'That way, you can just pay me one sum on the day. Now, when you're in town, you'll also need lodgings. For accommodation, I use Marietta Murdoch. She once trod the boards herself, so she understands our world. She's happy to book short stays. Her place is in Walmsley Mews. All respectable and above board.'

'And we pay you for her, as well.'

'Sign with me, Miss Warren, and you can empty your head of all concerns about money.'

'And what do we pay for *your* services?' Pearl enquired.

'Perhaps I'll get you a contract to read. It's all set out in there.' Gold got up from his desk and went to a filing cabinet in the corner. Flicking through the files, he stopped at one and withdrew from it a couple of documents. 'Detailed here are my terms. They're standard for this type of agreement.' As he handed a copy to Pearl, he met her look. 'And non-negotiable.'

She ran her eyes over the opening paragraphs; they appeared to explain who did what – in particular, what Gold, as their manager, would do for them. She turned the page; the next section explained what the client was expected to do. There was a lot to it; considerably more than she felt inclined to commit to there and then. When she turned the page again, the section containing figures leapt out at her.

She looked sharply up. 'Twenty per cent?' Beside her, she noticed Ivy shift her weight.

'Quite standard for a talent manager. And it's the same rate whatever the type of work I find for you. I don't charge more for, say, a personal appearance.'

Pearl didn't even know what that was. As far as she was concerned, every time she performed was a personal appearance; it wasn't as though someone else could turn up in her place.

She glanced to Ivy, who shrugged.

'You asked if I act,' Ivy said.

'It would help if you did. I would recommend lessons.'

You would, Pearl thought, determining to take Ivy aside as soon as she got the chance. 'Lew Robinson and his wife, Mary, that's who you want. Outstanding tutors of their craft.'

Ivy gave a woeful shake of her head. 'I'm not sure I can afford lessons.'

'It's normal for singers and actresses who are just starting out,' Gold replied without missing a beat, his manner matter of fact, 'to have a day job to cover rent, travel, tuition and the like. I can fix you up with employment, make sure it meets the criteria for a reserved occupation to stop you being called up. Plenty of things come to mind. As for the cost of acting lessons, well, we could always come to terms. I might, for instance, be persuaded to pay up front on the basis that you repay a sum each week...'

To her horror, Pearl saw Ivy's face light up.

'Really?'

'For a rising star? Of course. I would have to insist you didn't tell anyone outside of this room, though. It would be a private arrangement, not for broadcast.'

'I think, Ivy,' Pearl began, 'we need to talk about this.'

Ivy looked surprised. 'Well—'

'I'm not saying we shouldn't do it. Mr Gold seems very...' She looked at him across the desk. '...thorough. But there's a lot here to understand.'

'You won't get a better deal,' Gold said. 'Everyone in this business operates the same way. Some of us simply have better contacts, take better care of their starlets...'

Pearl frowned. *Starlets?* 'Mr Gold, I'm sure that's true. But while all of this—' she waved the contract '—is bread and butter to you, to us, it's a big step.'

'Miss Warren, your reservations are entirely natural. You are, of course, free to take my contract away with you, discuss it, and bring it back another day for signing.'

'Or I suppose we could sign it and post it back to you.'

Gordon Gold shook his head. 'You must sign here, on my premises, where I can make sure it's all in order and legally witnessed.'

While Pearl didn't know whether or not that was true, she did know that the look Ivy was sending her meant *We can't afford to come back and do this all over again*. And she was right. They couldn't.

'Look,' Gold picked up again. 'Your concern is to be commended. So, how about, I go through this with you, word for word, and you can ask me whatever questions you like. Whatever you wish to challenge, you'll have the opportunity.' Without waiting for them to agree, he got to his feet. 'Pop yourselves over there on the couch and I'll bring us some drinks.'

Feeling as though she was being herded into a corner of ever decreasing dimensions, Pearl sighed.

Apparently untroubled, however, Ivy shot to her feet. 'Thanks ever so. That would be real helpful.'

Pearl watched Gold go to a cabinet and select three cut-glass tumblers. Having set them on a tray, he removed the stopper from a decanter containing what she guessed to be whisky. If he was expecting her to drink it, he was in for a disappointment; she knew full well what he thought plying them with drink was going to achieve.

'Now then, girls,' he said as he carried the tray to where she was settling uneasily alongside Ivy on the couch. 'How about you make space for me in the middle, eh? That way, we can all look over the same document.'

Reluctantly, Pearl slid to her right and watched as Ivy moved away to the left.

In the resulting space, Gold landed heavily. 'One for you.' He placed a glass in front of Ivy. 'One for you.' He placed another in front of Pearl. 'And one for yours truly.'

'Thanks,' Ivy said, immediately reaching for hers.

'To a successful partnership. May your dreams come true.'

'Successful partnership,' Ivy agreed.

When he raised his glass, Pearl felt duty bound to reach for her own. But while the other two drank, she merely let the liquid touch her lips; the aroma from the glass brought to mind a winter's afternoon, damp earth underfoot, wood smoke coiling upwards from a cottage chimney. Did the drink taste as it smelled? She licked her lips; it did somewhat. The strength of it made her wince.

'So, let us begin with page one.'

Through the poplin of her shirt dress, Pearl could feel the heat of Gold's thigh. And no matter how hard she tried to ease herself away from him – the more she created a slender gap – the more he spread out to fill it. Every time he moved to gesticulate, his shirtsleeve brushed her arm. She could smell him, too; it wasn't the tang of body odour, in fact he smelled surprisingly clean and soapy. And of hair oil and something sweet – cologne, maybe?

To the other side of him, Ivy giggled. 'Oh, I see,' she was saying. '*That's* what that means.'

'And what about you?' Gold turned to Pearl to ask. 'Are you clear on this part?'

Meeting and holding his eyes, Pearl nodded. She had no idea to which part of the document he was referring; she'd been lost in thoughts of how to avoid – in particular how to convince Ivy to avoid – getting drawn into signing. 'Quite clear, thank you.'

'Excellent. Right. So, this next section…'

Again, Pearl stopped listening. It was plain that Ivy was being lured in, which left her, Pearl, with two choices: let her get on with it – Ivy was, after all, an adult – or try to talk her out of it, a course of action that carried the risk of incurring Ivy's wrath, possibly even spelling the end for their friendship. She did like Ivy, but would she miss her? Sometimes, she was a complete nuisance: she was untidy; she perpetually smelled of either cooking fat or cigarette smoke; and she seemed to want to become famous without actually making much of an effort. Oh, and she was always on the scrounge. *Can I use some of your Mum? Mine's run out. Can I borrow some shoe polish/nail varnish remover/Kirby grips?* When totted up, the cost of Ivy's friendship was not inconsiderable and continuing to mount. That said, she wouldn't want to see her make a mistake – certainly not one that could ruin her life. So, what was she to do?

By the time Gold had reached the last page of the contract, she'd made up her mind.

'Well, thank you, for that,' she said briskly. But, as she went to get to her feet, Gold extended an arm and, before she knew what was going on, his hand was pressing down on her shoulder. As she lowered herself back onto the couch, his fingers slid down to the curve of her waist.

'So, who's for a top up? Something to toast with before we all sign?'

Determining that if she was going to leave, it was now or never, Pearl shot to her feet, her shin clouting the edge of the low table, the resulting pain causing her to curse under her breath. More carefully, she edged away from the couch, tugged sharply at the skirt of her dress, and glanced back at Ivy. The hem of *her* dress was halfway up her thigh, Gold's fingers on her skin as the two of them clinked glasses.

'Ivy, I'd like to leave.' When Ivy turned slowly towards her, she went on, 'If we go now, we might make the earlier train.'

Carefully, Ivy replaced her glass on the table and, moving aside Gold's hand, got to her feet. 'Methinks you and I should have a little chat. Come on. Let's go out for a breath of fresh air.'

'Very well.' Collecting her handbag from the chair as she went past, Pearl followed Ivy from Gold's office, across the room beyond – where a girl with long hair was now slumped over the desk – and down the stairs to the alley.

'Pearl, listen to me,' Ivy swung about to say the moment they were outside. 'You won't have no trouble getting work. With your looks and your voice, you'll be on the stage whenever and howsoever you choose. You don't need me to tell you that. As sure as eggs is eggs, it's going to happen.' Pearl bit her tongue. She might as well hear Ivy out – hear her flawed reasoning for the mistake she was clearly about to make. 'But me, I don't have that luxury. Without your looks or your voice, I'm going to find it a lot harder. But sign with Gordon Gold—' for a moment, Pearl thought she was going to add 'Agent to the Stars' '—and I do at least have a chance. My dream comes within grasping distance. Who knows, work hard, and I might get a break. But if I don't take this chance, and no one else we go on to meet wants me, then I'm going to have regrets of the sort I don't know how I'll live with. And don't tell me you can't see that.'

Pearl was at a loss. Ivy *didn't* have a great voice, that was true. And she wasn't a beauty in the classical sense. But that didn't mean someone wouldn't see her for what she was. It took all sorts.

'I'm just not sure Gordon Gold can be trusted,' she ventured. It seemed better to lay the blame on Gold than on Ivy's short-sightedness for not seeing through him.

'Look,' Ivy went on. 'I know he's a slippery so-and-so. I've come across any number of Gordon Golds in my time. But at least this one has something I want. So, why not take what's on offer? Let's face it, I've neither the means nor the wherewithal to set up in London on my own.'

'I just don't want to see you out of pocket and upset. Or worse…'

When Ivy picked up again, Pearl noticed that her tone conveyed more than a hint of conciliation. 'Look, I know I came across in there as dippy, but that was on purpose. He asked me if I can act and, as I've just shown, I can. But, if he wants to pave the way for me to learn proper, I'm prepared to let him.'

'But—'

'I know you're only looking out for me. And for that I love you dearly. But I'm a grown woman. I've been taking care of myself a long time. I know what Gold is, but I'm going to sign with him anyway. Maybe he'll get me work, maybe he won't. Either way, at least I will have given it a shot.'

Pearl felt like crying. 'So… you'll be moving to London?'

Ivy sighed. 'I don't know. Not right away, I shouldn't think.'

'So, you're coming back with me to Exeter.'

When Ivy grinned and slung an arm around Pearl's shoulder, Pearl could smell the peaty aroma of the whisky on her breath. ''Course I am, you daft maid. And if you let me go back in and get this over and done with, we might still catch that earlier train of yours. Or, if you prefer, we could go and get a spot of late lunch somewhere.'

More than anything, Pearl wanted to go home. London wasn't turning out to be what she'd hoped for. 'Well, if you're going back in to sign with him, I think I'll wait here.'

'Sure? You don't want the satisfaction of turning him down?'

To Pearl's mind, that didn't seem like satisfaction at all. 'No. I'll wait here.'

'All right then. Back in two ticks.'

When Pearl heard Ivy clomp back up the staircase, followed by the groan of the hinge as she opened the door and went back into the office, she exhaled heavily. Ivy might be right to say she didn't have the world's best voice or the most beautiful looks, but she was sharp as a tack. She might even be right: perhaps Gordon Gold *would* find her work, maybe even stardom. And perhaps she, Pearl, would be the one left with egg on her face. On balance, she didn't think so. She might truthfully only be sixteen, but she'd been propositioned by any number of men promising her whatever they happened to think would wear down her resistance; unlike Ivy, though, she'd never, even once, countenanced stringing them along to get what they purported to offer.

Absently, she took a few steps along the alleyway and stared up at the narrow strip of sky. Since they'd arrived, it had clouded over. In fact, it looked to be threatening rain.

Equally absently, she turned and wandered back. As Ivy had pointed out, she was a grown woman and could do as she pleased. For her own part, though, what she, Pearl, was determined to do, was learn from the way this morning had turned out and hope that, for neither of them, this would someday all end in tears.

Chapter 14

Pearl sighed with disappointment. When she'd come tramping in through the front door and down the stairs, she'd been hoping to find she had the room to herself – at least for an hour or so. Today, for some reason, her feet were killing her, coupled with which she had a headache pounding away like a blacksmith's hammer. It had come on after her mid-shift break and had proceeded to grow steadily worse until, when it came to tallying her waybill, the pain had been so blinding she'd been unable to concentrate. Half an hour it had taken her to work out why her tickets didn't tally with her cash. Even Kath, who, by her own admission, was painfully slow at tallying her waybill, had come and gone in less time. The only thing that had kept Pearl going was the prospect of sitting quietly with her feet in a bowl of Epsom salts dissolved in warm water. It was a remedy her sister, May, swore by as a cure for all manner of aches and pains, claiming the salty water 'rid the body of impurities'. Sadly, with Ivy already home, peace and quiet was the last thing she was going to get.

'Are you going out?' she looked across at Ivy to enquire, more from hope than expectation as she closed the door behind her. To make matters worse, it was plain that Ivy had been smoking without opening the window, even though she knew it irked Pearl. With a huff, she strode across the room and wrestled with the sash.

'You should ask Old Mother Trude to get that seen to,' Ivy remarked of the window, her tone devoid of regret for not having struggled with it herself.

'I have. Many times.' Gritting her teeth in frustration, Pearl glanced to where, seated on her bed, Ivy was darning a hole in the sleeve of a sweater.

'I've not the least idea how I came to catch this. Still, once I start earning proper money, I'll be able to get a new one, won't I. Gordon knows theatre seamstresses—' Pearl shot Ivy a glance; she was already calling the man *Gordon*? '—who make clothing on the side, you know, *no coupons required*. Said he'll put me in touch. All hush-hush, of course.'

Unbuttoning the jacket of her uniform, Pearl shook her head in dismay. She didn't know which surprised her the least: that Ivy was already using Gordon Gold to get what she wanted – in this case, clothing made on the sly – or that she was on first name terms with him. Had he been *her* agent, Pearl was certain she would still be calling him *Mr Gold*, even if he'd suggested otherwise.

Realising Ivy hadn't answered her question, she put it to her again. 'You still haven't told me whether you're going out tonight.'

Hunched over her darning, Ivy shrugged. 'Maybe. Maybe not. Why? You after bringing a feller back?'

Pearl stepped out of her trousers. 'No, Ivy,' she replied. With the way her head was pounding, it was taking every ounce of her control not to snap at the woman. 'I just need some quiet to try and get rid of a headache.'

'Fresh air usually helps.' Failing to see the irony of her advice, Ivy cursed. 'Damn and blast. There's a second hole. And I'm running out of wool.'

Well, don't come to me for any, Pearl longed to warn her. Instead, she said, 'I've *had* fresh air. All day.'

'Aspirin, then.'

'Yes,' she said wearily. 'I know. I'm about to take a couple.' *But I'd still like to sit in the quiet and soak my feet.*

Her uniform hung up, Pearl stepped into her navy skirt, pulled it up over her hips and fastened the button on the waistband. Over her head she pulled the older of her two sweaters and then, spotting her washbag on the dressing table, unzipped the top and poked about inside for her box of aspirin. But when she found it and opened the flap, she was incensed to discover it was empty; she was certain there had been a couple of tablets left when she'd taken some the other day for cramps. She glanced across to Ivy. She wouldn't put it past the woman to help herself; she knew for a fact she frequently borrowed her shampoo – could smell the scent of it on her hair – and she didn't think twice about using her soap, either. In fact, these last couple of weeks, Ivy had gradually become less and less deserving of her trust, such that, were it not for the fact that she felt tense enough already, she would have a go at her. Since her headache was dreadful, though, she would try not to dwell on Ivy's transgressions and concentrate instead on feeling better. She would go for a walk, although not because Ivy had suggested it. She would go to the chemist on the corner and get some more aspirin. And then she would hide them somewhere Ivy wouldn't think to look.

As the week wore on, though, Pearl found herself growing evermore frustrated by her roommate's habits. If

Ivy wasn't going out, she, Pearl, wished she would; if she *was* going out, she regretted that the price to pay for a few hours of peace was being woken up by the inevitable racket that accompanied Ivy's return.

'Sorry,' Ivy would giggle as she tried in vain to silently close the door, or when she stubbed her toe on the foot of her bed. 'It's only me. Go back to sleep.'

With an exasperated groan, Pearl would lift her head, plump her pillow, and try to ignore the sound of Ivy getting undressed.

The same would happen in the morning. How the woman got through an eight-hour shift in the hospital kitchen without falling asleep, she had no idea. She certainly wouldn't mind a dose of her stamina.

'Is it four-fifteen?' she would groggily enquire when she was awoken in the early hours by Ivy trying to get dressed in the dark.

'Sorry,' Ivy would hiss. 'Did my alarm wake you? Forgot to put it under my pillow when I came in. And now I can't find my other... oh, never mind, here it is.'

In truth, it wasn't solely Ivy's lack of consideration that had begun to get Pearl down; not helping her mood was the fact that the evenings were growing shorter, the mornings darker, and the weather distinctly cooler. Already, summer had taken on the air of a distant memory; the one season that spelled freedom from the struggle to keep warm, to get laundry dry, and to go about one's business without getting soaked to the skin, had come and gone without her appreciating more than the odd moment of it. And all because the Germans had made her and her sisters homeless.

On the matter of bombshells, that was something else playing on her mind: the other day, she had bumped into

Clemmie who'd looked well – a little frumpy, perhaps, but glowing, nonetheless. And then her sister had shared her news. Their conversation – at least as she recalled it – still managed to make her feel a stab of envy even now.

'I'm glad I've bumped into you,' Clemmie had said, the warmth in her tone unmissable. 'Only... I'd like to invite you to come to tea.'

Since City & District had helped her to find lodgings, Pearl had given scant thought to Clemmie's own living arrangements. She had a vague recollection of her going to lodge with the woman who ran the WVS, which made her sister's invitation to tea all the more puzzling. 'What's the occasion?' she'd been forced to enquire.

Her sister's response, however, had been one she was unlikely to forget.

'Well, I've met someone...' Had it not been for the depth of Clemmie's subsequent blush, it would never have occurred to Pearl that the 'someone' to whom her sister referred was a man. When she'd gone on to elaborate, Pearl had been stunned. *Knock me down with a feather*, about summed up her reaction. 'And since he's asked me to marry him,' Clemmie had gone on to explain, 'I should like you to meet him.'

The only thing Pearl could think to say in that moment was, 'Does May know?' And when Clemmie had confirmed that she did, her next question had been, 'Who is he?' To then discover the feller in question had been an RAF pilot, whose service had been prematurely ended by an accident – such that he was now a tutor instead – oh, and that he was, to use Clemmie's words, 'a little bit older', she'd been left to stand there as dumb as a fence post.

It had to be down to the sheer depth of her astonishment that she was still grappling with the news now, almost a week later: gentle little Clemmie, who wouldn't say boo to a goose, was getting married – more remarkable even that that, she was going to be the first of them to do so, when common sense had always suggested she'd be the last – the realisation leaving her, Pearl, with no idea what to make of it.

At the time, for want of good reason to decline the invitation, she had somehow hidden her shock behind a smile and said that yes, of course she would go to tea with her. And her fiancé. At his house. But the nearer the afternoon in question drew, the more the prospect made her rue she'd been unable to think of a reason to get out of it. Why did she feel that way? She genuinely had no idea, but she'd like to believe it was for a better reason than that she simply envied Clemmie getting on with her life. Clearly, marriage was the last thing on her own mind; she had dreams to pursue. And therein, she supposed, lay the problem. May, by all accounts, was happily settled and enjoying life on the farm – and who'd have thought *that* when she'd first gone there? And now she'd found out that the very thing Clemmie had always craved – a husband and a family – was well within *her* reach, too. But here *she* was, the one with the gumption and the looks and the big dreams, barely an inch closer to achieving anything – certainly anything of note. In fact, having turned down Gordon Gold, and been left to watch as Ivy made grand plans, it could even be argued that she'd gone backwards. Small wonder, then, that she was peeved.

Unfortunately for Pearl, as September continued to unfold, events were to do nothing to cheer her up.

'Good grief I'm tired,' Ivy moaned one afternoon a few days later, as they both arrived home from their respective shifts.

'Hardly surprising. Talk about burning the candle at both ends.'

'What do you mean?'

Her instinct being to raise her voice, Pearl fought to remain calm. 'Up early in the morning, out late at night. I mean, where do you even find to go? Are you seeing someone?' Even as she asked, she thought it unlikely. 'Someone with his own place?'

From where she was pulling on a pair of slacks, Ivy shook her head. 'No, I'm not seeing anyone. A girl I know from the hospital has a brother up the rail yard. And he's got a group of friends. We go out together. They know a couple of clubs, one of them out at Heavitree.'

Pearl wondered, absently, whether it was the old ballroom. 'No wonder you're always tired. I don't know how you do it.'

'To be honest, it's why I've never asked you to come with us. Even *I* don't know how I drag myself out of bed some mornings. But at least my work is the sort I can actually do in my sleep. I don't think yours is.'

With a sigh, Pearl looked across at her. Sometimes, Ivy could be quite thoughtful. 'It's not. Come up short on my waybill more than once in a blue moon and I have to make up the difference from my wages.'

'That don't seem fair.'

'I didn't think so either, at first. But a threat like that hanging over you does tend to make you pay attention to what you're doing.'

'Suppose.'

'You out tonight then?'

But, before Ivy could answer, there was a rap at the door, followed by the shrill tones of Mrs Trude.

'You two decent in there?'

Waiting until Ivy had hastily pulled her sweater over her head, Pearl called back. 'We are.'

Without further ado, Mrs Trude opened the door and stood, hands on hips, surveying the room. 'I heard you come in, the pair of you.'

'Good afternoon, Mrs Trude,' Pearl greeted her. The look on the woman's face didn't bode well; she didn't appear happy at the best of times but, this afternoon, she looked even more browned off than usual.

'I've had complaints about the noise.'

As Ivy came to stand alongside her, Pearl frowned. 'The noise?'

'Clomping up and down these stairs all hours, slamming doors—'

'If you mean the door on the front porch,' Ivy said, 'it sticks. As you well know because we've both pointed it out to you. We neither of us slam it for the sake of it – it's just impossible to close quietly.'

'My other lodgers manage perfectly well.'

Liar, Pearl thought; she'd heard the door closing plenty of times. 'I think it sounds worse because we have to go out so early, when everywhere is quiet—'

'It's not just the mornings,' Mrs Trude replied shortly, 'though trust me when I say they're trying enough. Wasn't so bad when there was only the one of you. You on your own,' Mrs Trude went on, nodding her head towards Pearl. 'You weren't so bad. But now it's late at night as well.'

'We're sorry, Mrs Trude,' Pearl said. 'We'll be quieter.'

'Consider this a warning, then. One more complaint from any of my gentlemen lodgers and you're out. Both of you. Clear?'

Pearl nodded. By her side, Ivy did the same.

'Yes, Mrs Trude.'

'Quite clear, Mrs Trude.'

'Right, then, I'll say no more. But I'm warning you, don't test me.'

'We won't, Mrs Trude.'

'Old battle axe,' Ivy muttered the moment they heard Mrs Trude trudging back up the stairs.

Not wishing to fall out with Ivy – after all, they did seem to have been bickering a little less these last few days – Pearl paused for a moment to choose her words. 'Perhaps,' she said carefully, 'she has a point. Being down here, it's easy to forget other people live upstairs. And we do come and go when other people are trying to sleep.' By 'we', she knew she really meant 'you'.

'Yeah, well, war work doesn't keep regular hours. Maybe she should direct her gripe at Hitler.'

Pearl pressed her lips together against a smile. While she didn't want to be seen to be taking Mrs Trude's side, she knew their landlady's complaint wasn't without justification. *She* wished Ivy would come and go more quietly, too, or even stop coming and going quite so late, quite so often. 'Have you heard anything from Gordon Gold lately?' she asked as the thought went through her head.

'I had a note a few days back. Apparently, he has, as he put it, "some irons in the fire".'

'Heavens. Then I'll cross my fingers for you.'

'Thanks.'

More intrigued than she wanted to let on, Pearl went on to ask, 'Did he say what they were, these irons?'

Ivy shook her head. 'All right if I borrow some Vaseline?' Immediately, Pearl clenched her jaw. Almost as quickly, she tried to relax it; a scrape of Vaseline was hardly worth the two of them coming to blows over. 'My fingernails are all ridged and dry.'

'You should really put it on at night. And ideally wear gloves over the top. The warmth helps it to soak in.'

'Thanks, but I'll do it now. There's no chance I'll remember at bedtime.'

Reluctantly, Pearl unscrewed the lid from the little tin. 'Here,' she said, determined not to let Ivy loose with the minuscule amount that was left in the bottom; where she'd find another tub of the stuff she had no idea. She'd had this tin since before the air raids. 'Wipe your finger around in here, then, and spread it out over all of them. A little goes a long way. Make sure to get it into your cuticles, as well.'

'Thanks.'

To Pearl's ears, Ivy's reply was heavy with sarcasm – as though she thought she wasn't being trusted to only take a small amount. In that moment, it felt like the final straw. 'Maybe if you didn't keep buying cigarettes,' she said, 'you'd have some money for your own Vaseline. And you wouldn't have to keep using my shampoo, either… or my hair lacquer, which is almost impossible to get any more—'

'I don't keep using it.'

'And you *do know* soap is on the ration, don't you?'

'I only used it the one time. If you recall, I asked you beforehand. And as for telling me to stop buying cigarettes, well, frankly, you've got a nerve—'

'Oh, *I've* got a nerve, have I? I'd like to know how you work that out.'

'Well, who the bloody hell are *you* to tell me how to live my life?'

This was, Pearl knew, her chance to avoid stoking the argument; this was the point at which, if she was going to back down, she should do so. But why should she? She wasn't the one in the wrong.

'I'm *not* telling you how to live your life. Frankly, I don't care how you live it. But what I do know is that I'm weary of having you use my things when, with a little more thought on your part, you wouldn't need to. None of it grows on trees you know.'

'I hardly think one borrow of your shampoo, or one use of your soap is going to make a difference.'

'That's not the point,' Pearl said sharply. 'The point is that you never stop to think about who you might be putting out, do you?'

Ivy stopped rubbing her nails. When she looked up, her expression was one of fury. 'Who I might be *putting out*?'

'I invited you to come and live here. I didn't have to, but I did.' Adding *out of the goodness of my heart* felt over the top; Ivy's look was steely enough as it was.

'The saintly Pearl Warren, saving the urchin from the gutter.'

'Oh, stop it, Ivy, for heaven's sake. I'm not looking for thanks, and you know that. But I do think you could show some respect. It's bad enough that you borrow my things when I'm not here and think I won't notice. Maybe you *can't* help what time you have to start work but why, since you have to get up at four-fifteen every morning, can't you come home a bit earlier at night? Maybe, if you weren't half asleep when you had to get up, you wouldn't make such a din.'

'And here we are, back to you telling me how to live my life.'

'If asking you to show some respect for *my* way of life is telling you how to live *yours*, then yes, perhaps I am. Happen you living here in my room entitles me to that.'

'*Your* room?'

'I was here first. If I hadn't been, you wouldn't be here now. I didn't suggest you move in for my benefit.'

'Christ almighty—'

'And we both know who Mrs Trude was really complaining about, don't we? Who the real nuisance is. There's only *one* of us who rolls in, worse for drink, when the rest of the house is—'

The door flew open with such force it stopped Pearl dead. And when she swivelled towards the sound of it crashing into the side of the wardrobe, it was to see Mrs Trude, ready to spit blood. Shot through by a stab of fear, Pearl reached to the corner of the chest of drawers for support.

'Right!' Mrs Trude barked. 'That's it. I've had enough. I *told* you not to test me. But barely have I got back up those stairs than the pair of you start bawling. I will not have it. Friday night, seven o'clock, I want my keys back. Seven o'clock, I expect to come down here and find your things gone and the room spotless. I never wanted girls in the first place, but the bus company assured me you would be no trouble. *Clean and polite*, they said you were. And you,' she said, pointing to Ivy. 'You're only here because this one pleaded. I know you're the one to blame for all the slamming and the banging and the stomping. You should be ashamed of yourself. You're supposed to lead by example. And before *you*,' Mrs Trude went on, switching her attention to Pearl, 'try telling me I should let you stay on, I'll save you the effort. There are servicemen aplenty as would take this room in the blink of an eye. Just be grateful I don't go back to the bus company and let them know the reason you're out on your ear.' Unable to help herself, Pearl began to cry. 'Friday. Seven o'clock. I want both of your door keys back in my hand.'

With that, Mrs Trude swept from the room, the door trembling on its hinges in her wake.

'Happy now?' Ivy hissed. 'Now you won't have to suffer my smoking or my *stumbling about at all hours* anymore?' Continuing to weep, Pearl didn't even bother trying to reply. 'Because you're the one who's come worse off here, you know. What I've known for a week or more but held off telling you for fear you'd be upset is that I was about to move out of this place anyway. That letter Gordon sent wasn't about *irons in the fire* at all, it was to say he's got me a part in a musical. Rehearsals start in a fortnight. I would have been leaving soon anyway. Still, no skin off my nose if I go a week earlier. None at all. In fact, I might even start packing right now. Since I can go to a friend's place for a couple of nights while I work my notice at the hospital, I think I will. Trust me, the company there will be far less judgemental.'

Looking up, Pearl watched Ivy lift down her little suit-case from the top of the wardrobe and blow the dust from it. *Stop crying*, she willed herself, the irony of her situation piling anger on top of distress; Ivy was the one responsible for them losing their home, and yet not only had she been planning to leave anyway, but she had somewhere to go and stay in the meantime. By contrast, while Pearl had done nothing wrong, *she* was the one without a clue where she would find to go. To make matters worse, all the while she'd been having a go at Ivy about her habit of scrounging things, she'd been regretting not simply turning a blind eye – avoiding an argument to spare hard feelings further down the road. Well, too late now for regrets.

Swiping the back of a hand across her eyes, she looked about and, spotting her jacket hanging over the chair, snatched it up. Then she reached for her handbag and marched from the room. If Ivy wanted to leave tonight, that was up to her, but she didn't have to sit there and watch her go, especially if the woman was going to flaunt her good fortune in the process. As to where, exactly, she was headed, she had no idea. And on the matter of where she would go in the longer term, she had no clue about that either – and barely three days to work it out.

Oh, and while she was about it, that fateful moment she'd offered Ivy the chance to share her room would be the very last time she did a favour for anyone – even if they were supposedly in dire straits – because just look where she'd ended up for her trouble.

Chapter 15

She hadn't set out to go there. But, finding herself wandering aimlessly up St David's Hill, desperate, among other things, for someone to talk to, Pearl had gone up the path to Sylvia's front door and, after a moment's hesitation, summoned the courage to knock.

If Sylvia was surprised to find her in tears on her doorstep, she didn't show it. Instead, she stood aside and beckoned her in.

'Y-You're not in a lesson, are you?' Pearl asked as she stepped into Sylvia's hallway.

'No, dear. My last pupil of the day left a while ago. I was listening to the wireless. Go through and sit down.'

'I'm sorry to turn up like this. I didn't mean to. It's just that...'

'No matter. Come on. Take off your jacket for a moment and have a seat. Then if you want to pour out your woes, you go ahead.' Weighed by her despair, Pearl took a seat in one of two wingback chairs, each standing either side of the fireplace. As she did so, Sylvia went to the sideboard and turned down the volume on her wireless set. 'You know, rather than have the Home Service on all the time, I find myself increasingly turning to the Forces Programme. They seem to have more variety, and new ideas. This is the BBC Theatre Orchestra playing Elgar's "Sevillana"—'

'I'm sorry,' Pearl said. 'I should have thought—'

'Oh, don't worry. I don't mind missing it.'

Having only, until now, experienced the deliberately spartan surroundings of Sylvia's studio, the plushness of her drawing room came as a surprise; richly coloured rugs on the floor; plain velvet curtains in a deep shade of claret at the bay window; a large painting of a moorland scene in autumn on the chimney breast. The room was also home to a glass-fronted cabinet containing fancy chinaware and knick-knacks. There were side tables with lamps whose shades matched the colour of the curtains, while a length of wall next to the door was given over to shelves crammed with books. As rooms went, it was warm and welcoming and gave Pearl a sense of Sylvia as a person rather than as a music teacher, something about this new appreciation deepening her urge to confide in her. The problem was that, if she started, she might not stop.

'It's Ivy,' she eventually volunteered. When she glanced to the opposite chair, Sylvia showed no sign of surprise.

'I see.'

From there, the floodgates opened, and Pearl's jumble of woes tumbled out. She explained how she felt as though Ivy had been abusing her friendship; how, behind Sylvia's back, they'd been to see Gordon Gold; what had just happened with Mrs Trude and how, at that precise moment, Ivy was packing her things to leave. 'And I'm real sorry,' she mumbled when, feeling utterly drained, she had finished unburdening herself, 'but I couldn't think of anywhere else to go.'

For a moment, Sylvia didn't reply, nor did her expression give anything away.

When she did eventually speak, it was to say, 'I think, my dear, we're going to need some tea.'

With a handkerchief that was already sopping wet, Pearl dabbed at her eyes. 'I'm so sorry about this, truly, I am. And I'm sorry for coming to my singing lesson last week and not telling you we'd been to London. To be honest, with the way the whole thing turned out, I felt ashamed.'

On her way past, Sylvia touched Pearl's hand. 'It's all right. At least now I know why you were so quiet in your lesson last week. And why Ivy cancelled hers altogether. While it will probably be of no consolation to you at this precise moment, I can quite understand why you're upset. But I'm a firm believer in the proverb that a problem shared is a problem halved. So, you stay there while I go and put the kettle on.'

In many ways, Pearl couldn't believe what she'd done – either by coming here in the first place, or by telling Sylvia about Gordon Gold. On the other hand, how else could she have explained about Ivy? Besides, with Ivy on the verge of leaving, she could always claim it had been Ivy's idea to go and see him. Thinking back, Ivy *had* been the keener of them.

When Sylvia returned and set a tray of tea things on a little table she brought out from the corner of the room, her expression looked purposeful. 'I think,' she said as she lifted the lid of a dainty white teapot to stir the contents, 'the first thing you must do is cast Ivy from your mind. She has done what she has done, and you have been left in the lurch, so to speak. Nothing about either of those situations can we do anything to change. Am I disappointed with her? I most certainly am. But my sense of being let down does nothing to lessen your woes. Am I disappointed that the two of you went to see this Gordon Gold fellow without saying anything to me first? Not to the extent you might imagine. Hard though this might be for you to believe, I did plenty of hot-headed things when I was your age.'

It was a revelation Pearl indeed found hard to swallow. 'But you always seem so calm and sensible.'

'Take it from me, one can only be calm and sensible if one has finished being reckless and impulsive.'

Pearl could only suppose that was true. 'Mm.'

'Do I wish the two of you hadn't gone? Of course I do. There are so many ways the venture could have gone badly awry. Neither of you understand how the business works – who can be trusted and who are the snakes. More importantly, neither of you is ready for such a huge commitment.'

'I know that now,' Pearl confessed. 'To be honest, I knew it the moment we got off the train at Waterloo. If I was terrified by the idea of simply getting lost, how was I going to convince anyone to put me on a stage – and pay me to be up there?'

'I do understand why you went, though. You were restless.'

Pearl nodded. 'I was. Still am, if I'm honest with you.'

'Well, let us regard the episode as water under the bridge.'

Appearing to remember the pot of tea, Sylvia leaned towards the tray, set the strainer over one of the cups, and proceeded to pour. 'Please feel free to add milk and sugar.'

Pearl added a dash of milk but declined sugar; alongside the bowl of cubes lay a tiny pair of silver tongs, the two together appearing to offer the opportunity for all manner of mishaps.

'Thank you,' she said, picking up her cup and saucer. When a sip of the tea scalded her top lip, she carefully set the one back on the other.

'So, I think,' Sylvia picked up again, 'that Ivy's betrayal is something you must do your best to forget. In your path through life, you will come across good friends and bad. This particular incident you will eventually chalk up to experience. Your brush with Gordon Gold likewise. Perhaps look upon the entire episode as a glimpse of a world you're not yet ready to enter. Your need for new lodgings, on the other hand, we must resolve post-haste.'

Pearl sighed. 'It's a real worry, that's for sure. And I wish now I'd never tried to help Ivy out in the first place. Then I'd still be there. I mean, I know that, as rooms go, it was a bit gloomy but, before Ivy came, I had it to myself and could be as quiet as I liked. It was nice.'

'I imagine so.' When Pearl looked across at Sylvia's face, it was to see that she appeared deep in thought. 'You know, I have a spare room. Truth be told, I have two. And call me unpatriotic, but I've been resisting telling the council's housing department, largely for fear of ending up in the same position in which you found yourself with Ivy – saddled with someone whose habits don't fit with my own.' Pearl held her breath. 'But perhaps you and I might get along. I'm aware that we don't know one another very well but you have a care for your appearance, which I usually find a good indicator of a person's habits generally. I doubt my home is all that much further from the bus garage than you're used to walking. And other than my students coming and going, I tend to keep myself to myself. So, if it's peace and quiet you're after, there won't be an issue.'

Pearl could hardly believe her luck. 'How much rent would you want?'

'To be honest, I have no idea what would be reasonable to ask. The idea only occurred to me while I was in the kitchen making the tea. There would be the question of meals and so on to discuss, too.'

A room in a house like this, Pearl thought, would surely be out of her reach. And in which case, perhaps she shouldn't get too excited. But oh, if only this could be made to work out! Sylvia was right to say it wasn't much further from the bus garage. It would also mean she would be in a house filled with music. She might even be able to watch some of Sylvia's other pupils having their lessons and start picking things up more quickly as a result. In so many respects, it would be perfect.

'May I see the room please?' While she loathed being pushy, this felt like an opportunity she couldn't let slip through her fingers for want of using her tongue.

'Of course, dear.'

The room to which Sylvia showed her looked out over the back garden. It wasn't anywhere near as large as the basement at Mrs Trude's, but it was welcoming and far cosier. There was a single bed, small wardrobe, and chest of drawers. On the floor was a pretty rug with a fringe; at the window were plain curtains in a shade she thought might be called *eau de nil*; the wallpaper had sprigs of tiny flowers on a pale background. She'd never seen anything like it.

'It's...' As her eyes filled with tears, she felt a hand soothing back and forth across her shoulders.

'How about a week's trial?' Sylvia suggested. 'See how we rub along?'

Pearl sniffed. 'That would be lovely.'

'If we get along well enough, we can discuss the matter of rent. And once you're here, you can tell me how your shifts work, and about meals and laundry and so on.'

Pearl nodded her agreement. 'I can't believe you'd do this.' She remembered thinking Clemmie had been lucky to get that room with the WVS woman, but it couldn't possibly be as nice as this one.

'If you like, and you can manage on top of your other obligations, then when you come for your lesson on Thursday – I assume you wish to keep them up?'

With considerable vigour, Pearl nodded. 'Definitely.'

'Then how about you bring your things with you and make that your first night?'

Pearl exhaled in relief. This lovely kind woman had saved her bacon. 'Not sure I deserve this,' she admitted.

'Nonsense. We're all allowed the odd mistake. The critical thing is not to keep making the same sort, over and over again.'

Finally, Pearl smiled. 'No. I see that.'

'Then it's settled. Now, how about we go and finish that tea before it goes completely cold?'

A while later, walking back to her lodgings at Mrs Trude's, Pearl wanted to sing at the top of her voice. Everything was going to be all right – well, assuming Sylvia didn't find her too much of an intrusion, it would be. But at least her own behaviour was entirely within her own control, meaning that it was down to her, and her alone, not to squander the unexpected fresh start she'd so fortuitously just been handed.

Chapter 16

'If you don't mind my saying, dear, this evening, your thoughts would appear to be anywhere but on your singing.'

Pearl blushed hotly. Sylvia wasn't wrong. Try as she might, she couldn't keep her thoughts on the music. 'Sorry.'

'Let's try again, from "Don't want to feel this way," shall we?'

Pearl stared at the music on the stand in front of her, but it was no good; she wasn't in the right mood – not for this song or any other.

In her despair, she let out a lengthy sigh. 'I'm sorry. I just can't seem to concentrate.'

It was the Tuesday evening after Pearl had gone to live at Sylvia's and, although her singing lesson was usually on a Thursday, seeing her looking listless, Sylvia had suggested she might like to practise her two newest numbers. 'Looks like someone needs cheering up,' had been her actual words. 'Come on, there's nothing better than music – singing in particular – for lifting one's spirits.' On this occasion, though, Pearl knew it was going to take more than singing to improve her mood.

'Would it help if you were to tell me what's on your mind?'

Despite doubting that it would, Pearl nodded. 'Maybe. But only if you promise not to be appalled.'

'Goodness.' Sylvia raised an eyebrow. 'I can't promise you that, but I'll do my best.'

'And only if we can go and sit in the drawing room.'

Sylvia lowered the piano's fallboard. 'Come on, then.' The first time Pearl had set foot in Sylvia's drawing room, she'd been struck by how homely it felt, it having the feel of a refuge that invited the sharing of confidences; it was cosy, the weighty fabrics muffling sound, the door closing snugly against the rest of the world. Tonight, in her preoccupied state, Pearl found it particularly welcoming. 'I think we're going to need a lamp,' Sylvia observed of the failing light and moved to the window, where she pulled down the blackout blinds in the bay and then drew across the curtains. In the narrow band of light coming in from the hallway, she reached for the side table and switched on the nearest lamp. On her way to light the second, she closed the door. 'Whenever you feel ready,' Sylvia coaxed as she lowered herself into the chair on the other side of the fireplace.

Under Sylvia's steady gaze, Pearl felt a wave of mortification and took to staring into her lap. 'Can't say as I know where to start.'

'Well, is it just the one thing, or are there several?'

Despite being in no doubt about what was eating away at her, Pearl paused. 'There's two things.'

'Connected to one another?'

Pearl shook her head. 'Only in that they're both making me feel rotten.'

'Then how about we start with the one causing you the greatest distress?'

Distress. Yes, Pearl thought; distress was the perfect description for what she felt – certainly about what had happened just two days ago. 'On Sunday,' she began and then stopped to clear her throat. 'I went to see my sister, Clemmie.'

'I remember,' Sylvia replied evenly.

'My elder sister, May, she was there, too. Came down from where she works up near Crediton. I suppose I should tell you that we're not proper sisters, but half-sisters. My father married their mother – *my* mother, that is – who was widowed.'

Sylvia nodded. 'Go on.'

'Anyway, Clemmie had invited me and May to tea. All she'd said beforehand was that she'd met someone – a man, I mean – and that she wanted us to meet him because he'd proposed they get wed.'

'And that came as a surprise to you,' Sylvia observed.

Pearl nodded. 'Though not as much as when we walked up this nobby road past all these smart houses with grass out the front and a car parked down the side... and it dawned on me how that's where Clem would be going to live. Nor as much as when she put a key in the lock and let herself in.'

'That bothered you?'

'I think it was more a case that it pulled me up short – made me stop and wonder how Clemmie could have got to know some chap like that—'

'Like what, dear?'

'Someone so well to-do,' Pearl explained before continuing. 'That she could have got to know him so well in so short a space of time. It brought home to me how much she must have got on with her life.' Her confession barely begun, she paused for breath; what she had to admit next was the worst part. Own up to that, and she might feel less awful. 'Anyway, inside, the house was real nice. All clean and tidy and polished and... modern-looking. But then her chap comes through from the back and I couldn't have been more shocked than if he'd been King George himself.'

When she paused yet again, Sylvia encouraged her to go on. 'What was it that shocked you?'

'Well, see, this feller – nice looking and everything, smartly turned out – was on crutches. And you could see he was hardly using his legs at all. Anyway, Clem introduces us all – Andrew his name is – and we all traipse through into this posh drawing room. Whole wall full of books. And I'm stood there, looking around and thinking it must be a prank. Anyway, while Clemmie's gone to get us some tea, this Andrew starts telling us how he'd been a pilot in the RAF and had got shot at by a German... and how, when he got back, his plane wouldn't land... or something, and he ended up crashing into the ground. Did his spine in, and now he can't walk. And *then*, cap it all, Clemmie comes back, followed by this manservant type carrying a tray with a cake... and a tea service and napkins and everything.'

'And it made you feel uncomfortable?'

'I was flabbergasted. And it's not often I'm lost for words, as I'm sure you'd be quick to agree.'

'So, what happened?'

'We're all sat there, and while *I'm* thinking I must be dreaming, May starts making all this dainty conversation. "I understand you're a tutor now," she says to this Andrew, or something like that. And all I can think is what the devil is going on here? And why is May carrying on as though it's perfectly normal for your eighteen-year-old—'

remembering she'd lied about being eighteen herself, Pearl hastily backtracked '—nineteen-year-old sister to get mixed up with some posh old feller who can't get about without crutches? All I knew was that I couldn't sit there listening to them regale us with how the two of them met, as though it was perfectly normal. For a start, he was twice her age.' Sylvia raised an eyebrow. 'Well, thirty, if he was a day.'

When, after that, she was reluctant to go on, Sylvia leaned towards her. 'Did you say something to your sister? Something you perhaps now regret?'

In her mind's eye, as clear as though it was happening there and then, Pearl saw herself shooting up from the couch, storming from the drawing room into that gleaming hallway, Clemmie, all upset, coming after her and beseeching her not to be so mean.

'I said some things I shouldn't have.' *For crying out loud, Clem. You've no business in a place like this. Can't you see what's going on here? Can't you see his game?* Recalling the venom in her words, Pearl shuddered. *For Christ's sake, look around you. You're his little experiment. You're the little orphan he's going to clean up and dress nice and… and learn to talk proper to see if he can pass off for a lady.* Despite Clemmie pleading with her to stop, she'd gone on and on, spewing the most vile and hurtful accusations she could think of. *Either that, or it's you, trying to make up for never having a father* – Dear God, could she have been any meaner? – *it's as plain as the nose on your face. You're just something to occupy him, something to make up for the fact that no woman with an ounce of sense is going to sacrifice a normal life for him.* And on she'd pressed. *When the two of you go on a date, where does he take you, eh?* And when poor Clemmie had hung her head, she still hadn't eased up. *I mean, is he even able to, you know, do it?* It was at that point Clemmie had accused her of being crude. And rightly so.

The taste of bile from that afternoon back in her throat, Pearl looked up to meet Sylvia's gaze; Sylvia had to be the least judgemental woman she'd ever met.

'I said terrible, terrible things. And then I stormed out. Clemmie was sobbing. She said if that was how I felt, then she didn't think she'd be able to find it in herself to invite me back. And I didn't even care. Not one jot. I just said *fine.*'

'And since then, you've been going over and over it in your mind, feeling sick with shame?' Recognising the truth of Sylvia's statement, Pearl nodded. 'Having had time to reflect, you realise now how badly you behaved?'

Again, Pearl nodded. 'That's about the measure of it. And before you go on to say it, yes, I know I should go and apologise. Though I doubt she'd open the door to me. But the thing is, even though I feel terrible about the things I said, in my heart, I still don't think she should marry this chap. She's such a lovely kind person and there must be so many men out there who would fall over themselves to take up with her. Worst of it is, when we were little, and I was always talking about being a famous actress when I grew up, all *she* ever wanted to do was to get married and have a family. A *family*. And no matter how nice his house and all the rest of it, that's the one thing I don't reckon this Andrew will be able to give her. And of everyone I know, she's probably the person who most deserves to have their dreams come true.'

'The thing is,' Sylvia said carefully. 'While that might seem the case to you, it's your sister's life, and for no one but her to decide how she wishes to live it.' After a short pause, Sylvia went on, 'It sounds to me as though the three of you are close.'

'We were, once upon a time, until Hitler saw to it we lost our home, and we all got split up.'

'That's terribly sad. But you know, even the closest of sisters reach a point where they have to accept it's not their place to try and impose their views or opinions on the others. Express them respectfully if invited to, yes, but never to impose. But I think you already know that, which is why you feel so rotten. I also think you know what you have to do.'

Pearl hung her head. 'I do… but whether or not I can do it…'

'Do you still want to tell me about the other thing? You mentioned there were two matters on your mind.'

Pearl sighed. 'Maybe.'

'"Better out than in", as the saying goes.'

Overcoming her indecision, Pearl drew a breath and set about explaining how she felt about Ivy and Gordon Gold.

'I suppose I worry,' she said, her tone turning to one of exasperation, 'that *I* should have signed with him too. See, if I had, then, right now, I might be in London with her. We might both be in a musical stage show – who knows, I might even have got the part she did. Christ,' she muttered as the realisation dawned. 'What if it should have been me all along but now it's Ivy instead? What if, by taking this bloomin' part, she goes on to become famous? What if *she* goes on to become a star instead of me?'

'My dear Pearl, as I think you are coming to discover, hindsight is a harsh judge—'

'Instead, here I am, stuck doing the same old exercises just to go out and sing, unpaid, in an army tent. You know,

I often wonder what the point of it all is. Just my luck,' she said, gesturing wildly with her hand, 'that when I finally get to try and bring about my dream, a ruddy war comes along to ruin it. Had I been born five years earlier, I'd probably already be on the stage.'

'Pearl, dear, listen to me.' Sylvia's tone, Pearl noticed, had shortened. 'I know you're frustrated and cross, and impatient to be a success, but there's something it might help you to know. I wasn't going to tell you this, but Gordon Gold is highly unlikely to make Ivy a star. Nor would he have been likely to make one out of you, either. Until you told me you'd been to see him, I'd never heard of the man. Jack, neither. So, I wrote to a friend of mine in London. She's a dance teacher – albeit part-time these days. The rest of the time she drives an ambulance. Anyway, my point is that she didn't know of Gordon Gold either, but she did make enquiries. And I'm afraid it turns out that not only is the man small fry in the world of showbusiness, but he's also something of a charlatan.'

Pearl frowned. 'I don't know what that means.'

'Well, it's not a compliment, that's for certain. Let's settle for saying that he's known for being something of a fraud, a fake. Promises a lot but doesn't deliver.'

Sylvia's explanation didn't help. 'But if that's the case, then how does he earn a living? Surely, if what you say is true, he wouldn't make any money.'

'How, indeed. Tell me, did he ask you to pay to cover, say, expenses?'

'For a photographer and those sorts of things…' Unexpectedly, the penny dropped; she'd thought it odd when he'd said they were to pay him for things done by other people. 'So, if, as you say, he's no good, then what will happen to Ivy?'

'Perhaps, one way or another, she will fare all right. She always struck me as a sharp young woman, so, maybe she'll see through him and cut her losses.' Did Sylvia think Ivy would be back, then? After she'd burned her bridges? 'And I suppose there is always the faint possibility this Gold chappie *will* find her some work. But I have to say I'm doubtful. If I were you, I would consider I'd had a narrow escape, and stop regretting that you didn't sign his contract.'

'Hm.' Perhaps this new piece of information did lessen the blow. Poor Ivy, though.

'On a separate but not unrelated note, I happen to know that Jack is working on something new with the band. Something he'll want you to be a part of.'

At this news, Pearl hauled herself more upright in her chair. 'Oh?'

'But more than that it's not my place to say.'

'Oh.' While it had got to the point where she would take anything if it meant singing in more shows – and getting paid for her trouble – Jack having a new idea, whatever it might entail, was hardly the same as the chance of a part in a musical in London. And although it transpired she knew less than she thought about showbusiness, she understood enough to know there was also a considerable difference between working on something and having it in the bag. Jack's new idea could easily amount to nothing.

'So, my dear, tell me, do you feel any better?'

In truth, although it was a relief to have confessed about Clemmie, Pearl couldn't, hand on heart, claim to feel that much brighter. 'A little, thank you.'

'Then why don't you go and draw yourself five inches of bathwater and have an early night? You're bound to be grateful for it in the morning.'

Attempting to smile, Pearl got up from her chair. 'Yes. All right. Perhaps I'll do that. And thank you for listening to me moan.'

'Hopefully, in some small way, I have been of help to you.'

Sadly, Pearl thought as she trudged up the stairs, while it had been kind of Sylvia to listen and to sympathise, when it came to the matter of her behaviour towards poor Clemmie, she didn't feel any better at all. And she was starting to think that the only way she ever would, was by putting herself out and going to apologise to her. And to Andrew. And probably even to May. But how she was going to come across as contrite and sincere when, deep down, she still felt Clemmie needed to be taken by the shoulders and shaken until she saw sense, she had no idea. And as for Ivy, and the chance she'd failed to take to go with her to London, well, with the way things were, she could only imagine it would be a very long time indeed before she would know whether she'd done the right thing in that respect or not – and probably even longer before a chance remotely like it came her way again.

Chapter 17

'You were great tonight, as usual.'

Pearl smiled. 'Thank you for saying so.'

'Truly. No one would guess you're so new to this.'

'Hm.'

It was now Friday night and Pearl had just sung four numbers with The Tim Murrin Dance Band as part of their usual booking. While it was always gratifying to be complimented on her performance, she did sometimes wonder whether Jack would have said that anyway – purely to build her confidence. She liked to think not but, since she hardly knew him, was never entirely sure.

'You know,' Jack went on to say, 'I can't believe Ivy went off without so much as a goodbye. And yes, I do realise she was under no obligation to me, but she could at least have let me know she was leaving. I took a chance on her, and that's the thanks I get.'

'Sylvia feels the same way,' Pearl said. 'She might not let on, but I happen to know she's real hurt.'

'With good reason. Still, bonus for you I suppose – chance to take over her slot. By the way, your two new numbers have come on in leaps and bounds.'

Pearl smiled. 'To be honest with you, I still don't feel comfortable with either of them. I mean, I like the tunes and I know all the words but—'

'They don't feel like old friends yet?'

She laughed. 'Not in the least.'

'You slip into your old songs as though they were a pair of well-worn slippers, whereas these latest two feel more like brand-new shoes – stiff and uncomfortable.'

Pearl laughed even harder. 'I must remember that. It's so true.'

'Don't worry,' he said. 'It'll come. Practise, practise. It's only through singing them again and again that you'll find the phrases or sections to make your own. Once you're happier with them, Sylvia has a couple more we think would suit you.'

'More?' Goodness, he must have faith in her.

'Yup. I want you out there, up front. The audiences love you. But then you've seen that for yourself.'

'I do seem to get warm applause,' she said, feeling her cheeks colour. 'Does the band have many bookings coming up?'

To her disappointment, Jack's expression suggested not. 'Truth be told, it's gone a bit quiet. All the while this place stays open, we're assured of the one night a week here. And yes, I know that's not saying much. But doing this does get us seen. In fact, I've been talking to someone at one of the big hotels, who saw us play here a few weeks back. Something *might* come of it. For now, though, if you're after more than this, you'll have to make do with Cliff's concert parties.' Reading her disappointment, he grinned. 'Look upon them as a chance to break in those new shoes.'

Yes, Pearl thought, she would try and do that. But singing in a draughty army tent in the middle of a field to a crowd of baying soldiers was hardly glamorous. Noble, maybe – but noble didn't keep her in singing lessons; she might be Sylvia's lodger, but that didn't get her any favours, she still had to pay the going rate for her voice tuition – and rightly so, too.

'Well, goodnight, then,' she said with a smile to Jack.

'Goodnight. Watch out going home.'

Feeling immensely tired, Pearl left the back room and went along the corridor to what Jack laughingly referred to as 'the stage door'; in truth, it was merely an exit onto an alleyway that was used by the staff when the front entrance was locked. When she let herself out through it tonight, she came upon Ron Bachelor fumbling about with a torch. As her eyes accustomed to the darkness, she spotted that he was fastening cycle clips over his trousers.

In the name of making conversation, she gestured to where his pushbike was leaning against the wall. 'Do you have far to go?'

'Fifteen minutes or so. Depends how worn out I am and how many halves I've had.'

She knew, from having watched him, that Ron swore by a couple of halves of porter to lubricate his throat before he went on stage, followed by another couple afterwards to quench the thirst supposedly brought on by performing. *It's the smoke that does it*, he'd said one night to explain the number of empties in front of him on the bar.

'Well, be careful,' she replied as she pressed the little rubber button on her own torch and switched it on. It was the one Sylvia had given her on the night of her first performance. *Since I fear it might be a while yet before you have the luxury of a chauffeur*, she'd joked as she'd handed it to her, *you're going to need it to see where the bomb craters are*.

'You know,' Ron said as he cocked a leg over the saddle of his bike, 'I was surprised to see you still here. I thought you would have been lured up the smoke with that other one, what's-her-name.'

Lured up the smoke? Ron knew about Gordon Gold? How did he? She could only suppose he must have put two and two together when Jack told the band about Ivy, and about the two new numbers that she, Pearl, would be doing in Ivy's place.

'What makes you say that?' she asked, curious, nonetheless. In the narrow beam of yellow torchlight, she noticed that Ron had changed the black patent shoes he wore on stage for a pair of plimsolls. His dress shoes, she decided, must be in the rucksack on his back.

'The lure of the bright lights. Two girls together. I mean, this,' he said, nodding towards the back door of the club, 'is hardly glamorous, is it.'

'Everyone has to start somewhere,' she said, determining to divulge nothing of her reasons for still being there. Directing her torch down to the ground, she turned to set off along the alley. 'Well, goodnight, then.'

As she picked her way between the dustbins towards the street, she heard the tyres of Ron's bicycle crackling away over the gravel in the opposite direction. He was a strange fellow. But then it had to be hard to watch two young women turn up one week and steal the limelight – harder still, when his own set was reduced to make way for them. It must also require a particular doggedness to get up on stage each time, knowing that your best years were behind you – that if you hadn't made the big time by now, you never would.

Deep in thought, she paused momentarily at the kerb and then crossed the road. Ordinarily, on the way home to Mrs Trude's, she and Ivy would have discussed the night's performances. In her head, she could hear Ivy now: *I swear*

the band played 'Fools Rush In' more slowly than usual; I was
horrible flat on that last note; Was it just me, or did it take the
audience a long time to warm up tonight?

Directing the paltry beam of her torch a yard or so ahead of her, she sighed. It was a shame the way things had turned out with Ivy. Back at the beginning, she had been good company, her knack of finding the funny side in even the most miserable of moments marvellous for lifting her spirits. But, the moment they met Gordon Gold, everything had begun to unravel. She still hadn't worked out *why* he had turned up at the barracks that night? He claimed to have had a tip-off. But a tip-off from whom? She knew for a fact that it wouldn't have been from either Sylvia or Jack. But who else could it have been? It was a puzzle, all right. Sadly, once Ivy had got the idea of working in London into her head, nothing had been going to dislodge it – not even the realisation that Gold was someone they shouldn't trust.

Stepping into the road to skirt a length of hoarding erected in front of what, before the Blitz, she seemed to recall had been a public house, she let out another sigh. In a way, she supposed she should be grateful Ivy had left; had she not, the band wouldn't have had two numbers to fill. Jack *could* simply have reverted to Ron but, because he hadn't, she now had four numbers of her own. Moreover, she was now the only female, which meant that not only was there no competition, but also that she stood out. When Ron got up and sang, she'd noticed that, as far as the audience was concerned, he was largely background – no more than part of the music to which they were dancing. But when *she* slipped onto the stage, people looked to see who she was. She'd also noticed that, once she got into her stride, they smiled up at her as they whirled around the floor and applauded warmly at the end of every song. Perhaps, then, as her mother would no doubt have observed, every cloud *did* have a silver lining. If true, though, the silver lining attaching to Ivy's departure felt disturbingly flimsy; for all she knew, Ivy might only have a couple of numbers in a chorus line but, by now, she was at least on the stage – and in London, too, rather than in sleepy old Exeter, where she doubted anyone had even heard of a Talent Manager.

Looking ahead and realising that she'd reached the bridge over the railway, she let out another sigh. Allowing Ivy's success to rankle her was about as pointless as being continually down in the dumps about the war. Ivy was gone; had moved on with her life. And, since she knew to her cost that existing in a permanent state of grouchiness quickly became wearying, she was going to have to find a way to content herself with smaller pleasures – like singing with the band – and apply herself with even greater vigour to achieving her own dream, even if that would now take longer without the help of Gordon Gold.

–

The weather had been nasty the whole day – damp and dreary – and as she stood at the kerb, waiting while a coal lorry turned across her path into a side street, all she could think was that she couldn't wait to be home. The moment she was, she would change out of her uniform, wash, and then have another go at writing to May. It might be taking the cowardly way out but she'd come to think that, by writing to May first, she might find out how badly upset Clemmie was; once she knew that, she could work out the best way to seek her forgiveness.

Despite having confided her worries to Sylvia, neither of her concerns had gone away, not even a little. That she continued to envy Ivy her supposed success – and to regret not going with her – was a state of affairs she could do little about. Apologising to Clemmie, on the other hand, was something she *could* get on and do. And seeking May's counsel first ought to ensure that she approached Clemmie in the right way – as opposed to simply making matters even worse.

The coal lorry having finally negotiated the corner, Pearl crossed the road and continued on her way. But, at the next junction, her eye was caught by a blonde-haired woman in a smart navy coat scurrying along the opposite pavement. Was that— Frozen to the spot, she strained to make out the woman's features. It was. Oh, dear Lord, it was Clemmie. Now what did she do, pretend she hadn't seen her and keep walking? Or view it as serendipity?

In that same instant, Clemmie looked up and, appearing similarly stricken, slowed to a halt.

The decision about what to do seemingly out of her hands, Pearl glanced in both directions along the street and went towards her. 'Clemmie.'

Her sister responded with a single nod. 'Pearl. Hello.'

'How are you?'

'Fine, thanks. You?'

'Same, thanks.' Of all the people she could have bumped into… 'I'm on my way home.'

'Me too.'

'Miserable day.'

'Horrible.'

'What brings you all the way over here?' Pearl made her enquiry not just with a view to sounding friendly but to stall Clemmie for a moment while she decided what to do.

'One of our WVS members has been unwell recently. I popped over to see her.'

'Oh. I hope she's getting better.'

'She is. Well, I'd best be—'

'No, wait. Hang on a minute, Clem.' Sensing that her chance was about to slip through her fingers, Pearl drew a breath.

'What is it?'

Nothing ventured, nothing gained. 'I… want to apologise.' Regretting profoundly that she hadn't had time to think this through, she gave an exasperated little shake of her head. There were so many ways she could make a mess of this – so many, in fact, that her best bet seemed to simply be direct. 'I want to apologise to you for the things I said at your Andrew's that afternoon.' Golly, even simply saying the words made her feel lighter. 'I couldn't have been more in the wrong.' When Clemmie didn't immediately reply, Pearl went on. 'And please don't make out it was nothing just to be shot of me. It wasn't nothing. I've felt terrible ever since.'

'Very well,' Clemmie said evenly, 'I won't make out it was nothing. Nor will I claim I wasn't hurt by the way you behaved… because I was. But, having had time to reflect, I've come to realise that your reaction was just your way of showing your concern. You always did look out for me… and I did rather spring the whole thing on you. No doubt I would have felt the same had the boot been on the other foot, and it had been you breaking what was, after all, rather unexpected news.'

Pearl thought she might cry with relief. Trust Clem to look for the good in her vile behaviour. 'So—'

'So, thank you for your apology. It means a lot to me. But how about we just agree to let bygones be bygones?'

When Clemmie leaned across and kissed Pearl's cheek, Pearl sniffed. 'You're sure? Only—'

'I am.'

'Well… that's real generous of you.'

'Think no more of it. And perhaps, if there's a day sometime when you're not working, we might… oh, I don't know… try again?'

Pearl smiled warmly. 'I'd like that.'

Afterwards, when they'd said their goodbyes and promised each other they would keep in touch, Pearl was left trying to make sense of how she felt. Beneath her disbelief that they had so easily cleared the air, she was relieved – hugely relieved – not only to have lifted the burden from her conscience but because, while she might only recently have come to appreciate it, she knew she couldn't have asked for better sisters than Clemmie and May. Through the leanest of times, the three of them had always watched out for one another. Indeed, if it hadn't been for those ruddy Luftwaffe bombs scattering them to the four winds, they would still be looking out for one another now.

Her progress towards home ponderous, she frowned. Except, that wasn't true, was it? They weren't scattered, were they? Clemmie lived less than a two-mile walk from Sylvia's. And she knew for a fact that Clemmie and May exchanged regular letters. That she'd let herself become estranged from them was entirely her own doing. Through selfishness in the early days, and for want of a little more effort lately, she had let their sisterliness unravel. Well, as she had promised Clemmie not a moment previously, she would try a darn sight harder to keep in touch.

Enjoying the feeling of lightness arising from her relief, she sighed. Dearest Clemmie, if only everyone was so forgiving; in the same circumstances, she couldn't imagine her own response being anywhere near so gracious.

The spring back in her step, she allowed herself a wry smile. If only all her mistakes could be so easily put right. Unfortunately, the other regret weighing heavily on her mind was unlikely to be so simply resolved. By not signing with Gordon Gold, she might, as Sylvia had tried to get her to believe, have dodged a bullet. Deep down, though, she couldn't shake the feeling that, while Ivy was on her way to greatness, she, Pearl, was destined to remain stuck in Devon, her talent going undiscovered, her opportunities amounting to nothing more glamourous than singing for soldiers in chilly tents. No matter how optimistic she tried to be, she simply couldn't picture anything different. As things stood, even *hoping* for a change of fortunes felt like a waste of energy, which meant that perhaps it was time to accept she had missed the boat – and that, maybe, the least painful thing she could do was stop tormenting herself with her dream of becoming famous – kiss it completely goodbye – and come to terms instead with settling for what she already had.

October 1943

IV. Interlude

Chapter 18

'Thank goodness I've finally got the hang of that one.'

'Indeed. Now you've mastered that tricky little section in the middle, I'd say you're ready for Jack to include it in the show. He's asked several times recently how it's coming along.'

'Then he should be pleased to know it's ready.'

Watching as Sylvia closed the fallboard over the piano's keys, Pearl let out a contented sigh. She was enjoying the newer numbers she was singing with the band – not that she didn't have plenty of favourites among what Jack referred to as 'the classics'.

It was coming up to a year now since Ron had left what had, at the time, still been known as The Tim Murrin Dance Band. The circumstances of his eventual departure had been surprisingly acrimonious, with Ron accusing Jack of having had his head turned by a girl. Nothing, of course, could have been further from the truth; that Jack had steadily expanded her routine at the expense of Ron's was none of her doing – she simply sang the numbers she was given. When Jack had then secured their twice weekly booking at the swanky Castle Hotel, it had been Sylvia who'd suggested that, if the band was going to move with the times, they were going to need a new name. That was when Jack had come up with The Murrinaires, pointing out that, while it was both fresh and modern, it still gave a respectful nod to their founder, Sylvia's husband, the late Tim Murrin, without whom, the band would never have come into being.

On Saturdays, the band now had a permanent booking – well, as permanent as anything could be in this time of war – to play at the hotel's dinner dance, held in The Grill Room, where sedate but popular numbers were the order of the night. On Thursdays, however, they played the hotel's new Undercroft Club, which, as its name suggested, was in the basement, where the crowd was younger and more adventurous and clamoured for upbeat numbers to which they could dance and forget their cares. For several weeks before the club had opened, Pearl had gone with the band to rehearse in the empty venue, their audience comprising the odd tradesman or member of hotel staff who, upon happening to be walking past, would be drawn to see who, in an otherwise generally stuffy establishment, was belting out swing music. Together, the band had practised and practised until every one of their new songs was note perfect. Of the two nights they performed there, Thursdays were by far Pearl's favourite: her dress was racier, the patrons more youthful, the atmosphere electric. As Jack had said the first time they went there to play for real, The Grill Room was where a chap took his mother for her birthday; the Undercroft was where he took his girl.

Although great fun, the performances on Thursday nights were tiring, the morning after finding her grateful for the walk to work, the fresh air doing wonders for her head. She still loved being a conductress but, by mid-morning on a Friday, she found herself hoping that not too many passengers would want to sit on the upper deck, thus sparing her some of the traipsing up and down.

Despite near exhaustion, though, all the tea in China wouldn't have persuaded her to give up Thursday nights at the Undercroft.

Reflecting upon recent progress with her singing, she gave a satisfied smile. All in all, since Ivy had left – a little over a year ago now – and despite a short-lived wobble in her confidence about her own future, it had turned out to be quite the year. Alongside her own advancement, the country had also made steady strides towards winning the war. By virtue of living with Sylvia, who listened keenly to the evening news broadcasts, Pearl found herself understanding more about what was happening, her increased knowledge leading her to believe with greater certainty that the war would end in the allies' victory: not long into the new year, Russia, at great cost to its own troops, had destroyed two entire German armies, leading people to start talking about the end of the Third Reich; shortly after that, British and American bombers had wreaked havoc upon Berlin; more recently, Italy had surrendered and swapped sides. All in all, quite the year.

'I have some cocoa, if you'd like a cup.'

Realising she must have drifted off into her thoughts, Pearl looked down to see that, while Sylvia was busy putting away her music, she was also waiting for her to reply.

'Oh, yes please.' Drifting off was something that seemed to happen to her quite a lot lately. 'Cocoa would be lovely.'

'Come through in a minute then and I'll—' Her instruction to Pearl cut short by a knock at the front door, Sylvia changed tack. 'Be a dear and go and see who that is, would you? I'm not expecting anyone.'

On her way past the coat stand, Pearl grabbed the torch from the shelf, switched off the overhead light, and opened the door.

The pale figure she saw on the other side made her gasp and sent her reeling backwards in disbelief. Was she seeing things or was this— She raised the beam of torchlight higher. Good God. No, it really was Ivy, at her feet the same tatty suitcase she'd packed when she'd left last year, in her arms, a baby.

'Hello, Pearl.'

'Ivy.' She couldn't think what else to say; precisely as Sylvia had forecast all that time ago, the woman was back. She doubted even Sylvia had expected her to return with a child, though.

'Can I come in?'

'Well, I—'

'Who is it, dear?'

Moving aside, Pearl gestured Ivy into the hallway; over her shoulder, she called uncertainly towards the kitchen, 'It's... Ivy.'

'Ivy who?'

'Ivy Snell,' Ivy took it upon herself to respond as she set her suitcase down on the tiled floor. Ignoring Pearl's continuing bewilderment, she adjusted the weight of the baby on her arm and went in the direction of Sylvia's voice. 'I know it's late to turn up like this, but I'm in a bit of a fix.'

Hundreds of questions clamouring for answers, Pearl closed the front door. Ivy was back, the question of why clearly redundant: she was in trouble. She had a baby. And on her finger, she had a wedding ring. But, had she married and got pregnant – or got pregnant and then married? And if she *was* married, where was her husband, and what was she doing here, on her own?

Anxious not to miss what might be happening in the kitchen, Pearl hurried along the hallway to see; with her back to Ivy, Sylvia was pouring steaming cocoa into their two cups. Was she deliberately not looking at Ivy, Pearl wondered? It wouldn't surprise her; Ivy might have remarked upon the lateness of the hour, but she'd made no apology for it.

'There you are, dear,' Sylvia said, reaching past Ivy to hand Pearl her cup and saucer. 'Remember, it will be scalding hot.' Moving to lift her own cup from the table, she finally addressed Ivy. 'Well, this is unexpected.'

'That's one word for it.'

Still, Pearl noticed, looking Ivy up and down, the woman offered no apology, let alone an explanation.

Giving no indication of her thoughts, Sylvia blew across the top of her cup. 'What brings you back?'

'Suffice it to say... one set of unfortunate circumstances after another.'

'I see.'

While it was out of character for Sylvia to give anyone the cold shoulder, in this instance, Pearl was relieved to see that she wasn't welcoming Ivy with open arms. If nothing else, it put the onus on Ivy to explain herself.

Against Ivy's chest, the infant, wrapped in a greying shawl, wriggled, and shot out a fist. Then it made a noise of complaint.

'Do you think we might sit down?' Ivy said. When Sylvia nodded to the table, Ivy one-handedly pulled out a chair and sank onto it. 'I thought that bloomin' train was never going to get here.'

Clutching her cocoa, Pearl felt a twinge of meanness. Clearly, Ivy was worn out, the dullness of her complexion, combined with the untidiness of her hair and the absence of make-up, making her look considerably older than her mid-twenties.

On her arm, the baby started to struggle. Girl or boy, Pearl wondered idly. Perhaps of greater importance was the question of who – and where – was the father?

Eventually, it was Sylvia who broke the silence. 'So, what can we do for you, Ivy? Why are you here?'

Ivy exhaled so heavily that she sank several inches lower onto her chair. Finally, Pearl thought, she had the grace to look contrite. 'I was wondering whether I might stay for a few days.'

Ha! She knew it. Ivy was in trouble – and, by the look of it, not for the first time, either.

'A few days,' Sylvia repeated.

Ivy perked up a little. 'Like I said, I've had a spot of misfortune… one way and another. And I came to thinking how it might be easier to get back on my feet down here. London's… well, let's just say, if you hit on hard times, it can be an unforgiving sort of a place.'

'And the baby's father? Where is he in your hour of need?'

'Threw me out.'

'Well, since I can't have it on my conscience to condemn a baby to a night outdoors, you may stay. I'll sort out the spare room.'

'I'll help you,' said Pearl, largely because she didn't relish being left alone to make conversation with this new and bedraggled version of her one-time friend. Moreover, before showing her own colours, she could do with knowing Sylvia's thoughts on this unexpected turn of events.

'In the morning,' Sylvia moved towards the door and looked back at Ivy to say, 'you can tell me your plans.'

'Don't suppose you've got any evaporated milk?'

Pearl glanced to Sylvia, who appeared to be struggling to contain irritation. *Evaporated milk?* What the devil did Ivy want with that? And had she forgotten how to say please?

'Only a small tin. Are you no longer nursing?'

Ivy shook her head. 'Can't.'

'Do you have a bottle?'

This time, Ivy nodded. 'In my bag, but it'll need sterilising.'

'Kettle's there,' Sylvia said. Moving to the cupboard, she took from the shelf their only tin of evaporated milk.

'Any sugar?'

Christ, Ivy had a nerve. And still neither a 'please' nor a 'thank you' to be heard.

'In the caddy next to the tea. I'll go and make space in the spare room.'

Carefully, Pearl replaced her cup on her saucer and deposited them in the sink. Then she followed Sylvia up the stairs. When she arrived on the landing, Sylvia beckoned her into the unused bedroom at the front.

'What do you think has happened?' Pearl hissed.

'I imagine, precisely what it would seem.' From the end of the bed, Sylvia picked up her sewing basket and knitting bag and looked around for somewhere to put them. 'Can you reach to put them on top of the wardrobe for me?'

Pearl nodded. 'Of course.'

'That the bed hasn't been aired I can't help. As for where the baby is going to sleep…'

'I rather think that's Ivy's problem,' Pearl said. 'If you turn up, unannounced, at this time of night, I don't think you get to criticise whatever arrangements are made for you.'

'You're not pleased to see her either, then?' From a blanket box at the end of the bed, Sylvia produced two sheets and a pillowcase.

'Here, let me see to the sheet.' Having flapped it open, Pearl proceeded to spread it over the mattress. 'After the way she left us, there wouldn't be many a circumstance in which I'd want to see her anyway. But, like this, with a baby, and not so much as a word of explanation…'

Wrestling the pillow into its cover, Sylvia sighed. 'There's no rule that says she *has* to explain. Although common courtesy dictates that if you show up unexpectedly with the intention of asking to stay, it's poor form to say nothing at all.'

'And then to ask for both evaporated milk and sugar, both of which are on the ration.'

'I'm afraid that's Ivy through and through.'

Sylvia wasn't wrong.

'She's changed,' Pearl said. 'There's a hardness about her.'

'I should imagine having a child when you're not married will do that to you.'

Perhaps Sylvia hadn't noticed. 'She's wearing a wedding ring.'

'Pound to a penny it didn't come with a marriage certificate.'

'You think it's not a real one?' Across the bed from Sylvia, Pearl tucked in the top sheet and then reached for the eiderdown. Having given it a good shake, she laid it over the bed.

'It'll be brass. She'll have bought it from Woolworth's. Anyway, I suggest that, tonight, we let the two of them get some rest. Tomorrow, she can tell us her intentions.'

'You'll have to fill me in when I get back from work,' Pearl replied, rueing that, with tomorrow being Saturday, she would miss Ivy's attempts to explain herself.

As it was to turn out, Pearl didn't have to wait at all. In what seemed to be the middle of the night, she was awoken by the baby crying. Momentarily unable to work out where she was, she lifted her head from her pillow and, catching sight of her alarm clock, made out that it was four-thirty. Remembering the events of the previous evening, she groaned. Then, in case something was genuinely wrong, she folded back her bedcovers, swung her legs over the side of her mattress and pushed her feet into her slippers. From the back of the chair, she grabbed her dressing gown, put it on, and padded along the landing; the door to the spare room stood ajar, a shaft of light illuminating a strip of landing carpet.

At the door, she tapped softly.

'Who is it?'

'Me, Pearl. Can I come in?'

'Might as well. It's not as though I'm asleep.' In the little room, Pearl found Ivy sat up against the headboard, the baby, in its shawl, feeding from a bottle. In the sallow light from the single lamp, the bags under Ivy's eyes appeared even darker and gave her the appearance of being even more haggard.

'Is it a boy or a girl?' It seemed only polite to show at least passing interest.

'Girl.'

'What's her name?'

'Nothing yet.'

Last year, Pearl would have quipped something to the effect of, *Unusual choice for a girl*. But the Ivy slumped in front of her, barely able to keep her eyes open, didn't look as though she would appreciate the joke.

'Oh. Well, no rush, I suppose. How old is she?'

To Pearl's bafflement, Ivy shrugged. 'I hardly know anymore. I don't even know what day it is. Four-and-a-bit months, I suppose.'

Was Ivy affecting this vagueness, or did she genuinely not know the age of her own daughter? Either way, reckoning backwards, Pearl worked out that, if what Ivy said was true, then she must have fallen pregnant within a week or two of getting to London.

'And…' She didn't really want to ask but Ivy was the one who, despite showing up unannounced, had steadfastly failed to volunteer anything of her situation – other than that for some reason, she had nowhere else to go. '…the baby's father?'

'Wanted nothing to do with it.'

'So—'

'Look, to save you keep dancing about the matter, I got pregnant. No, the baby's father isn't already wed. No, he didn't offer to marry me when I told him. I didn't tell him for ages anyway. I didn't hardly show at all, and by the time I did, his ardour had already cooled, and he was onto the next one—'

'The next one?'

'Girl. The next girl.'

'Oh. Oh, I see.'

'Eventually, it was plain I had no choice but to tell him. When I first began to put on weight, the wardrobe mistress simply let out my costume. About a month later, when I had to ask her to let it out again, she must have

234

said something to the director because after that night's show, he took me aside and asked me straight up. I had no choice but to confess, and that was me finished – out of the show.'

Yes, Pearl supposed that would be the case. 'Oh.'

'And I was bloody good in it, too. Destined for bigger things. Everybody said so.'

'So… what did you do?' She was still having to coax Ivy to explain.

'Went and told the baby's father before he heard some other way, which he was bound to sooner or later. Tight knit lot, that cast. Verging on unhealthy.'

'He was in the same show?'

Ivy shook her head. 'Might as well have been. He knew everyone to do with it.'

'What did he say – when you told him?'

'Told me to get rid of it. When I explained how far gone I was, he turned purple and ordered me out. And when I said that, unless he gave me some money to find a room somewhere, I'd have to stay where I was, he said he wasn't giving me a penny – that for all he knew, I'd been sleeping around, and the baby wasn't even his.'

'Golly, Ivy.'

'Anyway, I reasoned with him – pointed out that since I'd lived with him throughout and he always knew where I was, I couldn't possibly have slept with anyone else. Not that he couldn't have worked that out for himself, anyway.'

'I see.' It wasn't a complete lie; she did understand some of Ivy's garbled tale.

'Once it was apparent which way the wind was blowing, so to speak, I told him I was going to give it up for adoption. That was when he agreed I could stay while I sorted out how to go about it – and when he said he'd give me money to make it happen. Not long after that, I left.'

'But where did you go?' So much of Ivy's story seemed contradictory that Pearl couldn't decide how much of it to believe. For a start, when Ivy had first arrived, she'd claimed the baby's father had thrown her out. Now, that no longer seemed entirely true.

'One of the other girls in the show told me about a Mother and Baby home.'

'And that's where you had the baby.'

Ivy gave a single nod. 'After I gave birth, I stayed until my money ran out. Give him his due, once her father did pay up, he gave me a fair sum. Made good and sure I understood there would only be the one lot, though. "Make it last. There won't be no more." That's what he said. So, I had to eke it out, watch every penny. When I got down to the last few quid, I had no choice but to leave the home and cadge a room or a couch wherever I could, mostly from women I'd met through the show. And then, well, no director's going to take on a woman with a baby. And trust me, I tried everything I could think of to persuade any number of them. Whenever casting opened somewhere, I went for an audition. Not a sniff. I was too old, I was too young. I didn't look right, I didn't look well. I needed to lose weight. You name it, I heard it.'

'So, the wedding ring—'

'This thing?' With a sour laugh, Ivy held up her hand. 'I bought this in a shop off Shaftesbury Avenue. Leave it on too long and it turns my finger green. One of the girls in the chorus had a sister who got caught out, and she was told to buy a ring and wear it before she had the baby so people wouldn't think she'd got herself into trouble. The same girl told me not to give my real name anywhere, either. So, I told everyone I was Florence Snelling. When I went into the home, I told them the baby's father had run off to the army. Trouble is, wearing this bloomin' thing still invites trouble.'

Pearl frowned. 'Trouble how?'

'People see it on my finger and say things like "Oh, a war baby. Well done, you." Like you might say to a woman who'd just signed up to become a FANY or a Land Girl.'

'Good heavens. People truly think like that?'

'It would seem so.'

Pearl felt sickened; babies to show Hitler that Britain wouldn't cave; more sons and daughters for the next war. After all, there was bound to be another one, as she'd overheard one of her passengers remarking just the other day, with each new generation came yet another reason for war.

'Well,' Pearl said, noting how the baby's bottle was now empty, the infant asleep. 'As you might recall, I have to make an early start. And since it's not worth trying to get back to sleep now, I might as well get washed and dressed.'

'Yeah,' Ivy said flatly. 'You're still a clippie, then?'

Pearl made her reply deliberately bright. 'Yup. And I love it.'

'Good for you. S'pose I'll see you this afternoon, then.'

'I imagine so – if you're still here.'

Despite Thursday being her night to perform with The Murrinaires at the Undercroft Club – something to which, ordinarily, she would be looking forward – as Pearl walked to work an hour or so later, she couldn't persuade her mind away from Ivy. In fact, the harder she tried not think about her, the more the woman kept intruding into her thoughts. She found it curious that Ivy wouldn't be drawn on the baby's father. Was she wrong to suspect Gold? A couple of things Ivy had said made it seem likely, and she'd seen for herself how creepy he was. But then, sometimes when Ivy mentioned *the baby's father*, there would be genuine warmth in her tone – and it was hard to imagine her feeling that way about Gordon Gold. She supposed it was always possible that, under his slippery exterior, he was a decent man.

As the morning wore on, Pearl couldn't shake the sense that what little Ivy had told her didn't add up. From that first afternoon she'd met her, Ivy had seemed as sharp as a tack and yet, the moment she'd got to London, she'd supposedly taken up with some fellow and got pregnant. That alone seemed odd. More peculiar still was the fact that, even with a baby on the way, she'd managed to carry on her role in the show without anyone becoming suspicious. What was more, despite not appearing to have a maternal bone in her body, and despite apparently knowing the baby's father wasn't going to do the right thing by her, when the chance had arisen for her to give the baby up for adoption, she clearly hadn't taken it. Examined more closely, little of what Ivy said rang true. But then who was she, a mere bystander, to judge? Moreover, if there was something Ivy wasn't telling her, who was she to pry?

Late that afternoon, her shift complete, Pearl trudged up the steps to Sylvia's front door, dismayed to hear the wail of a baby even before she'd let herself in. And when she went into the drawing room, it was to find Ivy in one of the wingback chairs, dead to the world, the baby in a sturdy cardboard box at her feet, her face purple from the effort of howling. Studying the contrasting pallor of Ivy's own complexion, she wished she could let her sleep on. But someone had to attend to the child.

'Ivy,' she said, gently nudging the woman's arm. 'Ivy, wake up.'

Ivy stirred. 'Christ.'

'Sorry to wake you but I don't know what to do with her.'

With considerable effort, Ivy roused herself from the chair, stretched her arms above her head and rolled her shoulders. 'God almighty.'

Glancing down at the writhing infant, Pearl took in her angry little face. The damp cowlick on her forehead was dark – almost ebony – but then Ivy's own colouring was of a tone she knew some people would call 'swarthy'.

'Is she hungry?'

Ivy shrugged. 'Christ knows. Hungry. Colicky. Hot. Cold. Dirty. Frightened. The list is endless, the racket the same no matter the cause.'

When Ivy lifted the infant from the box, the crying became less fractious.

'Is Sylvia not in?'

'Said she was going to the WVS to see if they had any nappies or baby clothes. As you might have noticed, I couldn't carry much.'

At least, Pearl thought as she spotted Ivy's hand, she'd stopped wearing the pretend wedding ring. 'That's good of her.'

'She also said I can stay until next weekend, you know, to give me the chance to work out what I'm going to do.'

The plummeting of Pearl's spirits was followed by a stab of guilt. 'She's very kind.' *Far kinder than I would be.*

'Yeah.'

About to turn away to go and change out of her uniform, Pearl hesitated. 'Ivy… can I ask you something?'

Against Ivy's shoulder, the baby seemed a lot happier. 'Why not.'

'Why did you decide against having her adopted?' Even before she had finished asking, she felt as though she had overstepped. After all, what business was it of hers?

Ivy, though, appeared unfazed. 'Don't think you're the first person to ask me that. Truth to tell, given my time again, I'd likely do so. As everyone at the time kept pointing out, it would have been the best thing for both of us – chance of a clean start, and all that. Fact is, right up until the last days before she was born, I was still in two minds. But then I began to think why go through all the upheaval – losing my part in the show, watching my dream fizzle out – just to have some official take the baby off me and give it to someone else to raise. 'Course, it's easy to have principles at the time, a good deal harder to live with them afterwards. Anyway, once she was born, well, call me stupid – because I know that's what you'll think when I say this—'

'Oh, no, I—' To disguise her embarrassment at having been caught out, Pearl gave a vigorous shake of her head. 'I wouldn't.'

'It's what *I'd* think in your shoes. Anyway, in the end, I suppose I didn't have her adopted because I was labouring under the ridiculous notion that, once she was born, her father would come and... well, that he would decide he'd made a mistake. It's pathetic, I know, but I couldn't let go of the idea that one day, he'd show up and take us home. And if I'd already given her up...'

'I see.' So, deep down, the cold and calculating Ivy Snell was a romantic? Who'd have thought it? Perhaps, then, she really had been in love with this man.

'They don't let you sign the papers for six weeks, anyway, even if you'd said all along it was what you wanted.'

And there she was: coldblooded Ivy was back.

'I see.' Surely, then, the father couldn't be Gold, could it? It was hard to envisage *any* woman getting all doe-eyed over that slimy character.

'It wasn't so bad in the home,' Ivy went on. 'They showed us how to do things like bathe them, change them, feed them. It's the only reason I know what to do.'

'Well,' Pearl said, unsure how to deal with the randomly switching sides to Ivy's character. 'She seems quiet now.' She had no idea what else to say. Everything about the situation struck her as both pathetic and yet painfully sad.

'Yeah. Now she's woken me up. I swear she waits until I nod off. Anyway,' Ivy said. '*You've* done all right for yourself in not much more than a year, haven't you? Room in a nice house. Steady job. The band doing two nights a week at some fancy hotel. Can't be bad.' Evidently noticing Pearl's expression change, Ivy went on, 'Sylvia told me.'

Pearl had to fight down irritation; she hadn't wanted Ivy to know about The Murrinaires. She was proud of how well she'd done for herself – of all she had gained through her own hard work. In fact, Ivy coming back made her feel the need to wrap her arms around the whole lot of it and draw it close, Ivy only ever being out for Ivy.

'I'm happy with what I've achieved, yes. And speaking of which—' she glanced to the clock on the mantel '—I'd best go and get ready. Last week, I noticed I'd caught the hem of my frock and so I need to put a stitch in it.' Not that she had to justify to Ivy why she was leaving her to it, she did have a life of her own to get on with.

As she slowly climbed the stairs, though, she was surprised to find herself beset by pity; Ivy had gone to London with such big dreams. And now, here she was, back again, her hopes smashed to smithereens by some chap she'd met.

Well, in there somewhere, she thought as she wandered into her room and closed the door, was a lesson: when it came to achieving a dream, there were no shortcuts. She just had to keep doing what she was doing and enjoy herself while she was at it. For the first time since that German bomb had turned her life upside down, she felt in control of where her life was going. That day in Gordon Gold's office, she'd trusted her instincts – and thank goodness she had. If Ivy's plight was anything to go by, then contrary to how she'd felt soon afterwards, heeding her guts and walking away had been the wisest thing she'd ever done. And, from now on, if she was ever tempted to ignore her feelings, she would picture Ivy and let nothing, and no one, persuade her to go against what she knew in her heart to be right. Oh, and no matter the sob story Ivy spun, she wouldn't let *her* do anything to ruin things for her, either.

Chapter 19

Golly, she'd be glad to get home. Such a dank and misty day had done nothing for anyone's already gloomy spirits, her passengers quicker than usual to moan; they were all either weary, chilled to the bone, or generally out of sorts. With any luck, Pearl thought as she left the bus garage in the direction of home, Sylvia would have lit the fire in the drawing room, meaning that she would be able to warm up with a cup of Bovril. This afternoon, especially, she'd come over all shivery.

With a long sigh, she turned onto St David's Hill; as though feeling under the weather wasn't bad enough, when she got home, Ivy would be there. She abhorred the way the woman had simply shown up, her brazen assumption that Sylvia would let her stay making what she was doing even worse. She had no sympathy for her whatsoever, she was a victim of nothing but her own carelessness. She did pity the baby, though. Ivy didn't have a maternal bone in her body, only ever troubling to do the minimum to keep the poor mite clean – clean*ish* – and fed. What's more, the week that Sylvia had agreed she could stay had been up a long time ago, and yet still Ivy showed no signs of doing anything to get back on her feet. In fact, she seemed to grow ever more lethargic while taking increasingly more and more advantage of their generosity. Sylvia had to practically bark at her to go and get a new ration book – her old one supposedly mislaid – and, even then, she'd had to lend her the shilling to pay the fine for its loss. It wasn't as though she even did any housework to repay Sylvia's kindness; she just slumped in the same chair in the drawing room every day, dead to the world until one of them roused her to attend to her child.

Drawing level with the gate to Sylvia's front garden, Pearl paused, her hand on the latch while she drew several breaths and reminded herself to stay calm. Getting wound up about Ivy's behaviour would solve nothing; she'd simply be left with her anger eating away at her insides. Of greater use would be to ask Sylvia what she was going to do about Ivy's reluctance to get off her backside and take responsibility for her situation. But not this evening. Right now, she felt as though she was going down with a cold, her most pressing desire at that moment being to get warmed up, have a bite to eat, and head up for an early night in the hope of feeling better tomorrow. Confrontation, of any sort, was most definitely not on her list.

Sadly, when she awoke the following morning, her throat felt no better. And, although she'd slept well, when she opened her eyes, she was disappointed to find she had a headache. Somehow, despite feeling gradually more and more awful as the day wore on, she managed to get through her shift, determination alone keeping her going.

'Have a teaspoon of Mrs Cottle's honey,' Sylvia said that evening when she saw Pearl massaging her throat. 'And take some aspirin. Are you sure you're well enough to sing? Let me hear a couple of *solfèges*.'

But even as Pearl tried to hit middle C, she was surprised by how much effort it took. 'I'll be all right,' she said quickly. There was no way she was going to miss

Thursday night at the Undercroft Club – and certainly not at this short notice.

Sylvia, however, appeared unconvinced. 'Well, only you know if you're up to it. If it was me, I'd think carefully. And if you do insist on going, then for goodness' sake keep sipping plenty of water – keep your throat moist.'

Pearl sent her a smile. 'I will. Promise.'

How she got through the evening, though, she had no idea.

'You feeling a bit off tonight?' Jack asked when they were taking a break halfway through their set.

'Just a bit of a cold coming,' she assured him as brightly as the rawness in her throat would allow. Tell him her throat was sore and he'd go into a panic about Saturday night.

By the time she'd sung her last number, though, even the generous applause didn't help to block out the pain. And by the time she'd walked home, grateful for the frosty night air to cool her down, she could barely swallow.

'You've overdone it,' Sylvia said shortly, taking in Pearl's pained expression as she stood in the hallway removing her coat.

'Did you… wait up?' The thought that Sylvia had been waiting for her to come home was both heart-warming and mortifying.

Ignoring her question, Sylvia pressed a hand to Pearl's forehead. 'And you're running a temperature. Go on, straight upstairs. Take off your make-up and get into bed. Put a damp flannel on your forehead and I'll bring you a jug of water and some aspirin. Since it seems to have come on quite suddenly, you're probably going down with the flu. Do you ache anywhere?'

Starting up the stairs, Pearl shook her head. 'No.' She would refrain from mentioning how, on the walk home, she'd felt earache starting. And she definitely wasn't going to let on that she was beginning to feel sick.

'Go on, then. I'll be up in a minute.'

'All right.'

Despite her physical exhaustion, Pearl found it impossible to sleep. She would get comfortable, close her eyes, try to empty her mind of concerns – of one new concern in particular – and try to slow her breathing. Next thing she knew, she was coming round from a vivid but nonsensical snatch of a dream to the sensation that her bed was swaying. Each time this happened, a check of her alarm clock showed she'd been asleep less than twenty minutes. Again, she would make herself comfortable, only for the same thing to happen, except that, each time she awoke, she felt worse: the pain in her ear had spread to her jaw; her head pounded. She was perspiring heavily, her hair sticking to her face; her throat felt as though one side of it was touching the other. Worst of all, in the crack of light from the bulb on the landing, the walls of her room kept appearing to rush towards her and then, just as quickly, to recede. The earlier fear she'd been unable to shake was proving well founded; she might be struggling to think straight but she knew what this was. She'd had it before – more than once. And as every singer knew, it carried real risks.

The night wore on. She was hot, she was cold. She was on a bus where she couldn't stop shivering and none of the passengers would pay their fares; she would teeter along the aisle in their direction, only for them to disappear the moment she drew level. Another time, she was on stage, in front of a microphone the size of a bicycle wheel; a piano would start to play but the notes were jangly, the tune not one she knew. When she turned around to see why the pianist was playing so badly, there would be no one there – no musicians, no instruments – but the music would continue, growing steadily louder and more distorted. When she turned back to the microphone, a face was staring down at her, grotesque and out of focus. And she was sweating profusely; her lovely dress would be ruined. Perhaps she should take it off.

'Refill the bowl, would you? As cold as it will run from the tap.'

Was that Sylvia? If so, why was she trying to stop her from undressing? Couldn't she feel how hot she was? Why was Sylvia even there, on the stage?

'Cold. Right.'

And who was that with her? The voice sounded familiar. Was it Clemmie? No, Clemmie had hair the colour of summer. This girl's hair was dark. It must be May. May had come. But now she was leaving – before they'd even had a chance to talk. She tried to call to her. 'May…'

'Shush, dear. It's all right. You have a fever.'

Who was this woman to tell her to shush? She wanted May to come back. Ah, here she was.

'This is as cold as it would run.'

She must sit up and talk to her. May lived on a farm, and she would have come a long way.

'Thank you, Ivy. That's good.'

'Do you think we should call a doctor?'

'I think we'll wait and see how she is in the morning. I don't want to make a fuss if it's nothing.'

'What do you think it is?'

Still unable to work out what was going on, Pearl strained to hear.

'Well, I thought it was flu. But, if it is, she seems to have caught a particularly bad case of it. As soon as it's a respectable hour, I'll pop next door. Mrs Cottle has a thermometer. If she's still running a temperature, I'll telephone Dr Eastman and ask if he can come and see her on his morning round.'

'All right.'

'Anyway, look, you go back to bed. You get little enough sleep as it is.'

'She does seem quieter.'

'I think the cold flannel is helping.'

'You'll come and get me if she worsens.'

'Ivy, I promise you, if she goes downhill, I'll come and get you.'

'All right, then. Goodnight.'

'Goodnight.'

Oh. That's a shame, May's gone home. Perhaps it's for the best, though, because I really don't feel very well at all...

–

'How long has she had the fever?'

'It came on late last night, doctor. She complained of feeling shivery and unwell. And then she woke us in the night, crying out about the walls moving.'

'Delirium. What did you say her temperature was this morning?'

'One hundred and two. We tried to cool her as best we could.'

Despite being able to hear voices, Pearl was struggling to work out whose they were. One of them, she thought she recognised as Sylvia's; the other belonged to a man, but it wasn't Jack. Nor was it Reg. Reg's voice was all rounded and homely. And he called her 'maid'. This man's voice was clipped and sharp and cold. He didn't sound like a bus driver, so she probably wasn't at work. In her mind, she laughed. At work in her bed? That would be daft. Ooh, perhaps he was an agent Sylvia had brought to hear her sing. If he was, she should probably warm up her voice. To that end, she tried to swallow but oh, dear God, her throat felt so sore. And her head – what had happened to make it hammer so?

'What do you know of her childhood illnesses?'

I had chicken pox. Definitely. I remember all three of us waking up one morning covered in spots. I was about six. I remember because I couldn't go to school, and I never didn't go to school. Oh, and I had mumps one time, as well.

'Very little, I'm afraid. I've only recently come to know her.'

'Age?'

'Nineteen.'

'Does she work?'

'She's a bus conductress.'

'Hm. Well, in itself, a fever isn't an illness, merely the symptom of one. And since, outwardly, she shows no evidence of a rash or inflammation but has a cough and complained of a headache, the list of possible causes is not overly long, particularly for an otherwise fit and healthy young woman. Draw back the curtain.'

'Of course, doctor.'

Pearl narrowed her eyes; Christ, that light was bright.

A blurry form leaned across.

'Can you open your mouth for me, child?' Pearl obeyed. 'Wider.' She did her best. 'Say *aah*.'

249

Her attempt came out as a whisper. '*Aah.*'

Fingers pressed her throat and then moved to beneath her jaw. 'Swallow.' She tried, but it was difficult. 'As I suspected. She has tonsillitis. Has she had it previously?'

At least twice. I don't remember the first time, but I got it again when I was ten. Mum said she knew straight away what it was from me having had it before.

'I have an idea she did mention it, yes.'

I did, yes, I did.

'Her tonsils need to come out.'

'There isn't another way? You see, she's a singer. A very good one.'

'I thought you said she's a bus conductress.'

Stupid man. Can't I be both?

'She is. But she also sings with a band. It's her dream to one day make a profession from it.'

'Singer or not, my diagnosis is the same. They need to come out.'

'Oh dear. There really is no other treatment?'

'There's a new drug called penicillin. However, its use is currently restricted to wounded servicemen.'

'So… she'll have to go into hospital?'

Hospital? No-no-no-no-no. No. I have songs to practise. Shows to perform.

'The hospital is full. Routine or minor operations we perform in the patient's home. My evening surgery finishes at six and I have a dinner to go to at eight. I shall be back as soon as I've seen my last patient of the day. Show me your kitchen. That's usually the best place to carry out the procedure. I'll tell you what you need to do to make it ready.'

'Very well. Please, follow me.'

Oh, good, Pearl thought, holding her eyes tightly closed against the light. *They've gone. Perhaps now, I'll be able to get some sleep. Then, when I wake up, I'll ask Sylvia to play a couple of numbers for me to practise. Only, as I recall, at the club last night, I was a little off my best…*

–

'Slowly, now. Watch you don't trip over your dressing gown.'

'Where… are we… going?' Gosh, Pearl thought as Sylvia helped her down the stairs, how badly it hurt to talk. Talk? Rasp, more like. Her throat was in agony.

'Just down to the kitchen.'

Through her dressing gown, Pearl could feel Sylvia's fingers pressing into the flesh around her elbow. 'Why?'

'Try not to talk, dear.'

'I feel… dizzy.'

'I'm sure.'

'And sick.'

'We're nearly there now.'

When the two of them eventually reached the hallway, Pearl could see movement in the kitchen. 'Who's… here?'

'Come on, you're doing so well. Not much further.'

Why was Sylvia talking to her as though she was six years old? And why wasn't she answering her questions? 'Who,' she repeated as forcefully as her throat would allow, 'is here?'

Just short of the doorway, Pearl felt her knees buckle, followed by Sylvia's grip tightening on her arm as she tried to hold her up. Why couldn't they have left her to doze? Get a good night's sleep and tomorrow she'd be as right as rain.

'Good. Remove her dressing gown and help her onto the table.' Despite feeling she might be sick, Pearl recognised the voice from earlier – although that might possibly have been in a dream; she'd had a lot of those. 'Good. Recline her with her head about here. You, young lady—' Young lady? Who was he talking to now, Pearl wondered. '—will need to hold her feet still. Make yourself comfortable. You are going to be there a while. Perhaps as long as an hour.'

From somewhere around her feet came the sound of chair legs scraping across the tiled floor. Then warm hands took hold of her ankles.

'Should I fetch something for the bleeding?'

Ah, now, *that*, she recognised as Sylvia's voice. But who was bleeding?

'No need. There won't be much blood and what there is, she'll swallow. Expect her to vomit afterwards.'

'Pillow,' she whispered, the table hard against the back of her head.

'You won't need a pillow. Now, Mrs… er…'

'Murrin. Sylvia Murrin.'

In her groggy state, Pearl wished she could see what was going on, but with her head tilted backwards, her view was confined to the kitchen ceiling. Oh, and whenever Sylvia drew near, straight up her nostrils. She giggled. *Nostrils.* What a funny word that was.

'Mrs Murrin, I am going to fasten this mask over the patient's nose and mouth. Onto the gauze inside of it, I shall drip chloroform at the rate of one drop for each of her breaths. Until she is completely sedated, which will take several minutes, she will most likely try to wriggle. That is when I shall need you to hold her shoulders. Do not allow her to move.'

Just as it was becoming interesting, Pearl felt something against her face. The pressure of it hurt her cheeks; the weight of Sylvia's hands hurt her shoulders. She sniffed. The smell was like nail polish remover. How odd when her nails were unvarnished. Now she could taste pear drops, very cold ones. She hadn't had a pear drop in ages. She supposed there weren't any; she must look next time she went past Long's the newsagent's. Yes, and if they had some, she would take her entire three-ounce sweet ration in one go. But now, at least for a moment or two, she might just close her eyes and have a little sleep...

–

'Pearl? Pearl, dear, can you hear me?'

The pain was horrendous. The back of her throat felt as though she'd swallowed a carving knife, the taste in her mouth bloody and metallic. And someone was talking to her, which was odd because, only a moment ago, she'd been thinking about pear drops. Desperate to see where she was, she tried to blink, but her eyelids felt like lead, the inside of her skull the same. She also felt as though she was about to— oh, dear God.

Once she had vomited, she felt unexpectedly better – at least, she no longer felt queasy. The cool flannel on her forehead was nice, too, as were the small sips of water. With a glance at Sylvia, she carefully opened her mouth. 'How—'

'Shush. Dr Eastman said you're not to talk. You're to have plenty of clear liquids and soft, cold food. He suggested ice cream, although where he thinks I'll get any of that, I have no idea.'

'I—'

'Shush, dear, *please*. The doctor has removed your tonsils. You won't remember because he sedated you beforehand. But it's all over now. Your fever has gone and all you need do for the moment is stay still. You're going to feel lightheaded for a while but, once the effects of the chloroform have worn off, he said you will be able to get up. He also said that, as long as you're not left alone, you can bathe and dress – if you feel well enough in yourself – and sit downstairs.' Since she wasn't allowed to speak, Pearl grunted. At that precise moment, all she wanted to do was go back to sleep. 'Dr Eastman is pleased with how it went. You'll have a painful throat for a few days but, because you're young and healthy, he expects you to be right as rain in no time.'

She'd had her tonsils taken out? Without anyone thinking to ask her first? What about the show? What about her voice?

She grasped Sylvia's arm and squeezed it hard. With her free hand, she gestured to her throat. 'Sing…' she whispered. 'Can… I… sing?'

'That's a matter for another day.'

'But—'

Sylvia's expression straightened. 'Pearl, you *must* stop trying to speak. Those were the doctor's orders. The more you rest your voice, the better it will be.' With a huff, Pearl conveyed her understanding. 'Good.'

Out on the landing, Ivy appeared. And when Sylvia went towards her and pulled the door part-way closed, Pearl strained to hear what they were saying.

'I managed to get hold of Jack.' That, she knew, was Ivy's voice. And if she'd been speaking to Jack, then pound to a penny, she was scheming. 'I told him you don't have a pupil until midday and so he said he'll be round in half an hour.'

Propped up against a couple of pillows, Pearl closed her eyes. She was so tired. But she also wanted to know what was going on. Keeping perfectly still, she tried to concentrate.

'That gives us a couple of hours.'

A couple of hours for what?

'That's what I said to him.' Ivy, again. 'In the meantime, I had a quick look down the running order. There's a few I recognise.'

'Good. If you can manage half a dozen or so, Jack can arrange the rest as instrumentals.'

'And of course, by next week—' *Next week?* Oh, this was exasperating. '—I will have had time to rehearse the others.'

Rehearse the others. In her mind, Pearl mimicked Ivy's tone. Being in a tin-pot musical had gone to the woman's head. And anyway, she'd been kicked out.

'You're going to be a lifesaver.'

'That's what Jack said. But as I replied, anything to help.'

Pearl scoffed. The only time Ivy Snell did anything to help was when she stood to gain something.

She tried to open her eyes; she wanted a word with Sylvia. She wanted to tell her she knew what they were plotting, and to point out that, while she was clearly unable to perform tonight, by the time Thursday came around, she would be fine; there was no need for Ivy to go to the trouble of learning new songs – songs that had taken *her*, with *her* talent, weeks to perfect. Most of them wouldn't suit Ivy's voice anyway. In fact, she was wrong for pretty much all of them.

Unfortunately, she was struggling to keep her eyes open, let alone hold a discussion. Perhaps, for now, then, she would have a little snooze. But, the moment she woke up, she would make it plain that the shows at the Castle Hotel belonged to her. Ivy Snell might have wrecked her own dream but, if that woman thought she was just going to waltz back in and take her place, then she really did have another think coming.

Chapter 20

'I'd completely forgotten how it feels to get up there in front of an audience and belt out a song.'

Across the table from Ivy, Pearl winced. Belt out a song? *Belt out a song?* For Jack's sake, she hoped Ivy was joking. If not, if Ivy really had stood up there and belted out one of the band's carefully rehearsed numbers, Jack wouldn't be at all pleased. On the other hand, might it not be – as the saying went – all grist to the mill: while she didn't like the idea of Jack and the band being left in the lurch, she didn't want Ivy getting on too well with them either, or for the band to start thinking too highly of her. The ungrateful woman already had her feet a little too far under Sylvia's table as it was.

It was now Sunday morning and, having spent the whole of Saturday dozing fitfully in bed, today, Pearl had been in the mood to get up. Last night, Ivy had stood in for her at the Castle Hotel Grill Room and, although it pained her to admit, she had woken up this morning desperate to know how she had got on. However, since she was forbidden from talking for another two days, she was hoping to glean what she could over breakfast, by listening to Ivy regale Sylvia.

At that moment, Sylvia came through the door into the kitchen. 'Goodness, Pearl, dear, I didn't expect to see you downstairs so early. Would it be safe to assume you're feeling better?'

Remembering the doctor's instruction – as conveyed by Sylvia herself – that to help her throat heal and to spare straining her vocal cords, she should speak only as a last resort, Pearl smiled. 'Better.' It was the first time she'd heard her voice since yesterday, when she'd attempted to protest about something, and she wasn't in the least impressed by how thin and weak it sounded.

'I should imagine you're hungry.'

Pearl nodded. 'Yes.' Golly, it was so hard to remember not to talk.

'Well, yesterday afternoon, when I popped along to the Co-op for the usual rations, I saw to my surprise that they had porridge oats.' Pearl's spirits sank. She'd been hoping for something more appetising. If swallowing food was going to be painful, she might as well at least eat something enjoyable and make the discomfort worthwhile. 'I soaked them, half milk – thanks to Ivy's extra rations – and half water. And I cooked them last night, so they could cool down. When Mrs Cottle next door heard what you'd gone through, she gave me a whole jar of honey for you. She waxed lyrical about its special healing powers and told me that you're to have four tablespoons a day. I thought you could have the first one in your porridge.'

Sylvia had gone to so much trouble that not only did Pearl feel genuinely touched, but she also felt obligated to eat as much of the porridge as she could bear. Perhaps, with honey, it wouldn't be too bad; she'd never tried it that way before – had rarely had honey at all.

'Thanks.' Whispering was the only volume she could manage.

'And at lunchtime, I have a little cheese to grate to make a sandwich for you. But I'll cut off the crusts. They might be too jagged.'

'Don't suppose she can have tea,' Ivy surmised as she got up from the table. 'Only, I'd been just about to put the kettle on.'

I *am* in the room, Pearl wanted to yell at her. *It's my tonsils I've had removed, not my hearing.*

'She can have a cup if she's prepared to let it go cold first. But I rather think milk would be better, especially as, for once, we have enough.' When Sylvia looked across at her, Pearl mimed being sick. 'Nonsense, dear. What you need now is vitamins and goodness. I'll pour you a small glass. And this evening, I thought we might try a little mashed potato and sardines. Both are soft and the sardines are in oil, which will surely aid swallowing. Don't worry about bones, I'll check them thoroughly first.' Sylvia was being so kind to her; far more kind than Mrs Trude would have been. That witch wouldn't even have called a doctor for her. 'What about you, Ivy? There's a box of cornflakes or a loaf for toasting. And what about the little one? Have you fed her yet?'

'She was still asleep. I've left her.'

'That's good – if she's begun sleeping through, I mean.' Sylvia, Pearl noticed, seemed to be going to great lengths to sound encouraging. 'So, how did it go at The Grill Room last night? Your first Saturday night back on the stage?'

Ivy grinned. 'It went well. I was expecting to be dead nervous. But once I started warming up, I just felt eager to get out there. What was it Jack said? Oh, yeah, that I was a real trooper.'

Jack said I was a real trooper. Honestly, if the milk Sylvia was forcing her to drink wasn't already making her feel sick, listening to Ivy talking about Jack certainly would. Was it wrong that she couldn't bear to support Ivy in her delight? Did that make her a bad person? She supposed, in the circumstances, it was a good thing she *couldn't* speak; confined to sending Ivy little more than the odd smile at least meant she couldn't be accused of being mean-spirited.

'Fortunate you had a cocktail frock,' Sylvia observed as she came back to the table with the rack containing several slices of toast. 'It's difficult enough getting a plain blouse at the moment. You would have stood no chance of getting an evening dress.'

On the one hand, Pearl wanted to hear what Ivy would come out with next; on the other, she didn't think she could stand much more of her smugness. *Don't get too cosy,* she longed to warn. But why waste her voice? The only way to cut short Ivy's spell as her replacement with the band was to get better – and to do so as quickly as possible. Allow the situation to go on too much longer and the woman might prove harder to budge. And there was no way she was going back to sharing the stage with her. No, thank you very much.

Catching Sylvia looking across the table at her, she tried harder to finish her breakfast. At least the honey was nice. But the only way she could eat the grey-looking porridge without retching was to think of it as medicine – medicine that would help heal her throat and get her back on the stage at the Castle Hotel quicker than if she refused it. She would use Ivy's boastfulness as a spur: if ever she felt the hard work of recuperating was getting too much for her, she would picture the stage in the Undercroft Club, and redouble her efforts to get back there.

–

'There you go. Don't drink it too fast.'

When Sylvia placed the glass of Benger's Food in front of her on the kitchen table, Pearl acknowledged her instruction with a nod.

It was now a week since Dr Eastman had come to remove her tonsils – a week of being subjected to endless remedies, all aimed at helping her throat to heal and her strength to return. At least the preparation Sylvia had put in front of her this morning was tolerable, the taste of the creamy coloured liquid making her think of biscuits – a glass of Benger's Food was certainly more palatable than some of the things Sylvia had tried to press upon her, a dose of Parrish's among them. The latter might be rich in iron, but it tasted like rusty nuts and bolts.

Having finished the glass, Pearl took it to the sink and swilled it out with water before returning to sit at the table. It was the morning after Ivy had sung for the first time at the Undercroft Club. And, just as with The Grill Room last Saturday, she hadn't stopped going on about it. *Jack said this, Jack said that. Cliff said the tone of my voice made some of the songs sound quite different, that my inflection was fresh and interesting.*

Having to sit there and listen to Ivy rattling on caused Pearl more pain than having her tonsils taken out in the first place. And that was why, with Ivy having gone back to bed to catch up on her sleep, Pearl was now seated, notepad in front of her, hoping Sylvia would answer the questions she'd jotted down to ask her.

'This,' she whispered and pointed to her first question: *Is Doctor Eastman coming back to see me?* If he was, she would have a chance to ask him when she could start singing again. And yes, she knew that wouldn't be for a couple of weeks yet, but simply the act of knowing would give her something to which she could look forward.

Before answering, however, Sylvia paused. 'Last week, when he was leaving, he said he might come back on Monday to see how you were doing but, since he didn't, I suppose we must assume he didn't consider it necessary.'

In her head, Pearl cursed. She'd been hoping to question Dr Eastman directly, rather than make do with Sylvia's interpretation of his instructions from last week. And yes, she did know that without Sylvia she would have been stuck.

She pointed to the next of her questions: *When can I talk again?*

'He said a couple of days.'

'So why...' Pearl said softly, tossing down her pen in frustration, '...do you keep telling me...' To her annoyance, she found that she had to pause mid-sentence to swallow. '...not to. It's been... a week.'

'Because I can imagine how desperate you are to get back to singing and I merely thought the longer you rest your throat, the quicker you'll be able to do that.'

Pearl sighed. It was clear Sylvia only wanted what was best for her. But *she* wasn't the one who had to sit and listen to Ivy talking about singing songs Jack had specifically chosen for her own register − not Ivy's − and how everyone was apparently treating Ivy as though she was their saviour.

Meet halfway? Pearl scribbled on the page and slid it across the table.

'What do you have in mind?'

Very carefully, she cleared her throat. 'That I speak… a sensible amount.'

'Very well. Does it hurt to talk?'

Pearl shook her head. 'Not to talk. More… to keep swallowing.'

Sylvia got up from the table, reached to the dresser for a glass and went to the sink. The glass filled with water, she returned and put it down. 'Then we must increase the amount you drink. The more liquids you take, the easier it will be on your throat. But don't down the entire glass in one go.'

Pearl reached for the glass and took a sip. 'All right.' If all it took to ease the rough feeling in her throat and enable her to talk was to keep drinking water, she would do it.

On her sheet of paper, she wrote, *Will my throat be scarred?*

'Turn to the light and let me look. I ought to be keeping an eye on it anyway.' Sylvia peered into Pearl's mouth. 'You would seem to have some robust looking scabs, which is a good sign as they will protect the wound while it heals. They'll fall off when they're ready. That being the case, why don't we agree that, once they're gone, we consider you're back to normal?'

Pearl went to scribble on her paper but changed her mind. 'How long?'

With a smile, Sylvia shrugged. 'I should imagine every individual is different. I don't know anyone who's had their tonsils removed but I suppose it's much like healing anywhere else on your body – a week to ten days?' Having got into the habit of writing things down, Pearl scribbled, *Jack knows I'm coming back?* To her relief, Sylvia nodded.

'He does. I told him what the doctor said about getting plenty of rest in the early days and then taking things slowly. I also explained that he'd advised three months before you can start—'

'*Three months!*' Her resolve not to overdo it having deserted her, Pearl blushed.

'If you're going to try and screech at me, then yes, all twelve weeks of it.'

'Why?' she whispered in despair. In the space of three months, Ivy would have made the show her own. The band would have got used to her and have forgotten they'd ever played with anyone else. They'd pretty much wiped Ron from their memories – and he'd sung with them for years. Three months would also mean Ivy continuing to live with them. She could just hear Sylvia now: *No, of course you must stay on here, you're the only reason the show can carry on.* It would be too much to bear.

'Pearl, dear. Look at me.' Pearl stopped tracing the grain of the tabletop with her fingertip and raised her head. 'I know this is disappointing for you. Scarcely had you got underway with Jack and the band at the new venues, and this happened. You're upset, I know. In your shoes, I imagine *I* would be, too. But I only have your best interests at heart. You want to go back to singing. I want that for you, too. To that end, the other day, I telephoned a friend of mine, Celia – the one in London I think I told you about previously.' Assuming Celia to be the woman Sylvia had asked about Gordon Gold, Pearl nodded. 'I remembered that both of her brothers are surgeons, one in the army and the other in a London hospital. So, I enquired whether she would mind asking one of them how best I can assist your recovery. It's not that I don't trust Dr Eastman, but the poor man is clearly rushed off his feet and I didn't want to risk bothering him solely to have him bark down the telephone at me that all you need is rest.' At this, Pearl smiled. 'Anyway, a couple of days ago, Celia telephoned me back.'

'What did she say?'

'According to her brother, it's usual for your throat to feel painful for up to three weeks. Early on, a couple of days after the operation, the pain might appear to fade. But it's quite usual that, as it starts to heal, pain will return, more severely, and for it to persist anywhere up to a fortnight. The good news is, after that, you should be able to swallow and eat normally. Which is why, since in order to keep your throat moist enough to hold a conversation you must keep swallowing, I've been urging you not to talk.'

Pearl exhaled heavily. Another two weeks of hardly talking, another two weeks of having to put up with Ivy singing with the band.

'But then can I—' Remembering what Sylvia had just told her, Pearl closed her mouth and instead wrote on her pad, *start singing practice?*

'Let's wait and see, shall we?'

Pearl shook her head. Immediately, she wished she'd done so with less vigour. 'I have to know.' God, it hurt to keep swallowing – a fact she couldn't afford to let Sylvia see.

'Look, dear, I'm afraid this is something we simply mustn't rush. Singing is hard work on your throat – you don't need me to tell you that. The reason I'm not prepared to commit to an amount of time is because, before we start any form of practice, however modest, you need to be able to speak normally and without pain, and we don't know when that will be. Even then, I will only allow a few light exercises each day, to test your throat little by little. You will know in your heart when you feel ready. And I'm sure I will be able to tell from how you sound when you speak. You have a wonderfully warm voice. There is no reason to think the operation will have done it any harm. But be too hasty to sing, and who knows what might happen.'

Pearl knew Sylvia was right. But three months? *Three whole months?* The matter of Ivy notwithstanding, being unable to sing for three months meant she would miss the build up to Christmas, with all the dances and parties that Jack had told her were not only great fun to do, but handsomely remunerated as well.

The matter of money put another thought in her head. 'Go back to work?' she whispered.

'A couple more weeks. I'll telephone today and tell them how you're coming along.'

It seemed, then, that she had no choice. There was nothing she could do to speed things up. She would have to grin and bear it – look forward to the distant day when she could start strengthening her voice. Oh, and try not to let Ivy's supposed success get her rattled in the meantime.

–

'I can't help it if I'm tired.'

'My dear, all women are tired. It's the way of the world. But to speak frankly for a moment, I'm beginning to think that, in your case, claiming to be continually tired is merely an excuse.'

'*For what?*'

Halfway down the stairs, Pearl paused to listen. By the sound of it, in the kitchen, Sylvia and Ivy were having an argument. Eager to know what it was about, but careful to avoid the penultimate tread of the staircase for its propensity to groan under her weight, she crept on down and went along the hallway. The door to the kitchen stood slightly ajar, and through the narrow slit she could see Ivy with her hands on her hips.

'There must be thousands of women across the land who'd give their eye teeth for a child but here *you* are, barely able to look at yours.'

In the hallway, Pearl blanched. She'd never heard Sylvia speak so directly. In the normal course of events, she was one of the most mild-mannered people on earth. She could only imagine that Ivy had done something Sylvia considered beyond the pale – either that, or else she had tested her patience once too often.

'*What did you just say?*'

'Ivy, there's no need to affect umbrage. You know well enough by now I speak as I find.'

'And what *you* should know is that—'

'Poor child. You feed her – in as much as evaporated milk, sugar and water can possibly constitute feeding—'

'It's not my fault she didn't take to me—'

'Her to you? Or you to her?' Crikey, Sylvia *was* being frank. 'Look, all I'm saying is that while it's good of you to stand in for Pearl – and I know Jack is immensely grateful – your responsibilities to your child must come first. Despite your claim of being constantly tired, you have more than enough time to see to her. Until she was struck down by tonsillitis, Pearl managed six days a week on her feet as a conductress and still found the time for two shows – and all that on top of learning and rehearsing new songs in between.'

'Yes, well, Saint Pearl doesn't have a baby.'

Saint Pearl?

'Indeed, she does not. But it's *your* choices that have brought you to this point.'

'Huh.'

'It's not my place to judge. And I have never discussed your situation with anyone outside of these four walls – not even Jack. However, since you are living at my expense, in my home, I feel I have the right to speak my mind. You are an unmarried mother. Whether you like it or not, you have responsibilities. If you choose to have nothing to do with the baby's father that is up to you. However, by doing so, you are making your life doubly hard, which, I shouldn't have to point out, requires that you sort yourself out. You asked if you could stay here while you got yourself on your feet. From that, I rather supposed you had a plan for doing so. It would seem, however, that I was mistaken. So, for your own good, and to be fair to Pearl, who pays her way in my household, I am going to say this. From now on, the money you earn performing two nights a week, you are to pay to me as a contribution towards your keep. You are also to find work and, in order to do so, find someone to care for your child while you earn a wage to support her.'

'Pearl's not working. She can mind her.'

In the hallway, Pearl curled her hands into fists. Had Ivy really just said that?

'Pearl will be going back to work inside a fortnight. If, in the short term, you would like her to look after the baby while you attend interviews, it's possible she might help you out. It will fall to you to ask her for the favour.'

When Pearl noticed that the room had fallen silent, with no wish to be caught eavesdropping and her fists still clenched at her sides, she backed along the hallway and slipped into the drawing room.

Finding the curtains still drawn, she dragged them aside, raised the blackout, and stared out at the street. Ivy really did take the biscuit. She was glad Sylvia had been straight with her; while she didn't wish Ivy undue hardship, it was time the woman started taking responsibility. It grated to see her slouching about, not even doing the clearing up she created from eating and drinking, not thinking to offer to do the laundry or run the sweeper over the carpets – especially since she had yet to give Sylvia a single penny for her keep. In fact, if Ivy did ask her to look after the baby, she had a good mind to refuse. Unfortunately, while it might be satisfying to see the expression on the woman's face when she did, the chance of Ivy getting back on her feet and pulling her weight if she did so, would only recede even further. And that would help no one – least of all that poor child. Ivy was lucky the little girl had such a contented and apparently undemanding nature.

Continuing to stare out at the greyness beyond the window, Pearl heaved a lengthy sigh. Since she was stuck having to convalesce, all she could do was wait and see what happened. In the meantime, since she felt better with each passing day, she would show her gratitude for the kindness Sylvia had shown her this last fortnight by resuming doing her share of the housework. Ivy, on the other hand, she would leave to stew in her own juices.

V. Lament

Chapter 21

'Fares, please.'

'Church Street, please, love.' When Pearl's passenger glanced up as he handed her the tuppenny fare, his face lit up in recognition. 'Well, hello, maid. I haven't seen you in weeks. You been on a different route?'

Returning his smile, Pearl handed him his ticket. He was the third passenger to remark upon her absence and they were barely a mile along their route.

'No, unfortunately I've been unwell.'

'Oh dear, no. That's a shame.'

'But I'm better now, thank you.'

'Well, you take it easy, love.'

Pearl smiled. Take it easy? There was slim chance of that. Still, it was good to be back at work. She might moan about her feet aching, and rue how cruel these cold and foggy December mornings could feel, but she'd missed being out and about. She'd missed seeing her regular passengers and chatting with Reg – or sitting in the canteen, with a steaming hot mug of tea, and laughing with other conductors about the daft things that happened along their routes. It was nice, too, that passengers seemed genuinely glad to have her back. From what she'd gathered, in her absence, her route had been covered by pretty much anyone wanting to work an extra shift or, when that had failed to produce a volunteer, by one of the inspectors. That, she would very much like to have seen.

Her fares collected, she went to stand on the rear platform and craned to see how far along the route they were. These pitch-black mornings made life particularly difficult; Reg had to drive at a snail's pace, and, thanks to the blackout, the interior lighting was so dim she had to rely on a torch to punch tickets, and on her memory to call out the stops for passengers who might otherwise lose track of where they were. At least her earlier worry that she would have forgotten the fares had proved unfounded – she might have been absent for the best part of four weeks but, now she was back on her bus, it seemed as though she'd only been gone a couple of days.

By the time she was on her final run back to the bus garage that afternoon, though, she was so exhausted she couldn't wait to tally up and go home. Fuelling her impatience was the fact that, tonight, Sylvia had said she could try a few simple exercises for her voice. Finally, she would get to find out how long it might be until she was ready to start performing again.

When she eventually arrived home, as had become her habit, she called out to announce her arrival. That there was no reply didn't surprise her. If Sylvia wasn't in a lesson with a pupil, she was probably out trying to buy food. Of late, getting even the most basic items required not only the patience of a saint but a considerable dose of good luck as well.

Having hung her coat on the stand, she went to the drawing room and looked in, the sight that greeted her making her grimace: slumped in one of the chairs was Ivy, her state of dishevelment suggesting she wasn't long out of bed. What was wrong with the woman that she couldn't even bother to wash and dress? If nothing else, where was her pride?

Despite feeling an urge to give Ivy a good shake, Pearl knew the only way to avoid a full-blown argument would be to soften her approach. To that end, she paused to draw a calming breath and then said, 'How have you been today?'

Ivy didn't even turn to look at her. 'What's it to you?'

No matter Ivy's lack of grace, Pearl resolved not to lose her temper. Moving to sit in the other chair, she said, 'Seriously, Ivy, please tell me you haven't spent all day sitting here in your nightclothes.'

Ivy didn't move. 'Like I said. What's it to you?'

Pearl exhaled in frustration. 'Other than concern for the wellbeing of a friend, absolutely nothing. So, since you won't tell me what's on your mind, and I'm desperate to have a wash and get changed, I'll leave you to it.'

On her way up to her room, Pearl shook her head in despair. Over the last few days, she and Sylvia had tried everything they could think of to coax and cajole Ivy into action. They had tried asking her what was wrong, they had tried telling her to snap out of it. It was almost as though the more they tried, the more belligerent Ivy became and the further she slipped from their grasp. But if she wouldn't tell them what was wrong, how were they supposed to help? Ivy's behaviour might be stretching their patience to its limits, but Pearl would still help her if she could – if the woman would simply stop rejecting the hand of friendship and explain what was wrong.

Reaching the landing, and seeing the door to Ivy's room ajar, she pushed it further open and crept in. On her back, in the cot Sylvia had borrowed from a neighbour – and had somehow wedged into the tiny room – the baby was gurgling at the ceiling. She was a pretty little thing, with dark eyes and a shock of ebony hair. How could Ivy not want to fuss and coo over her, cuddle her? She might not neglect the little girl's physical needs, but she certainly didn't show her any affection. Moreover, what woman had a child for four or five months without even giving her a name? She was pretty enough that there ought to be plenty of choices to suit.

At her wits' end, Pearl let out another sigh. The only thing that seemed to get Ivy out of that chair was going out to sing. If it hadn't been for doing the two shows each week, she probably wouldn't trouble to wash or dress, let alone leave the house. She'd heard talk about women who had difficulties taking to their babies; there had been one in Albert Terrace. What if that was how Ivy felt, but was too ashamed to tell anyone?

It was a thought she would put to Sylvia when, a few minutes later, she arrived home with two bags of shopping.

'I fared reasonably well this afternoon,' Sylvia said as she put down the bags. 'What about you? How did you get on today?'

'Pretty well, thanks. I'd say I'm almost back up to full steam.'

'That's good to hear.'

In truth, towards the end of her shift each day, Pearl felt utterly exhausted – but had no intention of telling Sylvia. 'I'll put the kettle on – if you managed to get any tea.'

'In the grey shopping bag. I managed to get the full six ounces.'

Once the tea was brewing in the pot, Pearl studied Sylvia's expression. Since she didn't look particularly frazzled, she decided to risk sharing what was on her mind.

'You know, I'm worried about Ivy.'

'I must confess,' Sylvia replied as she went to place a box of All Bran in the larder, 'I, too, find myself at a loss to know what to do for the best. If I thought she'd talk to Dr Eastman, I'd take her to see him. But if you and I can't work out what's going on, I'm not sure he'd be of much help.'

Pearl didn't disagree. 'He'd probably simply remind her there's a war on and tell her to pull herself together.'

'That's my fear. When I was passing the chemist, I almost went in to get her a tonic. But then I thought she probably wouldn't drink it. And that's another thing. Since you're asleep by the time she comes home from doing the shows, you wouldn't know this... but she reeks of drink.'

Into Pearl's mind came an image of being in Gordon Gold's office and how, when he'd poured them both a whisky, Ivy hadn't hesitated to drink hers.

'I know she's partial. Though I can't rightly think who'd be buying it for her.' Lowering her voice, she went on, 'She certainly doesn't have the money to buy it herself.'

'No. It went through my mind to ask Jack to keep an eye on her. But I'm not sure I feel comfortable. In any event, I can't think anyone from the band would be encouraging her.'

'No.' Pearl wasn't so sure, though. From the odd occasion when they'd talked about men, Ivy did seem to have a 'type', older being one of her preferences. And Fat Harry had been after her from the off. 'Perhaps it's her way of escaping the mess she's in – you know, drinking enough to deaden her feelings.'

'Perhaps. We can none of us know what goes through another person's mind.'

Moving to pour the tea, Pearl felt no less uneasy. 'I'll take her in a cup. Do you think I should try again to talk to her or leave her alone? With each new day, I resolve to stay out of it but it's hard to see her so miserable.'

Accepting the cup and saucer Pearl handed to her, Sylvia's expression didn't change. 'I know. But try encouraging her too often, and she might clam up altogether.'

'Mm.' It was hard to imagine Ivy being any *less* communicative.

'Perhaps let me have a think.'

'All right.'

'On an entirely different note,' Sylvia began with a smile. 'How about, once we've finished our teas, we go through to the studio and see how you get on trying a few—'

'Yes please!'

'—exercises.'

'Yes.'

'Solely on the understanding, mind, that if I say you are to stop, you do so without a word of dissent.'

'Of course. Yes. Without question.'

'Very well. Then I'll see you through there in a while.'

Goodness, Pearl thought. Finally, she was going to hear how she sounded – discover what she was up against. And while, for the moment, Sylvia might only let her exercise for ten minutes at a time, it was better than nothing, each and every minute representing one small step back to singing and, ultimately, towards reclaiming her place with the band.

Pearl sighed in exasperation. It was no good. Any hope of being able to sing at the Christmas parties at the Castle Hotel had been well and truly dashed. Practise as she might, her voice wasn't getting any stronger. She would admit to being quite taken with the warmer, richer tone it seemed to have developed but, when it came to strength, it showed not one jot of improvement. Instead, it continued to sound wavery and unreliable.

Seated at the piano, Sylvia reached across and patted her hand. 'Don't lose hope, dear. It's still early days. As I've said to you throughout, your recovery will take time.'

'But I can't bear it,' Pearl moaned. 'Not being able to sing like I did is horrible. It's knocking my confidence.'

'I don't doubt it. Trust me, if I could wave a magic wand for you, I would.'

'Is there *nothing* I can do?'

'There *is*...' Sylvia said. 'But you won't like it.'

Pearl clasped her hands together as though in prayer. 'Please, I beg you. Tell me. I'll do anything.'

'Well, firstly, give your voice plenty of rest—'

'Easy for you to say. I have to talk to passengers all day.'

'But you can rest it in between.'

'I suppose.' Bracing for disappointment, Pearl asked, 'What's the second thing?'

Sylvia smiled. 'The second thing is to be patient.'

Pearl's expression collapsed. 'That's not funny.'

'My dear, it wasn't meant to be. Look, why don't you pull up that chair and sit down for a moment.' Having fetched the chair, Pearl complied. 'Now, listen to me. Perhaps, instead of getting hung up on all the things you *can't* do, you might be better served showing gratitude for what you can.'

279

'Hm.' What she *could* do wasn't enough. Not by a long way.

'As I understand it, the critical time for someone who has had their tonsils removed is the week or two immediately afterwards, when there is a significant chance of bleeding from the incisions. I can't profess to understand the finer points, but I am familiar with the anatomy of the throat. Your tonsils sit or, in your case, sat, on top of your throat muscles. With your tonsils gone, those muscles are exposed, and remain exposed. So, as you eat and speak and stretch, there is an increased likelihood they will bleed. Thankfully, you followed the doctor's instructions and took care, so that hasn't happened.' Evidently deciding Pearl wasn't convinced, Sylvia went on, '*So what?* Is that what you're thinking?'

Pearl giggled. 'You read my mind.'

'The point is this. For a singer, the throat muscles are terribly important, both for the palate and for the vocal tract, the movement of which alters resonance. So, perhaps try to look upon where you are now as having overcome that first hurdle. Not only did you suffer no bleeding but, as you have recently begun to show, you are able to produce a relatively true note. Given Dr Eastman's rather no-nonsense approach to the operation, that was by no means a foregone conclusion.'

'Wasn't it?' Thank goodness, Pearl thought, no one had told her that at the time.

'A tonsillectomy for a professional singer would have been carried out with, well, shall we say, rather less speed and considerably more care.'

'So, what you're saying is that I was butchered by a quack.'

'On the contrary. Dr Eastman would appear to have done a remarkably good job, given the crude conditions in which he had to operate.'

'So, I *will* get back to normal? I *will* sound as I did before?'

'I have every confidence, yes. What we must do in the meantime is find songs that suit your voice to the extent that you are currently able to use it – songs that rely less upon you having full ability to move your palate.'

'Right…'

'If a song suits you, you will be less tempted to strain or try and compensate.'

That did at least make sense. 'Right.'

'My suggestion is that we continue with ten to fifteen minutes of exercises a day, our aim being to build up to thirty minutes at a time, and then take it from there. And yes,' Sylvia said, evidently seeing Pearl's face, 'I know you're disappointed. In your shoes, I would be, too.'

'I'm not going to be ready for Christmas, am I.'

Slowly, Sylvia shook her head. 'I'm afraid not, dear, no.'

'I'll have to suffer the agony of Ivy telling me what I've missed.'

'Well, it's altogether possible that Ivy won't—'

'You know as well as I do how insufferable she'll be.' Insufferable – always a favourite word of her sister, May's – felt particularly apt. Ivy was going to sing at the Christmas parties, the mere thought making Pearl seethe.

But what if that wasn't the worst of it, Pearl wondered? What if her voice never grew any stronger than it was now? What if she was destined never to sing again? What if Sylvia was simply saying all of those things about time being the best healer, while covertly crossing her fingers for it to be true?

Slowly, she got to her feet and returned the chair to where she'd found it. Well, she wasn't ready to give up. Ivy continuing to stand in for her with The Murrinaires might be making her tetchy, but she would grasp what she saw as the injustice of the situation and use it to push herself. She would practise. She would exercise. And before too much longer, she would cast out the usurper Ivy Snell and reclaim her rightful position with The Murrinaires. Just watch her and see.

Chapter 22

'What do you think is wrong with her?'

Bleary-eyed, Pearl watched as Sylvia rocked the little girl in her arms and hummed softly.

'Given her age,' Sylvia whispered over the baby's head, 'I suspect she's teething.'

'Oh.'

'Which is painful.'

With the baby's cries piercing her exhausted brain like the point of a knife, Pearl gave up bothering to whisper. 'Is there anything we can do?' The last thing she needed, having been awoken around four o'clock that morning by crying, was to now suffer a horribly late night as well. She glanced at the clock. Unable to believe what she was seeing, she moved closer for a better look. *Twenty to one?* 'Ivy should have been home well before now.'

Without ceasing in her attempts to soothe the infant, Sylvia returned Pearl's look of exasperation. 'When *you* sang at The Castle, you were always in by midnight. I used to hear you latch the door.'

'Sorry. I tried to be ever so quiet.'

'Trust me, I'd happily swap.'

Pearl smoothed a hand over the baby's head. Momentarily, the infant stopped grizzling. 'Is there anything we can give her? She feels hot.'

'When my two were little, we used to get teething powders. But I seem to remember hearing some time back that they're no longer sold because they contain all manner of things a baby shouldn't have, including morphine.'

Pearl continued smoothing her hand in light circles over the child's head. 'She seems to like that.'

'She does. But we can't stand here stroking her head for the rest of the night. I recall trying mine on gripe water, which was supposed to help – but I don't seem to remember it doing any good. I know some people smear butter over the gums but that might make her sick. I also remember trying a cold finger. Oh, and when I was truly at my wits' end with Jonty a couple of times, I resorted to putting brandy on his gums. Now that *did* work.'

'Do we have any brandy?' At this point, Pearl was prepared to try anything.

'There's a bottle in the sideboard.'

'Do I go and get it? Are you at your wits' end yet?' *Because I know* I *am.*

'Perilously close.'

'I'll go and fetch it.'

It was two-thirty when Ivy eventually came home. Pearl knew this because she awoke to hear a heated exchange taking place in the hallway. With a groan of despair at finding her sleep disturbed so soon after managing to get back to bed, she wrestled with the eiderdown and turned onto her side. Moments later, she turned back. Since she was awake now anyway, she might as well hear what was being said.

Lowering her feet to the floor, she pushed her toes into her slippers and felt about in the dark for her dressing gown. Pulling it over her nightdress, she went to the door and crept out onto the landing.

'That is indeed true,' she heard Sylvia say, her tone short. 'I am *not* your keeper. But, by that same token, neither am I your child's nanny.' Whatever Ivy said in reply, Pearl couldn't make it out. She did, however, hear Sylvia pick up again. 'For heaven's sake, Ivy. Whether you like it or not, you are her mother, the person responsible for her care and well-being. And that means you simply cannot stay out all hours. When I agreed that you could stay here, it was because I wanted to help you get back on your feet. But, as far as I can see, the longer you're here, the less of an effort you seem to be making to bring that about.'

Still unable to hear Ivy's reply, Pearl frowned. What should she do? Did she go down and side with Sylvia? Or should she keep out of it? If it wasn't for Ivy leaving them holding the baby while she was out, she wouldn't be so concerned. But Ivy had once been her friend. And she clearly needed help – either that, or she needed a boot up her backside.

Cautiously, she edged her way down the first few stairs. Ivy looked dreadful: beneath her eyes were smudges of mascara; at the shoulder of her dress – which looked far more badly creased than when she'd gone out – the strap of her brassiere was showing; as for her hair, that was all over the place. She was the epitome of May's expression about looking like she'd been dragged through a hedge backwards – which raised the question of what she could have been doing to get in such a state. And with whom? The possibilities made her shudder.

'Oh, here we go,' Ivy said when she caught sight of her on the stairs. 'I suppose *you've* come to berate me now as well.'

Pearl winced. Since she'd been spotted, she might as well go on down. In her sleep deprived state, she was certainly in the mood to let Ivy know how utterly brassed off she was by her behaviour.

'Well, you can hardly say it's none of my business,' she replied. 'Do you *know* how long it took us to get your baby to stop crying?' There was no need to disclose that, in the end, it had only been by rubbing brandy on the poor child's gums that they'd finally got her down at all. '*You* might not have to go to work in a few hours' time, but *I do*.'

'Oh, for Christ's sake,' Ivy rounded on her. 'It's not as though I asked either of you to wait up for me. And not that it's any of your business but all I did was stay behind after the show for a drink or two. How else do you expect me to let off a bit of steam after being stuck in this place all day long? It's all right for you, with your cushy little job, swanning about in your uniform with your pretty hair—'

'*Pretty hair?*'

'—floating through the days without a care in the world—'

'Ivy, you're tired,' Sylvia broke into Ivy's tirade. 'And you've clearly had too much to drink. Go to bed. And if your baby cries, get up and see to her. We'll finish this discussion tomorrow.'

'Finish it whenever you like,' Ivy said shortly as she started up the stairs. 'Won't make no difference. By the sound of it, you two make a far better job of looking after that baby than I ever could.' When Ivy then swung sideways and leaned over the banister to jab her finger, Pearl shrank several steps backwards. 'It's not like I'll ever be able to compete with Goody Two Shoes there, is it. And don't think I don't know what the two of you say behind my back. So, come on, one of you say what you're both stood there thinking – that the baby would be better off without me.'

'That's *not* how we think.' In truth, Pearl didn't know how else to respond. She could only suppose it was the drink leading Ivy to make such accusations. She certainly reeked of it. She'd also stunk out the hall with the smell of cigarettes.

'In fact, no.' To Pearl's dismay, Ivy started back down the stairs. Arriving in front of them, she went on, 'Tell you what, no, let's *not* wait until tomorrow, let's have it out, here and now. Right this minute. You're both clearly in the mood to run me down so, go on, call me all the names you use when I'm not here. I know you're thinking them. Don't hold back on my account. I'm a big girl. I can take it. Give it your best shot. Let's well and truly knock Ivy Snell to the ground, shall we? And once she's down, let's kick her a couple of times for good measure. Come on.'

Pearl struggled to fight back tears. How had Ivy ended up like this?

'Ivy, please, why don't we all—'

'Oh, yes, go on. It's all right for you. By the way, you do know how it was Gordon bloody Gold came to be watching us that night in the first place, don't you? You remember – that night, summer before last, when we did that show at the barracks?'

Pearl shook her head. '*What?*' What on earth was Ivy going on about now?

'Ron Bachelor. *He* was the tip-off. Gordon told us someone tipped him the wink to come and hear us sing, remember? 'Course you do. Well, it was ruddy Ron Bachelor. Turns out, him and Gordon go right back to the old days. "You want to come and hear these two young girls. Right up your street, Gordon." True as I'm standing here.'

'Ron?' Well, *that* didn't make sense. 'But he didn't like us – couldn't stand us. Was simply watching and waiting for us to fail.'

'Christ, you can be slow sometimes, Pearl Warren. Which is precisely the reason he told Gordon about us. He knew Gold couldn't resist a pretty face. He knew, full well, that by telling Gordon, it would get us out of the way – out of the band.'

'I think you're making it up,' Pearl said stiffly. 'No one would do such a thing. Even grouchy old Ron.'

'Think what you like if it makes you feel better. Keep imagining, if you want, that it was all down to your voice.'

'Ivy, go up to your room.' The ferocity of Sylvia's command made Pearl start. 'I will not put up with this. Go on, right this minute. And remember what I said about your daughter. She's your responsibility. When she cries, get up and see to her. And since we're airing our grievances—'

'Airing *your* grievances, more like,' Ivy scoffed from halfway up the stairs.

'You might as well know that Jack has enquired about Pearl's progress with her recovery, to which end I've suggested he come here tomorrow afternoon to hear for himself.' For Pearl, the news was tremendous – scary but hugely welcome; to invite Jack, Sylvia must believe she was almost ready to go back to performing. Better still, Jack must be desperate to have her back. 'I'm only telling you this now,' Sylvia continued, 'because when I see him, I've a mind to suggest that, after Saturday night, he drops you from the band anyway – if for no other reason than to give you the chance to sort yourself out and care for your child.'

'Do what you want,' Ivy replied without stopping to turn back. 'I don't give a damn.'

Pearl was no longer really listening; her thoughts were on Sylvia's news about Jack. His view would be so helpful – would give her a second opinion about her voice, and how well it was recovering. That she should have learned the news in such awful circumstances did take the shine off it. Ivy was sliding further and further down a slippery slope, losing rapidly the sympathy of the very people trying to help her. Keep going and, at this rate, she would soon have slipped from their grasp altogether.

With a long and weary sigh, Pearl turned to Sylvia. 'Is that true – about Jack?'

Sylvia nodded. 'He'll be here at five o'clock tomorrow.' Screwing up her eyes, Sylvia peered at the face of the grandfather clock. 'No,' she corrected herself, 'he'll be here at five o'clock *today*. So, you'd better go and try to get some rest. I'll make sure you don't oversleep and end up late for work.'

Pearl frowned. 'You're not going back to bed?'

'I'll take a nap later. I'm too infuriated to sleep.'

Pearl knew the feeling. But, despite thinking it unlikely she would sleep now either, she had no choice but to try because, in a few hours, she would be clocking on for her shift. And, after that, it turned out she would be singing for Jack...

Chapter 23

Pearl smiled. She was glad she'd bothered to make the detour because now she knew that not only was Jack the brother of the man who owned Bassett's Music Shop on Longbrook Street, but also that he was Master of Music at the boys' grammar school. How she hadn't discovered that before, she had no idea. She could only think she'd become so consumed by her desire to sing that she'd never stopped to show interest in the people helping her along the way. Sylvia was a case in point: she'd always known Sylvia was a widow, she even recalled her saying she had two grown-up sons. But, for all she knew, they could be serving overseas with the army or navy, their involvement in the war giving Sylvia grave cause for concern. Or they could be pilots, risking life and limb in the air. Realising she'd never bothered to ask after them made her feel shamefaced. Even what she knew of Ivy and *her* background was only superficial. And what about Clemmie and May? Despite promising both of them – the only blood relatives she had left – that she would keep in touch, she'd done nothing of the sort. She really must make more of an effort to take an interest in other people.

Anyway, since, at Jack's suggestion, she'd called into Bassett's on her way home from her shift, she was now in possession of sheet music for the half dozen new songs he wanted her to learn in preparation for her return to the band. She'd reminded herself not to get too excited; Sylvia would only let her tackle one piece at a time – and only then in short lessons – but a chance to learn anything new was a start. She was certainly raring to get stuck in.

In the rapidly failing afternoon light, she flicked through the sheets of music, studying the titles as she walked. Ooh. 'Stormy Weather'. What a song. True, it had been around a while – first performed, according to Jack, more than a decade ago. But he'd also remarked that, in her newest film, Lena Horne sang it as though she really did have a broken heart. Clearly, it was a number she was going to love.

Excitement mounting, she flicked on through the pages, the title of another of the tunes making her gasp: Jack had only chosen the Mack Gordon and Harry Warren number 'At Last', from the musical *Orchestra Wives*. Gosh, what a song *that* was. In the film, it was performed as a duet but, in her head, she could already hear it arranged as a solo. In the growing darkness, she allowed herself a grin; these new numbers were going to be so much fun. They were also going to require discipline to learn, but she wasn't afraid of hard work. She would practise diligently; she would not become distracted – by which, she meant avoiding getting bogged down in whatever drama currently surrounded Ivy.

There was a chance Ivy might be gone soon, anyway. Over the weekend, Sylvia had read her the riot act – again – things having once more come to a head when, having thanked Ivy for stepping in at such short notice, Jack had gone on to confirm that, going forward, he wouldn't be needing her. If, after the latest row with Sylvia that had ensued, Ivy didn't pull herself together, she never would. Did she feel sorry for the woman? Not really. She'd lost count of the number of times she'd exhausted herself trying to help, repeatedly extending, without judgement, the hand of friendship, only to have Ivy rebuff or berate her. *What would you know about it, Goody Two Shoes?*

Looking up and realising she was almost home, Pearl slipped the sheets of music back into the envelope and reached to unlatch the gate. On the front step, she poked her key into the lock and opened the door but, before she had even stepped inside, the distressed wailing of the baby set her teeth on edge. With an irritated shake of her head, she closed the door and bent to take off her shoes.

Overhead, the wailing continued. Where the devil was Ivy? Surely, even *she* couldn't sleep through *that* ear-splitting racket. Bracing herself for an onslaught of abuse, she pushed open the door to the drawing room. To her surprise, not only was the room empty but it was immaculate: no blanket screwed up in a heap on the chair or discarded on the floor; no half-drunk cup of tea abandoned on the side table, not even an empty glass or series of water rings where one had stood. Almost as astonishingly, the blackout had been lowered, a single lamp had been lit, and the fire had been laid ready. Sylvia must have grown so utterly brassed off with Ivy's mess that she'd taken matters into her own hands and given the room a thorough going over. She couldn't blame her. While it was one thing to stick to your guns and refuse to clear up behind the woman, it was quite another to put up with the resulting disarray.

On the point of heading upstairs, Pearl changed her mind and went through to the kitchen, where she found the table cleared of clutter and not a single item of dirty crockery littering the sink. Wherever Sylvia was now, she could only hope that, by the time she returned, the fury that had fuelled her tidying spree had blown itself out.

Unsure what to make of things, she started up the stairs, calling ahead as she went. 'Ivy? Ivy, are you up here?' Undoubtedly, she was wasting her breath. To put up with that volume of wailing, Ivy would have to be passed out drunk.

The door to Ivy's room standing partly open, Pearl peered in: no Ivy. Returning to the landing, she went to her own room at the back of the house, where she put the envelope of sheet music on the top of her chest of drawers and dumped her handbag on the bed. Then she unwound the scarf from her neck and unbuttoned her jacket. With a weary sigh, she retraced her steps to Ivy's room, squeezed along the side of the cot and leaned over the rail. As she lifted the baby, she recoiled from the stench of soiled nappy. No wonder the poor mite was crying, she was lying in her own mess. Moreover, although the room felt cold, the poor child's face was burning hot, her cheeks on fire.

As though astonished that someone should have picked her up, the little girl fell still and locked her eyes onto Pearl's.

'There, there,' Pearl soothed. 'Now where's that mummy of yours, hmm?' More softly, the baby resumed crying. 'Hold on, poppet. I know you need attending to, but we've got to find Mummy.'

Reaching over the cot to the window, Pearl pulled down the blackout, switched on the light and glanced about. Ivy's cocktail dress was hanging, as it always did, on the outside of the wardrobe. From the partly closed bottom drawer of the chest, one of the sleeves of her dark green sweater was spilling out onto the floor. On top of the chest, cosmetics were strewn about – lids open, tops unscrewed. On the rug by the wastepaper basket, balls of used cotton wool that had failed to make it into the bin lay where they had fallen. To behave in such slatternly fashion in someone else's home really was beyond the pale. Slattern or not, though, where was she now?

With her free hand, Pearl reached to open the wardrobe door. The only thing unaccounted for was Ivy's coat. Was she to believe Ivy had gone out and left the baby alone? She would like to think Ivy wouldn't do such a thing but, since the woman was nowhere to be found, it appeared that she had.

Negotiating the end of the bed, she returned to the cot and lowered the infant back in. 'Sorry,' she whispered. 'I know you're dirty, but I need to find your ma.'

When the little girl took to screaming again, Pearl closed her eyes and kept them firmly shut while she tried to think. Where the ruddy hell could Ivy have gone? And what was she supposed to do if she couldn't find her? She didn't even know where Sylvia was – or how long she would be gone.

The child's screams continuing, Pearl reopened her eyes. As they acclimatised to the light, she caught sight of something in the cot. It appeared to be a scrap of paper. Leaning over the rail, she fished it out. It was part of a page torn from an exercise book. Assuming it to be rubbish, she went to screw it into a ball, only to find herself drawn to Ivy's handwriting. Moving away from the cot, she smoothed out the piece of paper and held it beneath the overhead light.

> *Do what I should have done all along and find her a home.*
> *I won't be back.*

She re-read the words. What the blazes did Ivy mean? *I won't be back* from *where?* Where could she have gone? Back to London? Hardly – unless she'd stolen some, she wouldn't even have enough money for the train fare. And what on earth did she mean by 'find her a home'? A home where? With whom? Trying to work out what was going on, Pearl stood, shaking her head. Had Ivy left this note deliberately – as an instruction? Or was this a scrap of rubbish she'd intended for the bin? If it was a note, it was neither addressed to anyone nor signed.

In her mystification, she spun about, clouting her shin on the bedstead as she did so. Cursing the pain, she limped to the chest, where she tugged open the top drawer and stared at the contents. Knickers. Socks. Brassiere. An odd stocking. Where could Ivy go without taking underwear? Ramming the drawer shut, she yanked out the one beneath it. Slip. Nightdress. Scrap of towel. Incomprehension turning to panic, she went back to the wardrobe and pulled open the door: a couple of pairs of slacks; her corduroy skirt; the dark green dress she'd worn on stage before she'd got the slinky black number. But no coat. It hadn't been hanging in the hall, either – when she'd come in just now, the coat stand had been empty.

She glanced back at Ivy's note. *Do what I should have done all along and find her a home. I won't be back. For God's sake, Ivy, where have you gone? Where, on a bitterly cold December day, have you gone with only your coat and your—* Struck by a thought, she reached to the shelf at the top of the wardrobe. Her hand struck leather. Ivy hadn't even taken her handbag.

Fingers trembling, she lifted it down. To look inside felt like prying. But what choice did she have? To stand any chance of working out where Ivy had gone, she needed to know what she'd taken with her. Inwardly begging Ivy's forgiveness, she clicked open the clasp. Inside was Ivy's purse, along with it, the horrible orangey lipstick she'd told her to stop wearing and a twelve-pack of Craven 'A'. She flipped open the carton: three left. She opened the purse: two farthings. Not even enough for a bus fare. If Ivy *had* decided to run away, she most certainly wouldn't have left behind three cigarettes. Not a chance. So, where had she gone?

Hearing the front door creak open, she held her breath.

'Hello? Anyone home?'

In her dismay, she exhaled: Sylvia.

She hurried down the stairs anyway. 'Have you seen Ivy?'

'Not since late morning, before I went into town to collect Aunty Winn's wristwatch. I think I've told you she lives down on Bonhay Road with her daughter – that's my cousin, Ann. Anyway, Aunty Winn had broken the strap and I'd taken it in to be fixed. I only intended dropping it back into her, but she insisted I stop and have some soup with them. All that nattering and the afternoon completely got away from me.' *Yes, yes*, Pearl thought, not wanting to interrupt Sylvia but wishing she would stop talking. 'Even on the way back,' Sylvia resumed as she stood unbuttoning her coat, 'I got side-tracked by taking a detour to see what was happening on the riverbank.'

'The riverbank?'

Sylvia hung her coat on the stand and removed her scarf. 'I should think every policeman in town must be down there.'

Pearl stiffened. 'Why? What was going on?'

'Someone I spoke to said they'd found a body… but you know how grisly some people's imaginations can be.'

Feeling a rush of light-headedness, Pearl shot a hand to the newel post for support. The sensation easing, she reached into her pocket and withdrew Ivy's note. 'Look,' she whispered, and held it out for Sylvia to see.

Sylvia strained to read Ivy's handwriting. '"I won't be back"?'

'It was in the baby's cot.'

'But—'

'Are you sure she was still here when you went out?'

'I know for certain she was. I poked my head into the drawing room, and she was slumped in the chair as usual.'

'And she didn't mention anything about going out? *Please*, Sylvia. *Think*.'

When all Sylvia did was shake her head, Pearl bent to retrieve her shoes. 'Where did you say the police were?'

'Bonhay Road… about halfway between the weir and the railway bridge. But surely you don't think—'

'I don't know *what* to think,' Pearl said shortly, ramming her feet into her shoes before wrenching her coat from the stand and thrusting her arms into the sleeves. 'I hope to high heaven—' she paused to tie her shoelaces '—I'm wrong. But I have a horrible feeling, right here.' She pressed a hand to her midriff. 'And unless I go and check, I doubt it will go away.' Grabbing the torch from the shelf inside the door, she turned back. 'I'll take this. I'll try not to be long.'

'Yes. Yes, of course, dear.'

When Pearl switched off the light and opened the door, it was to find the fog from earlier had thickened noticeably. 'Oh, and I'm sorry,' she said as she stepped outside, 'but the baby needs changing.'

In a daze, Sylvia turned towards the crying. 'Changing. Right. I'll see to it.'

The fog closed around Pearl like a damp cloak, the beam of light from the torch swiftly proving useless. Stopping only briefly at the kerb to listen for traffic, she crossed the road. She would cut down through Peep Lane, which, she'd discovered while out walking one afternoon, led straight down the hill to Bonhay Road and the riverbank.

At the bottom of the last of several flights of steps, she emerged from the alleyway onto the pavement. Down at the same level as the river, the fog was even denser. Turning up the collar of her coat, she went left, the brick arch of the railway bridge looming out of the fog only when she was almost beneath it. Somewhere beyond it had to be where Sylvia had seen the police.

Her hands thrust deep into her pockets, she strode on. From further along, she caught the odd snatch of voices: commands, shouts. Drawing closer still, she heard ripples – the sort that might be caused by someone wading through water. Her throat tightened. *Please*, she willed. *Please let this be nothing to do with Ivy. I might have said some harsh things about her, but* please, *let her be safe, let her be passed out drunk in an alley somewhere, or wandering the city to clear her head, even with some man in a hotel. Anywhere but in the river...*

She was close enough now to make out a huddle of people, their coats pulled about them, the ends of cigarettes glowing red in the dark. With no idea how to find out who was in charge, she continued as far as the first of two vehicles parked at the kerb. Alongside one of them she made out a police constable. Clearing her throat, she went towards him.

'Um… excuse me.'

The constable turned towards her. 'Miss?'

'Is it true they've found a body?'

'I'm afraid I can't tell you that, miss.'

Oh, for goodness' sake. 'No. I appreciate that.' In the bitter cold, she felt her teeth rattle. 'And I w-wouldn't n-normally ask but you see my friend's gone missing.'

The constable straightened up. 'Male or female friend, miss?'

'F-Female.'

'Wait here, please.'

Without actually telling her anything directly, the constable had given her two pieces of information: firstly, that there was indeed a body; secondly, that it belonged to a woman. Had it been a man they'd found, then by now she would have been on her way home, no longer fearing the worst.

After what felt like ages, the constable returned with an officer Pearl assumed to be his superior.

'Sergeant Woodridge,' the second man greeted her. 'Constable Jephson tells me you're looking for a friend.'

Pearl nodded. 'I am.'

'You've reason to believe she's gone missing.'

'Yes. You see, she's taken her coat but not her handbag… which has her purse in it. And her cigarettes. And she'd never go anywhere without those.'

'And this friend—'

'Her name's Ivy Snell. She's in her early twenties. Brown hair, brown eyes. About my height.'

'Does she reside nearby?'

'On St David's Hill. She lodges with Mrs Sylvia Murrin, at her music school. I live there too.'

'You say she took her coat. Can you describe it?'

'Grey wool. Like a blanket. Three buttons down the front. And she was probably wearing brown ankle boots.' Yes, Pearl thought, she must have been because they weren't in the hall, and wherever they landed when Ivy kicked them off was where they stayed until the next time she wore them.

'Anything else she might have had about her? Anything distinctive?'

'Um…' Growing evermore stiff with cold, Pearl tried to picture Ivy dressed to go out. That the sergeant was asking such specific questions had her so fearful she could barely think. 'Yes. On her coat, there would be a little pin – a brooch.'

When the sergeant motioned to the constable, the latter moved away. 'Can you describe it, this pin?'

'It's in the shape of a musical note. A crotchet. Silver… badly tarnished.'

The constable returned and handed something to his sergeant.

'Like this one?'

Into Pearl's ears came a noise like the rushing of a train. With seemingly no control over her body, her head fell forward. Someone grasped her arm. And the last thing she saw as her vision became blurred was the pavement hurtling up towards her.

Chapter 24

'Pearl? Dear? Can you hear me? Can you wake up?'

With a sense that someone was talking to her, Pearl opened her eyes; leaning across her was an indistinct form – probably, she decided, Sylvia. The trouble was that her eyelids felt so heavy she couldn't seem to keep them open, and what she really wanted was to go back to sleep. Instead, by forcing her eyes wide, she was gradually able to make out her surroundings. Seemingly, she was in bed. What she couldn't work out was why.

'Have I…' To test her throat, she swallowed. 'Have I got tonsillitis again?' It was the only explanation she could come up with for why she was in bed.

'No, dear, it's all right. You're quite well.'

'Then why—' She tried to lift her head from her pillow. Outside, it appeared to be daylight. 'What time is it?'

She saw Sylvia turn to check the clock. 'Five and twenty past ten, dear. Can you sit up?'

Still struggling to keep her eyes open, Pearl hauled herself upright. Goodness, she felt groggy. Was it Sunday? Since she wasn't at work, she supposed it must be.

When Sylvia turned back to face her, Pearl saw that she'd been crying. *Crying.* Oh, dear God. Ivy. The police had found her in the river.

'Ivy,' she ventured. 'She's—'

'Yes, dear. I'm afraid that's right. You went down to the riverbank. When they showed you her brooch, you fainted from shock. A bystander had some sal volatile. A few breaths of that brought you round enough for a policeman to bring you home. Fortunately, you'd mentioned where you live.'

'I had?' How come she didn't remember any of this? Closing her eyes against the jagged brightness of the daylight, she tried to think.

'When they brought you in, you were distraught. Inconsolable. I called Dr Eastman. He came and gave you a sedative. You've been asleep ever since.'

'But—' A sedative. That must be why she was struggling to recall any of this. How, for instance, had Ivy ended up in the river? Why had she even been down there in the first place? Had she gone for a walk to clear her head? It seemed unlikely; if she remembered correctly, it had been a raw kind of a day – grey and damp and foggy, and certainly not an afternoon for taking a stroll.

'Please say if you don't feel up to it, dear, but I've woken you up because Sergeant Woodridge is downstairs, and he would like to talk to you. He has a few questions he'd like to ask you about Ivy.'

Pearl raised herself more upright. 'Then I should talk to him.' She might be having trouble piecing together what had happened but, if there were questions, then she owed it to Ivy to answer them if she could.

'If you don't feel up to it, I'll see if he's willing to come back later.'

'No.' By way of emphasis, Pearl shook her head. Best to get it over and done with. 'I'll get dressed.'

Sylvia, though, was already holding out her dressing gown. 'I don't think you need go to that bother. Take it slowly as you get up, and I'll help you into this.'

Moments later, with Sylvia's help, Pearl was seated by the fire in the drawing room, in the chair opposite her, Sergeant Woodridge. He was a large man, and the sight of him squeezed into one of Sylvia's wingback chairs reminded her of a cartoon drawing of someone in a fix. The notion made her want to giggle.

'I apologise for calling upon you so soon, Miss Warren,' Sergeant Woodridge began. 'But while events are fresh in your mind, I was hoping you might be able to tell me a little about Miss Snell's movements, in particular, those of yesterday afternoon.'

To show that she understood, Pearl nodded. She supposed this was what the police did when someone died unexpectedly. ''Course. I'll do my best... but I'm a bit foggy.'

'Naturally.' The sergeant's initial questions weren't unduly taxing. How long had she known Miss Snell? How had they first met? Did Ivy have a boyfriend? To the latter, Pearl had replied that she didn't think so. 'And yesterday,' Sergeant Woodridge proceeded to ask. 'How would you describe Miss Snell's mood?'

Ivy's mood. She tried to remember. Unfortunately, where her head was concerned, yesterday afternoon might as well have been last month. Gradually, though, several things came back to her.

'I didn't actually see her. When I left for work in the morning, she wasn't up – I started work at six. And when I came home, she wasn't here.'

'What time would that have been – that you came home?' When she told him, he went on to ask, 'And it would be normal for Miss Snell to be here at that time of day?'

'Normal. Yes. She's… not working at the moment.'

'So, her not being here would be out of character?'

'No… I mean, yes.'

'Miss Warren, it *was* out of character, or it wasn't?'

Pearl frowned. What did it matter now? The thing that was out of character was that Ivy was dead.

'She'd never gone out and left the baby alone before, if that's what you're asking.'

'Ah, yes. The baby.'

Slowly, Pearl was starting to remember. 'Soon as I came through the front door, I could hear her crying – the baby, I mean. She's been crying a lot lately. She's teething. I looked for Ivy. I looked everywhere. When it was plain she wasn't down here, I went up to her room to try and work out where she might be, you know, to see what she'd taken with her.'

'And what did you find?'

'I found her coat gone but not her handbag.'

'And that struck you as peculiar.'

Was it odd that the sergeant never seemed to blink? 'Well, yes. Especially since by then I'd found the note.' Now why the devil had she gone and mentioned *that*? She was pretty certain Ivy had meant that to be private. Next thing, he'd be asking to see it – and she didn't like the way it made Ivy look. Still, it was too late now. She could hardly backtrack.

'The note,' Sergeant Woodridge repeated.

'There was a note in the baby's cot. I didn't find it at first but when I did I—'

'Do you still have it, this note?'

It went through Pearl's mind to say that she'd thrown it away; she was bristling with disloyalty as it was. Ivy might have been unbearable at times, but she didn't want her going down on record as a poor mother. *Never speak ill of the dead*.

When Pearl agreed that she did still have it, Sylvia, who had been standing at the window, said, 'Can you remember where it is, dear?'

'In my coat pocket, I think.' She was pretty sure she'd taken it with her when she'd gone haring down Peep Lane.

'I'll go and fetch it, Sergeant.'

'Thank you, Mrs Murrin.' To Pearl's mind, the sergeant looked displeased. 'It would have been helpful to know about the existence of a note before now.'

'I've only just remembered it.' It was the truth. It had taken until a few moments ago for her to recall how, in her panic, her only concern had been to get down to the river and reassure herself that if there *was* a body, it wasn't Ivy's. 'Whatever the doctor gave me last night seems to be making it hard for me to think.'

When Sylvia returned and handed Ivy's note to the sergeant, Pearl was taken aback by the speed with which he read it, folded it up, and tucked it inside his pocketbook. When he then looked back at her, she was even more convinced that mentioning it had been a mistake.

'The wording of Miss Snell's note casts her actions in a particular light wouldn't you say? Closes down certain avenues of enquiry.' When Pearl frowned, Sergeant Woodbridge went on, 'Removes the need to expend any more valuable constabulary time.'

Pearl directed a glance at Sylvia, who, standing behind the sergeant, responded with an expression that suggested she could be of no help.

Pearl sighed. 'I don't understand.'

'When we find a body in the water, Miss Warren, our first question is always to ask how it got there. Did they fall in? Did someone push them? Did someone put them in the water to conceal evidence of a previous wrongdoing? Or did they go into the water of their own accord? And if so, was it their intention to take their own life?'

Pearl gave a little moan. 'No-o…' Hearing the possibility set out so starkly was heartbreaking.

From his pocketbook, Sergeant Woodridge extracted Ivy's note and held it up for her to see. 'And yet, we have this.'

'She might have been down in the dumps of late,' Pearl ventured, her voice trembling, 'but I think it completely wrong to suggest she scribbled a note, left it with her little girl, and then went down to the river to do away with herself.'

'Forgive me, Miss Warren, if I disagree with you. You see, in my experience, the most obvious answer to a conundrum is usually the correct one.' With difficulty, Sergeant Woodridge levered himself up from the chair. 'And in this case, it is my firm belief that Miss Ivy Snell, being, as you put it, "down in the dumps of late", did precisely that. She left a note in the one place she could be sure it would be found and set out to do exactly as she describes here: not come back. Indeed, that we have found no evidence to the contrary – no signs of foul play – would support that view, would it not?' When Pearl couldn't bring herself to agree, the sergeant went on, 'In fact, there is not a shred of doubt in my mind that further investigation into the circumstances of Miss Snell's death would amount to anything other than a waste of manpower. That being the case, I shall recommend to my inspector that the case be considered closed.'

As Sylvia left the room to accompany the sergeant to the front door, Pearl hung her head and stared through her tears into her lap. Impossible though it seemed, she had to accept that the sergeant was probably right. Ivy had gone to the river with one thing in mind, and the guilt that accompanied the realisation made her feel sick. It was bad enough that the last thing she said to Ivy had probably been hurtful and mean. Worse still, had she stopped wishing the woman would simply pull herself together and behave in a more considerate manner – had she done more to help and encourage her friend to that end – then Ivy might still be there with them now, and the little girl upstairs might not have been condemned to growing up without a mother. And the more she gave into the thought, the more she knew that nothing and no one would convince her otherwise.

–

'I've never said this about a funeral before but that was awful, wasn't it?'

Seated opposite Sylvia at the kitchen table, her hands wrapped about her cup of tea in the hope of getting them warm, Pearl gave a single nod. 'It was horrible and… bleak.'

With a lengthy sigh, Sylvia replaced her cup on her saucer. 'The worst funerals are always those where there's hardly anyone to mourn.'

'Ivy told me she lost her parents when she was small, and that she had neither brothers nor sisters. But for there to have been just the two of us and Jack is heartbreaking.'

'We did the best we could, in the circumstances.'

'Yes.'

'And I know this is going to sound trite but, now that it's over, I genuinely believe she would want us to put it behind us and get on with our lives.'

Would she, though, Pearl wondered? Or had she done what she did so that the two of them would examine their consciences and then, concluding that they had failed her, be forever burdened by their guilt? Ivy always had seemed the sort to hold a grudge.

With a sad shake of her head, Pearl sighed. While part of her wished she'd been kinder to Ivy – despite the way Ivy had often made that nigh-on impossible – she wasn't sure she would ever be able to forgive her for abandoning her daughter. Having known what it was like to grow up without parents, how could she have wished that same fate upon her own child? And yes, it was true that she didn't know the circumstances in which Ivy had become pregnant in the first place. But, whatever the situation, surely it didn't excuse leaving a child to grow up alone? There were so many people in the land who wanted children but, for whatever reason, never had any come along. Perhaps that very fact would eventually help the baby's chances of finding new parents. Although, who, with all the attendant uncertainty of this war, would feel able to commit to raising someone else's— But wait; *so many people who wanted children but, for whatever reason, couldn't have them*.

Raising her head, she studied Sylvia's expression. 'I recall you saying,' she began, aware of what was at stake, 'that once the funeral was over, you'd go and talk to the authorities – about the baby, I mean.' Noticing how her hands had begun to tremble, she plunged them into her lap.

'I know it sounds heartless, but it's all we can do. You and I can't raise her. And with Ivy appearing to have had no next of kin—'

'But what if I knew someone who might adopt her? Properly, I mean. A married couple who can't have children of their own but might take in an orphan?' Seeing the doubt that came over Sylvia's face, she hurried on, 'They've a lovely home – and they're not short of a bob or two.'

'Well…'

'I'm not suggesting we do it on the quiet. They wouldn't go for that anyway. No, I mean for it all to be above board. You said yourself, only the other day, about how there's so many children orphaned by those raids last year, that there's not enough folk to give them homes.'

'Perhaps…' Sylvia said as she got to her feet, 'I should see whether I can squeeze any more tea out of the pot. Only, if you're going to try and explain to me what you have in mind, I've a feeling we might be here for a while…'

–

'Thanks for coming,' Pearl said as Clemmie approached the table in the corner of the tearoom. To make certain she wouldn't be late, she'd made a point of getting there early and had, as a result, been sitting there for ten minutes, gradually losing all the feeling from her toes.

It was late one afternoon in the week after Ivy's funeral, another damp and foggy day, conditions so bitterly cold that, despite the cloak and dagger way she'd worded her message to Clemmie, she'd still been less than certain her sister would come. *Dear Clemmie*, she'd written. *Meet me at Farthing's on Tuesday at four o'clock. It's important. Your sister, Pearl.* With hindsight, she could have been a mite less abrupt.

'From your note it sounded urgent.' Pulling out the other chair, Clemmie sat down and pulled off her gloves. 'I ordered a pot of tea. I think we'll need it to keep warm.'

Pearl smiled. From her appearance, Clemmie looked really well. She had an air of being 'cared for'.

'Marriage obviously suits you, then. You look very... neat. Very... wifely.'

'*You* look very glamorous. But then you always did.'

'Seen May lately?' The recognition that she'd failed, yet again, to keep in touch with either of them, brought Pearl not only feelings of guilt but also of regret.

'Not since the christening back in the summer. But we write.'

'She okay? And the nipper?'

'Seems to be. She wrote just last week to say that any day now George will be crawling.'

'Suppose he would be.' Pearl tried to recall when May had written to announce that she had married Dan and was expecting a baby. It couldn't have been that long after Clemmie had married Andrew.

While they waited for their tea the two women made small talk. Yes, the weather recently had been awful; yes, they were both working hard at their various endeavours; yes, they couldn't wait for the war to be over.

When the waitress arrived with their tray, Clemmie poured their teas. 'So,' she said. 'What is it you wanted to see me about?'

Recalling her decision not to give away anything of her purpose until she had satisfied herself that it was the right thing to do, Pearl drew a breath, exhaled slowly, and said, 'Are you happy with Andrew? The two of you together, I mean?'

Clemmie looked affronted. 'Of course I am. Why would you ask such a thing?'

'Because I wouldn't tell you what I'm about to if... well, if you had regrets.'

'Regrets?'

Crikey, she was making a ham fist of this.

'Look,' Pearl picked up again, at pains this time to soften her tone. 'The reason I ask, is because—'

From there, she found it easier to explain than she'd been anticipating, the look on Clemmie's face as she sat listening to the story of what had happened to Ivy changing from shock to hesitation to disbelief – but the good kind of disbelief, Pearl decided as her explanation petered out, the *can this really be happening* sort of incredulity.

'You thought of *us*,' Clemmie whispered.

Pearl nodded. 'To be honest, until Sylvia began talking about going to the authorities to see about putting the little girl into an orphanage, I hadn't given thought to her future at all – other than to feel sorry for her. But the moment Sylvia started talking about what would have to happen, I thought of *you*. And knew I had to give you the choice. You and Andrew would be perfect parents.'

'Goodness,' Clemmie said. 'I... well, I don't know what to say. I'm trying not to become too excited because I've no idea what Andrew will think. We've talked about not being able to have a child of our own, but we've never talked about adopting one. I'm not even sure I know how to raise the topic to start with.'

'I've a feeling,' Pearl said with a smile, 'you'll think of a way.'

'How long do I have before we must make a decision?'

Pearl shrugged. It was a good question. 'Since no one seems to know the child exists – apart from the police, who, to be honest, couldn't seem less bothered – I don't see Sylvia being in a hurry to do anything, not while there's a chance of finding the poor mite a decent home.'

'All right. Well, on my way home,' Clemmie said as she got to her feet, 'I'll try and work out how to tell Andrew. I'll settle up for the tea and go straight back and talk to him. And then I'll let you know. Perhaps... tomorrow?'

Joining Clemmie in getting to her feet, Pearl smiled warmly. After so much gloom, to feel hopeful made a nice change – to do something so extraordinary for both Clemmie and the little girl, even better.

'All right. And I'll tell Sylvia.'

Leaning across, Clemmie kissed Pearl's cheek. 'Heavens, Pearl, what a thing. Thank you. Thank you so much.'

'I'll keep my fingers crossed for you.'

Yes, Pearl thought, waiting while Clemmie settled the bill before accompanying her out into the foggy night. What she'd done today was a good thing. Now she just had to hope nothing would get in the way of it being allowed to happen.

VI. Solo

Chapter 25

The dress was spectacular. When Clemmie had telephoned her late one afternoon from the WVS shop in Heavitree to say that, among the contents of a donated suitcase of lady's clothing, she'd found a dark blue evening dress – and would she like her to put it by for her to have a look – Pearl would admit to having been doubtful. Nevertheless, heartened that Clemmie had thought of her at all, after work the next day, she'd gone to see it, only to be lost for words. The gown was stunning, the style unfussy and elegant.

'Don't take this the wrong way,' Clemmie had said, 'but I almost didn't telephone. I thought you might say it was too old-fashioned.'

To Pearl, the gown was anything but. True, the straight cut of it harked back to before the war but its simple lines made Pearl love it all the more. Besides, as she'd once read in a woman's magazine, style never went out of fashion.

'It's like something Jean Harlow would wear,' she'd said. 'Glamorous but not gaudy. Slinky but demure.'

'So, are you going to try it on then?' Clemmie had asked with a laugh.

The fit hadn't been perfect; the woman who'd worn it before had clearly been broader across the chest but, having examined the seams, Pearl could see how, with a couple of darts let in, it could be made to fit like a dream.

'I'll take it,' she'd said when Clemmie had covertly scribbled a price on the corner of a slip of paper.

And now, here she was, at the Undercroft Club's New Year's Eve party, sheathed in the column of midnight blue silk, her hair piled on top of her head, the cloud of butterflies once again flitting about in her stomach as she waited to join The Murrinaires for the medley of five songs Jack had put together for her. She knew she looked the part, she knew the songs. And both Sylvia and Jack had agreed that her voice was ready – a little different to before her operation, in that it appeared to have a greater fullness, but all were agreed she need have no qualms.

Stood beside her, Sylvia caught her eye and smiled. 'Still excited?'

Pearl grinned. 'I've had to force myself not to sing along to everything they've been playing.'

'I don't doubt it. But maybe settle for tapping your foot, instead.'

Bringing her forefinger to her lip to signify that she would be quiet, Pearl nodded. It was almost impossible to believe she was finally back there. After her operation, Dr Eastman had said it would be three months before she could sing again and, initially, Sylvia had thought him right. Still, as long as he wasn't in tonight's audience – given the man's advancing years, it seemed unlikely he would be – he need never know that she had gone against his instructions.

When the moment came for her to join the band, Jack came across the stage, took her hand, and led her to the microphone. From the floor came a couple of wolf whistles along with a ripple of applause in recognition; it was comforting to know she hadn't been forgotten.

Drawing a deep breath, she looked out across the audience and leaned towards the microphone. 'Good evening, ladies and gentlemen. It's lovely to be back at the Undercroft Club.' And when Cliff, on piano, played the first few notes of her introduction, she was gladdened to feel her butterflies starting to settle.

Quickly lost in the music, she allowed her eyes to rove the room, the swirl of gowns glittering like jewels against the sharp black and white of evening dress. She caught the sparkle of necklaces and the glint of earrings, now and again the blur of a beaming face. Within moments, it was hard to believe she'd ever been away, Jack's arrangement of the five numbers into one continuous piece flowing as smoothly as silk.

'Clearly, you've some fans in tonight,' Jack observed when he came to stand beside her at the end of her performance, and she took yet another bow. 'If you're up to it, I reckon we can just about squeeze in "The Lady Is a Tramp" and still be in time for the countdown to midnight. But we'll have to start right this second. What do you say?'

Pearl shot a look to where she'd left Sylvia, only to see that she was no longer there.

'Love to,' she replied. 'Although, if Sylvia asks, I'll say you twisted my arm.'

'Fair enough.'

That she hadn't sung a note of her favourite song in more than two months didn't enter her head; within a couple of bars, it felt as though she was simply catching up with an old friend: same come-hither dip of her shoulder, same tantalising smile, same knowing wink. The audience's whoops of delight confirmed she was back. And as she and the band brought the number to a close, all thoughts of Sylvia being cross were drowned out by the roar from the audience, the countdown to midnight, and all hell letting loose. Champagne corks popped, couples embraced. Releasing her from a hug, Jack loosened his collar and signalled to the band. People crossed arms, grasping the hand of whomever was within reach.

'*Should auld acquaintance be forgot…*' The club was filled with voices.

When it was all over, Jack gave her another hug. 'What do you wish for in the year ahead? Or is that a silly question?'

'For this war to be over?' she raised her voice to say, thinking it hardly silly.

'And if you could wish for more than that?'

'Good health. The chance to perform. And yes, I know that's two wishes, but I need the one for the other.' What she wasn't going to admit – for fear of appearing pushy, ungrateful, even – was that, for her, a return to performing was only the first step, her aim for the coming year altogether more ambitious. By this time *next* year, she wanted to be well on the way to doing this for a living – but properly, not through the antics of some grubby little fraud like Gordon Gold.

Behind them on the stage, the band were preparing for their final few numbers. Faced with the prospect of a normal day's shift starting in a few hours, though, Pearl knew it was time to find Sylvia and head home – or else suffer the consequences tomorrow.

Submitting to a hug and a kiss from each member of the band, she left them to it and went to collect her coat. It had been the best New Year's Eve ever. Hardly surprising: in previous years, she'd been too young to celebrate – technically, still was. It was such a shame that neither

Clemmie nor May and their husbands could have been there. When the three of them had gathered together at Clemmie's on Boxing Day, she had extended invitations to all of them but, since both her sisters now had babies – and since, in May's case, the journey would have been pretty much impossible – both had been forced to decline. She was glad to have seen them, though. And to see how well Ivy's baby had settled with Clemmie and Andrew. Penny, they'd named her, Andrew explaining that, despite the number of forms they had already filled in, and the various applications they had lodged, it seemed they had barely scraped the surface of what was required to make her officially theirs. It was, though, he had gone on to reassure her, just a matter of being patient.

Given the year she'd had, Pearl was quietly thrilled by how things were working out; being able to return to singing was an achievement in itself, there having been moments when she'd truly believed it was never going to happen. But, by recovering from her operation with her voice in good shape, she felt as though she had been given a second chance. And a second chance, especially in this time of war, was a rare thing. Incredible, then, that a completely different, but no lesser miracle – one born out of tragedy and sadness – should rank even higher on her list of achievements during the last year. Thinking to tell Clemmie about Ivy's baby eclipsed everything else by some measure and was, by far, the best thing she had ever done. Even if she was one day given star billing at The Palladium – always assuming that, once this war eventually came to an end, the poor old place could be patched up and reopened – she still might not experience quite the same glow. As Sylvia had said, it was an act of which she should be justly proud – and one she would go a long way to better.

–

'Pearl, dear? Pop in a minute, would you? I've some news.'

It was late Friday afternoon at the end of the following week and Pearl had just arrived home from her shift. Barely had she got over the late night – early morning? – of the New Year's Eve party when Thursday had come around, and she'd been back at the Undercroft to perform with The Murrinaires in their regular spot. And she didn't mind admitting it had taken it out of her.

Having unwound her scarf and taken off her coat and shoes, she went through to the drawing room, approached the fire, and offered her hands towards the warmth.

'Walking home on days like this,' she said, feeling the heat of the flames on her palms, 'I get frozen to the bone. But anyway,' she said, casting over her shoulder and, noticing Sylvia's unusually broad smile, continuing warily, 'I'm home now. And you said you have some news?'

'I have indeed. And I think you'll agree it's rather exciting.'

Her interest piqued, Pearl turned fully about. 'Then I'm all ears.'

'In the audience at the club on New Year's Eve was a man named John Worth.'

John Worth. Pearl frowned; was she supposed to know that name?

'Right…'

'He'd spent Christmas down here with friends. And, on New Year's Eve, those same friends took him to the Undercroft… where he heard you sing.'

Pearl frowned. 'And?'

'And he was so impressed, he returned last night for another listen.'

She did wish Sylvia would get to the point; while the warmth from the fire was lovely, she was desperate to have a wash and get out of her uniform. 'So, I've got a fan.'

'He's a little more than a fan, dear. He's an agent. And at the end of the night, after we'd left, he spoke to Jack, who referred him to me. Turns out, he'd like to meet you.'

Pearl's frown deepened. 'An agent? What, you mean, a proper one? All above board? Not some dubious Gordon Gold type?'

'A bona fide agent. His offices are in London – the Williams Worth Agency. I made a few telephone calls to check that he is genuine, and everyone I spoke to said that his firm is highly reputable. His agency isn't huge, but neither is it insignificant.'

After so long spent wishing for precisely this moment, Pearl was having trouble taking it in. An agent had heard her sing – had even gone back for a second listen – and now he wanted to meet her?

'I don't know what to say. It feels too good to be true.'

'After your experience with Gordon Gold, it's only natural you should be cautious. But I assure you, this man is different. And this time, you and I will see him together.'

'You said he's in London.'

'Yes. At the moment, though, he's still here, in Exeter, but intending to catch the train back to London on Sunday. So, I suggested that before he does, he might like to come here for the three of us to have a chat.'

'And he agreed?'

'He'll be here at ten o'clock Sunday morning.'

The significance of what was happening beginning to sink in, Pearl realised that, without having even put herself out, she'd attracted the attention of an agent – a London agent – who, it appeared, wanted to represent her. And on Sunday morning he was coming to meet her. In her mind, she ran a hasty eye over her wardrobe of clothes – first impressions were important.

'What should I wear?' Belatedly, she wondered what it said about her that her first concern was for her appearance.

'Well, dear, since he's already seen you on stage, I think all you need be is clean and tidy. Perhaps your dark skirt and that pretty jumper you bought from the WVS.'

'Yes, of course.' Now she just felt silly. 'Sorry, it's nerves getting to me.'

'At ten o'clock on a Sunday morning, the man's not going to expect glamour.'

No. No, of course he wouldn't. But what *would* he expect? She would certainly need to make an effort with her hair. And her tatty slippers were a definite no-no. And if he wanted to hear her voice without the band, what should she sing? Which of her numbers would show her to best advantage with only Sylvia to accompany her on the piano?

With seemingly hundreds of questions clamouring for answers, she sank into the empty armchair and shook her head in disbelief. Just six days into the new year and one of her wishes might be on the cusp of coming true; she might be about to climb the next step of the ladder to her dream, and from there to who knew what dizzying heights? Obviously, she shouldn't count her chickens – that was a sure way to court disaster – but it just went to show what you could achieve by working hard for what you wanted and sticking at it, come what may.

Still not quite able to believe what was happening, she exhaled a long sigh. By this time on Sunday, she might have an agent – by the sound of it, a proper one who would get her bookings. This really was it. She was on the brink of achieving her dream. And, just this once, she had no words to describe how that made her feel.

London

1946

VII. Ensemble

Epilogue

May Beer tried desperately to wriggle her toes. She knew it had been a mistake to borrow a pair of shoes from her sister; while they might both take the same size, her own feet weren't used to such daintily shaped footwear. Well, more fool her for forgetting to pack her own. Standing there now – and especially given the length of the evening gown she'd hastily run up from an old pair of damask curtains – she was minded she could have got away with the pair she'd travelled up in because no one would have been able to see them.

She'd never been to London before. But then, apart from being taken by the school to see a pantomime of *Cinderella*, when she'd been about six or seven years old, she'd never been to the theatre, either. If it hadn't been for Pearl getting tickets to this new show, they wouldn't have been there now. She still couldn't work out why Pearl had been so insistent they all see it. *Please come*, she'd written to say. *The three of us together, doing something fun, will be a proper treat.* Given the disruption it had caused on the farm, and the upheaval for the children, she hoped it didn't disappoint.

Shifting her weight to ease the discomfort to her poor toes, she looked around the foyer. With so many lights burning, and so many people dressed to the nines, the plush surroundings were a stark contrast to so much of the rest of the West End. This morning, when their train had been trundling the last few miles into Waterloo station, she'd been shocked by the extent of the destruction. She'd seen bomb damage in Exeter, of course she had; she was unlikely to forget the devastation caused by the air raids that had destroyed their home. But, up here, in the capital, the ruins seemed far and away more dreadful. It just made her all the more glad the war was finally over – although when the bomb sites would ever be demolished and new houses built in their places, was anybody's guess.

'All right, there?'

May turned her attention to her husband. The only time she'd seen him wearing a collar and tie had been the day they'd got wed, him in full evening dress was something she'd never thought to see. His outfit was borrowed, of course. The day he'd tried it on for size had also been the day he'd realised he needed to visit the barber. Months of nagging hadn't got him there but one smart suit and off he went, quick as you like. *Can't take you up the smoke looking like a bumpkin, can I?* he'd said upon catching sight of himself in the mirror.

Look at him, handsome devil. When it came to husbands, she'd done all right for herself. She was glad their little George took after him, with his strong looks but gentle nature, that boy was going to be a heartbreaker one day – she just knew it. Have all the girls after him, he would. By contrast, the only traits their little Jenny had inherited from the Beers was an unfortunate dose of their stubbornness, her looks drawing more upon the Huxford side.

Looking back up to find Dan examining her expression, she recalled him asking her a question. 'Sorry, love, what did you say?'

'I asked if you were all right.'

'Fine, thanks. Bloomin' cross I didn't think to bring shoes to go with me frock, though.'

'That pair of your sister's pinching your feet?'

She nodded. 'Something chronic.'

With a grin, he leaned towards her. 'Once we're sat down, happen you can kick them off.'

'Trust me, I'm banking on it.' She cast about the foyer again. It was now so crammed with people, she had to raise her voice to make herself heard. 'I don't see Pearl anywhere.'

'No. I've been looking out for her, too. It's not like she won't stand out.'

May glanced at her wristwatch. 'Well, I suppose there's still a good while yet. She always did keep everyone waiting.'

'What was it she told you to do when we got here?'

'She said to go to the box office, tell them our names, and someone would give us our tickets and show us to our seats.'

'Well, we're almost at the front of the queue. So, not long now.'

'I do hope your ma and pa aren't having any bother with the children. Jenny's been that clingy lately.'

She felt Dan take hold of her hand. 'For once in your life, May Beer, would you just stop fretting. Jenny will be fine. They both will. You know how they love their Granny and Gramps.'

''Course.' Even if George and Jenny *were* playing up, there was nothing she could do about it now. For just this one night, she would try to put their naughtiness to the back of her mind and enjoy the show – not to mention the night in the hotel afterwards, booked for them by

Pearl. Of everything, what she was looking forward to most was a soak in that lovely bath, and the luxury of having breakfast laid on in the morning. And no washing up afterwards. And no one pulling anyone else's hair or throwing their sibling's shoes down the lav. Yes, even if, after all this palaver, the show turned out to be something of a let-down, she would make the most of Pearl's generosity and thank her profusely for it afterwards – assuming, she thought as she turned yet again to scan for any sign of her, the girl actually turned up…

–

Taking in the sight of the staircase rising away in front of them, Clemmie Dunning sighed. While it was wonderful that Pearl had chosen seats for them in one of the theatre's boxes, she couldn't help but think the stalls would have been more practical for Andrew.

'I'm afraid, sir,' the theatre's front of house manager addressed her husband, 'there's rather a lot of steps. But the rise is quite shallow. Will you be able to manage?'

By his wife's side, Andrew nodded. 'Might take me a while,' he said, gesturing with his head to his sticks, 'and thank you for your concern, but yes, I shall be fine.'

'But perhaps we could go on ahead,' Clemmie suggested to the manager. 'Before everyone else is making their way up?'

The manager signalled his consent with a nod. 'Of course. These are your tickets, then, Mrs Dunning. You're seated in the Prince's Box. The other four members of your party went up a few moments ago. If you would like to follow me, I will take you up.'

'Thank you,' said Clemmie, passing ahead of her husband as the manager held open the door.

The other *four* members? She could only think Pearl must have brought someone. A young man, perhaps? She hadn't mentioned anyone – but then it must be more than a month since she'd seen or spoken to her; Pearl's last letter had said only that she was training in London and would catch up with her when she got back. The next thing she'd heard had been when Pearl had telephoned one day to ask, in an oddly breathy and excited voice, whether, if she made all of the arrangements for them, she and Andrew would be able to travel to London and meet her to go to a show. *A very good show*, Pearl had seemed to think it necessary to add.

And now, here they were, in the West End of London – being shown up to the Prince's Box, no less – with still barely any idea of what was going on. The room in the hotel Pearl had booked for them was the height of luxury, her gesture beyond generous. She could only suppose this training Pearl had been doing had resulted in a promotion for her – or maybe even a completely new job; thinking back, Pearl hadn't specifically mentioned the training having anything to do with the bus company.

Earlier this afternoon, she'd been struck by the notion that Andrew somehow knew more than he was letting on – and that possibly even Andrew's help and general assistant, Pearce, was in on it, too. Although, in Pearce's case, that could only be because Andrew had told him. Her supposition had been strengthened by the fact that, when she'd asked Andrew to check theatre listings in the copy of the *Evening Standard* he'd picked up at Waterloo, he'd said he would rather not as, on this occasion, he would prefer the evening to be a surprise. As a rule, Andrew hated to be surprised by anything. In fact, he took surprises as a personal affront to his ability to plan for any and all contingencies.

May was as much in the dark as she was; she'd said as much when Clemmie had telephoned – several times – to compare notes about their sister's curious invitation.

Following Andrew slowly up the stairs, Clemmie let out another sigh. After all this fuss, whatever the show turned out to be, she would do her best to enjoy it – *and* their night in the hotel. She hadn't stayed in one since that funny little place in Exmouth where they'd gone on their honeymoon. Of course, they hadn't had Penny then. Dear old Pearce, they were so lucky to have him. *Nothing would give me greater pleasure*, he'd said when Andrew had asked whether he might look after their daughter for the night. Of course, it helped that Penny adored 'Ears', as she called him, having been unable, when she'd first started talking, to correctly pronounce his name.

At the top of several flights of plush-carpeted stairs, they were shown to their box. To Clemmie's surprise, May and Dan were already there, and got up to greet them. Also there, was Sylvia Murrin – Pearl's landlady and singing teacher, who Clemmie had met on a previous occasion – and a debonair older gentleman who introduced himself as Jack Bassett, the leader of the band with whom Pearl sang – or, as Jack had actually said, 'used to sing' – in Exeter. This last piece of information came as news to Clemmie, Pearl having given her no indication that she'd stopped performing. She could only suppose it had something to do with her being in London.

Once settled in her seat, Clemmie ferreted about in her evening bag for the pair of opera glasses Andrew had given her. Peering through them at the people in the circle, she concluded that, despite clothes rationing still being in full force, there were some marvellous frocks; she could only suppose some lucky women had a wardrobe from before the war and had simply dusted off something suitable. She scanned the rows of seats, the auditorium was pretty much full, the last of the stragglers being escorted quickly to their rows. And yet *still* there was no sign of Pearl. Much longer and she would genuinely start to worry. Hopefully, she would get here before the curtain went up. Having made all these elaborate arrangements for everyone else, it would be a dreadful shame if she was the only one of them to miss the start of the programme...

–

Pearl Warren smoothed a hand over the front of her dress. She'd never worn anything in a deep green colour before. But the wardrobe manager had been right, it set off perfectly her ivory shoulders and flaming hair. Besides, it was more than just green, when it caught the light, it shimmered with the iridescence of a peacock's feather. And her hair! Gone was her victory roll, in its place a sleek chignon, seemingly secured with a single pin of at least twelve inches in length and whose tip held a sparkling emerald-coloured gemstone. The truth of the matter was rather less glamourous: the knot of her hair contained more than two dozen Kirby grips; the whole creation set in place with at least half a can of lacquer.

Behind her, a tap at the door brought her thoughts back to the present. 'Five minutes, Miss Sweeting.'

She turned away from the mirror. 'Coming.'

Well, this was it. Opening night. *Opening act.* The audience would be filled with anticipation. All eyes would be on her. She'd rehearsed and rehearsed and rehearsed. She'd got used to the band, and they to her. She was opening a show in a West End theatre and would be doing so for two nights each week for as long as the show ran – or until John Worth found her something even better. It wouldn't be long, he'd assured her. Once word got round about her voice, directors and producers would be clamouring to work with her. But even just thinking about that was getting ahead of herself. As Sylvia had once told her, you were only as good as your last show, and the only one that mattered was the one you were about to go and do.

A short walk from her dressing room, she arrived in the wings, the show's producer coming to stand next to her.

'Ready?'

She nodded. 'I am.' *I've been ready for this moment since I was old enough to hum a tune.*

On the auditorium side of the curtain, the compere for the night – a household name from wartime entertainment shows on the wireless – was welcoming the audience with jokes and witty one-liners to warm them up. Listening to the outbursts of merriment, Pearl hoped her flight of butterflies wouldn't cause her any trouble.

'Thirty seconds.'

She crossed the stage to the microphone.

'Ladies and gentlemen, put your hands together and give a warm welcome to Miss Sadie Sweeting!'

The audience applauded, the orchestra struck up. The curtain rose and she tapped her foot. Against the lights, she saw the silhouette of the compere standing, arm outstretched towards her, before he disappeared into the shadows away to her right. The music built and she drew a breath. Then she hit her first note and sang. She'd made it. She was singing on a London stage, and it was almost impossible to believe.

Once into her stride, she flicked her eyes to the Prince's Box, high up on her left. And while she couldn't be sure, she thought she saw Clemmie and May staring down at her – no doubt speechless in their disbelief.

Not so long ago, she and her sisters had been homeless and penniless, with no earthly idea what lay in store for them and little reason to look to the future with any hope. But, in a way, their misfortune at the hands of those enemy bombers had been the making of them: May had fought tooth and nail to save an ailing farm, unexpectedly finding love and happiness with the man who had gone on to become not only its owner but her husband, the pair of them finding even greater happiness with their children; Clemmie had found purpose through her voluntary work, through which she, too, had met her husband, and gone on to adopt their daughter, whom both of them adored and who adored them back. And then, here she was herself, her long-held dream finally taking flight.

Best of all, though, she knew that, when it mattered most, her sisters would be there for her, as she would be for them. They might live apart, and lead very different lives, but in times of need – or, indeed, in moments of celebration – the three of them would come back together to help or to share in each other's achievements. And she knew she wasn't the only one of them to think that, as it happened, things simply couldn't have turned out any better.

Historical Note

At the outbreak of World War II, the British government mandated that all 'places of entertainment' be closed. This included the country's cinemas, of which there were, at that time, more than four thousand. It was a period when, with no television, and only a very limited choice of radio programmes, going to see a film was an immensely popular pastime. Indeed, an estimated one-third of the population went to the cinema at least once a week. Within a fortnight of the restriction being brought in, the government recognised the role cinemas played in keeping up the nation's morale, and the order was withdrawn. As the war continued, cinema audiences grew even more.

At the same time, dancing also saw a surge in popularity. For young people especially, dancing offered not only the chance to forget about the war for a few hours and enjoy themselves, but also to meet new people. A couple of years after war began, American servicemen started arriving in the UK, bringing with them new and exciting types of music, along with fast and energetic dance styles to go with it.

At the start of *These Wartime Dreams*, it is May 1942 and Pearl is just beginning her journey to achieve her ambition of performing. At this point, the American influence on music has yet to take hold, and most of the songs Pearl knows would have come from the musicals she would have seen over the previous few years. All of the songs, films, and performers I've mentioned in this book are real and would have been well known at the time. I list them in full on my website – rosiemeddon.com – but further information about them is widely available.

Acknowledgements

Throughout the writing of this trilogy, I have been fortunate to have the assistance of people without whom, my task would have been immeasurably more difficult.

Kiran Kataria, of Keane Kataria Literary Agency, has been her usual fount of technical advice and pragmatism.

Emily Bedford, at Canelo, has shown enthusiasm for my characters, my plots, and my writing in general. Receiving her feedback each time has spurred me on and given me the confidence to continue.

Closer to home, my husband has been steadfast in his belief in my abilities, has listened while I have bemoaned my latest struggles, and has never stinted in his all-round support and willingness to pick up the slack of everyday life so that I might plough on regardless.

To these kind people, and to everyone else who has helped to make this trilogy possible, I extend my deepest thanks.